HIDDEN CROWN

THE GATEKEEPER'S TRIALS: BOOK ONE

EMMA L. ADAMS

This book was written, produced and edited in the UK, where some spelling, grammar and word usage will vary from US English.

To be notified when Emma L. Adams's next novel is released, sign up to her author newsletter.

PREFACE

"And see you not yon bonny road
That winds across the ferny lea?
That is the road to fair Elfland
Where you and I this night must be."

Thomas the Rhymer

If faeries loved one activity more than they loved enthralling mortals, it was admiring their own reflections.

Elegantly dressed faeries occupied the entire row of mirrors in the ladies' bathroom at the nightclub, touching up the glamour on their already-perfect faces. Shifting colours, bright flowers woven into curling hair and glittering wings caught the garish lights above the mirrors, while in the background, a lilting tune played through loudspeakers at top speed, like a modern remix of a traditional faerie ballad.

On another night, I might have come here looking for a good time, not a murderer, but I made a point of preparing for both possibilities. Ducking into a vacant stall, I reached into my bag for an iron dagger and carefully slid it into the sheath on my thigh, hidden under the hem of my dress. Then I threw on a glamour of my own. My blond-tinted hair darkened to black, my face altering imperceptibly. I kept my rounded ears—passing as a regular human would be an asset for once—and trusted the neon lights in the nightclub to hide my magic-tinted eyes and the swirling silver mark on my forehead beneath my newly glamoured curls.

My phone buzzed with a message from my sister —*where are you?*

Right. I was *supposed* to be meeting Ilsa at the pub across the road, but the instant I'd heard the lilting music from inside the nightclub, I'd known someone was up to no good. Suppressing a sigh, I turned my phone to silent and left the cubicle.

Nobody noticed I didn't look like the same person who'd walked in, but glamours were second-nature to the fae. As prey walking among predators, I had to be alert for every small change in my perception, but the fae had the luxury of taking what they saw at face value. A lilac-haired half-faerie with furred fox-like ears looked up, her confused gaze flicking from my glamoured reflection to my rounded human ears, but I was already walking away.

The thrum of the music swallowed me up along with the heaving, sweating crowd. Glamoured half-faeries danced with humans, the latter distinguished by their glazed, vacant expressions. Nobody could say they hadn't been warned. Every human these days knew not to dance with the fae, but peer pressure was as powerful as the faeries' ability to play on human desires like a well-strung harp. Even half-faeries weren't immune to the magic of their Sidhe brethren, though they liked to think they were.

All it took was one promise, one detour into the wrong part of the forest, one dance—and then you were theirs. Forever.

On the stage, DJ Thorntooth cranked up the music to twice its previous speed. The screeching ballad mingling with modern auto-tune created an eardrum-melting combination even by nightclub standards, but I resisted the impulse to buy a round of shots to numb the oncoming headache. I needed to be at my sharpest if I wanted to take down my target without more bloodshed than there needed to be.

As his name suggested, DJ Thorntooth wasn't human, even if he was wearing the skin of one. Damn unhygienic, if you asked me. Since most people in here were either drunk, stoned, couldn't see through glamour or just plain didn't give a crap, they had no idea how much danger they were in. On the plus side, that meant I'd have less panicking to deal with.

The music sped up, and so did the crowd, their movements turning jerky, robotic. They would dance until their screams drowned the sound of the bass and their blood soaked into the beer-drenched floor. I wove through the haze of magic, pretending to be enthralled, while my own magic lurked beneath the surface. It didn't make me completely immune to the effects of the music, but the green glow at my fingertips helped me focus on what I needed to do.

I inched closer to the stage, creeping up behind the DJ. Then, threads of magic lashed from my hands, yanking him off his feet and onto the filthy floor. His startled cry was lost in the clamour as I aimed my next attack right at the stage. Thorny stems burst from floor to ceiling, cutting off the music with a spluttering crash.

"Show's over, folks," I shouted into the microphone. "DJ Thorntooth will be taking a long-term hiatus."

The DJ wriggled free from my magic and dove off the stage, knocking humans and half-faeries aside like skittles. The bewildered clubbers hindered his escape entirely by accident, allowing me to grab his wrist and drag him towards the back door.

"You can't have magic!" he yelped. "You're human."

I didn't argue that I wasn't human, because I was. Instead, I pushed my curls aside with my free hand and let the symbol on my forehead do the talking.

The mark of the Summer Gatekeeper.

He gave an uncomprehending blink. Then the pieces clicked into place. "I wasn't doing nothing wrong! I'm an innocent bystander!"

"And that human skin you're wearing just leapt off of its own accord, did it?"

"They planted it on me!" He squirmed, fighting me all the way out of the back door and into the alley behind the nightclub. "I'll tell on you to the Seelie Queen. She's a good friend of my mum's, she is."

I dropped my voice. "Really? Because I'm in the employ of the Summer Court, and if you'd ever set one foot there in your miserable existence, you'd know the Seelie Queen is currently in jail for treason. And you—" I jabbed him in the chest—"Will soon be joining her."

"I didn't do anything!" he shrieked. "You'll never get away with this."

I pulled a pair of iron handcuffs from my purse. "Time for a one-way trip to the Ley Line."

He screamed as the iron made contact with his skin, latching his wrists together. His face turned greyish, his knees giving out as the iron ate away at his magical defences.

"Hazel!" My twin sister's voice came from the mouth of the alley. "What are you doing? I thought you were supposed to be meeting Morgan and me at the pub."

"I was." I gave a sharp tug on the DJ's wrist, and he whimpered. "Before I got side-tracked by this lowlife human-killer."

"Ugh." Ilsa pulled a face at the sight of the DJ's human-skin coat. "Are you taking him to Faerie?"

"Unfortunately." Human prisons might have upgraded since the faeries had revealed themselves to the world, but the Sidhe were supposed to be responsible for punishing their wayward kin, even if they made every effort to evade that responsibility most of the time. "I'll message you when I'm done. This won't take long."

"Sometimes I think you go looking for trouble on purpose," Ilsa said.

"I don't need to look too hard, do I?" For all that the faeries claimed our realm was a poison to them, they were the ones who'd let their outcasts invade earth and spread chaos and destruction over the past two decades, and since humans were woefully behind on effective methods for dealing with fae criminals, it fell to me to dispense justice in my own way.

I dragged DJ Thorntooth through the cobbled, winding streets until I came to the shimmering line that divided our realm from Faerie. The Ley Line was invisible to most, including the DJ himself, and he gasped in surprise when the cobbled street vanished from sight.

An instant later, we appeared on a country lane outside the Summer Lynn house. Ivy cloaked the walls of the manor, giving it a dark and forbidding appearance without the usual soft sunbeams highlighting the garden's vibrant colours. The house might be stuck in perpetual summer, like the Seelie Court, but the clocks ran on the same time as the human world outside, and a crescent moon hung in the sky overhead.

DJ Thorntooth eyed the wide gardens, their flowerbeds bursting with night-blooming flowers. "Nice place you've got here."

I gave him a smack on the back of the head. "Shut it."

I opened the gate and pushed him through into the garden, steering him around the side of the manor towards the black mass of trees towards the back of the lawn. Behind those trees lay the forests of the Winter Court, and the house belonging to the other branch of the Lynn family.

Don't let the Seelie/Unseelie divide fool you. The Summer Court is as ruthless as Winter, and its inhabitants just as devious. I should know, because I dealt almost exclusively with the little bastards.

I reached the tall, wide gates that marked the end of our garden. Flanked by eternally blooming flowers, the Summer gate was one of the only known passages from the human realm directly into Faerie. Legend told that the gate—and its Winter counterpart—had sprang into existence in the same spot where my ancestor, Thomas Lynn, had crossed into the faerie realm for the first time.

Unlike most humans, he'd walked out again. Some stories said the Sidhe themselves had gifted him with extraordinary powers. Others claimed he'd fled with the Wild Hunt snapping at his heels. Whatever the case, all the versions of the tale I'd heard told me Faerie's influence had remained, lingering over his shoulder as he re-integrated into the human realm, married his childhood sweetheart, and had children.

That's when the Sidhe came back. Thomas Lynn, it seemed, had sworn to come to the aid of the Courts whenever they needed him, and the Sidhe had taken him at his word. They'd woven a spell so deep that it filtered through the bloodline of any person born into the Lynn family, choosing one host for each Court with every generation. His twin daughters became the first Gatekeepers: one for Summer, one for Winter. And now, centuries later, it was my turn.

I rapped on the moss-covered bars of the gate, which made a hollow, echoing noise. "One criminal, coming right up."

The Sidhe had made no secret of their disapproval of my using the gate as a depository for their rule-breaking brethren, but since Mum had been forced into early retirement by an attempted coup in the Summer Court, they'd been in no rush to officially crown me as Gatekeeper. As far as I was concerned, that meant they'd have to deal with any criminals I tossed their way in the meantime.

I pushed the gate inwards, and the DJ made a desperate bid for freedom. Handcuffed hands outstretched, he leapt headfirst into the hedge with surprising agility, vanishing in a shower of leaves.

"Hey!" I ran to the gap between the neat hedges that led into the Inner Garden. The unfortunate DJ flailed upside-down for a moment before crashing into the glowing pool of water in the grove's centre.

Crap. That's probably bad luck. The pool contained healing magic from the heart of the Summer Court itself

—not that it would be of any use to the DJ when the Sidhe got hold of him. I grabbed his flailing arm and fished him out of the pool, dragging him after me with a firm hand.

"What magic was that?" he spluttered, his hair sopping wet and his skin glistening with droplets of silvery water.

"There's no point in asking. You'll be dead in five minutes." I gave him a sharp kick through the gate, and he landed in a heap beneath his human-skin coat.

"You said I was going to jail!" He scrambled upright, his eyes wide with alarm. "Please—"

I slammed the gate closed, cutting off his pleading. As far as I was concerned, cowardly shits who murdered innocent people deserved no leniency. I turned my back and headed home to get a drink.

Even cast in darkness, the Summer Lynn house was impressive, its ivy-curtained walls resembling a fairy-tale cottage blown up to manor-size. I entered through the back door and conjured up a glass of wine. Whether it came from inside Faerie or was simply a creation of magic, I hadn't a clue, but with the faeries, it was usually better not to ask.

Light glimmered in the corner of my eye. I lowered my glass and damn near threw it at the person standing in in the darkness like a living statue. The mark on my forehead pulsed with magic, alerting me to the threat. *Little too late there.*

"Your Gatekeeper's Trials will begin tomorrow," the man said, his voice soft and yet precise, layered with the hint of a threat.

My grip tightened on the glass. I could have layered the house in a thousand alarms and tripwire spells and none of them would have kept out a Sidhe messenger from the Summer Court. They owned the place, after all.

"At least turn on the light if you're going to interrupt my evening," I said to the intruder.

The house obliged, the kitchen lights flickering on and illuminating a tall, lean faerie, clad in green attire that marked him as a Seelie messenger. His eyes glimmered with a greenish-blue sheen as he ducked his head, allowing locks of pale silver hair to fall over his sculpted cheekbones.

Don't let their pretty faces fool you. Sidhe magic was designed to draw humans into their orbit and ensnare their senses until by the time the claws came out, it was already too late.

The same curse that bound my family to serve the Sidhe gave me some degree of immunity to their charms, enough to tell me this dude was half-human. Sidhe magic caused human senses to short-circuit from sheer over-whelm and all descriptions to slide through my fingers like sand. Half-Sidhe didn't have quite the same dazzling effect on the senses, and my annoyance at this rude arse-hole who'd broken into my house won out over the primal terror inspired by the sight of an otherworldly visitor.

I propped my free hand on my hip. "You could have come through the gate instead of sneaking in here and lurking around in the dark, you know. I was standing right there."

Not that it was really a surprise. The Sidhe, as a rule, did not pass up an opportunity to make a dramatic entrance. Besides, I was glad nobody had witnessed the DJ's attempted escape into the grove. Nobody outside of my family was supposed to know the Inner Garden existed.

"Did you hear me?" he said. "Tomorrow, you'll be inducted as Gatekeeper."

I returned his scowl with a smile. "Heard you loud and clear. Might you elaborate on the time? I was hoping to enjoy the rest of this."

I lifted the wine glass and took a measured sip, gaining some measure of satisfaction out of winding up the dickhead who'd kept me waiting in limbo for months and then decided to wreck what was left of my evening.

A muscle ticked in his jaw, as though he found me as irritating as I found him. To most fae, my very *existence* was an inconvenience.

"Nine in the morning by your time," he said. "If you're late, you will find yourself transported directly into the Summer Court no matter where you happen to be, if you're thinking of shirking your duty. If you're asleep, or in the mortal realm, the same rule will apply."

"Really." I lowered the glass. "What if I was in the middle of a threesome? Would the other people be transported into Faerie, too? Because that would get kind of awkward for all of us."

His eyes narrowed. "If you are with another person or persons when the hour strikes, you will all be transported to Faerie. Unlike you, no other humans will be protected against harm. If you would like to begin your Gatekeeper's training with innocent deaths on your conscience, by all means, do as you like."

"No need for that," I said. "I'm impressed you know what a conscience is. I assumed the Sidhe thought it was just another name for a weapon."

"Is it not just that?" he said. "Feeling pain for others is as damaging as any wound inflicted with a blade and may prove equally fatal."

"Remind me not to hire you to write me a motivational speech." I gave him an eye-roll. "Relax. I won't be late, and I won't bring any friends. Faerie's not on anyone's bucket list as a tourist destination."

Including mine, for that matter, but I hadn't exactly had a choice. And now my short-lived freedom had come to an end.

"See to it that you keep your word, human."

He turned on his heel and left, vanishing into thin air.

"Great to meet you, too," I said to the space where he'd vanished. *Sidhe.* For beings who prided themselves on impeccable manners, they seemed to take pleasure in making an exception for me. I didn't blame Dad for leaving when I was a kid, because being around the Sidhe was a lot to handle when you were human.

I glanced at my half-full glass, tempted to switch it for a bottle, but I needed to be in top shape for my induction. Besides, Mum was going to be thrilled to know one of *them* had slipped by the house's defences.

Putting down the glass, I turned off the lights and then crossed the kitchen to the back door. Judging by the steady thumping noise from the shed adjacent to the house, Mum was still up. I'd more or less forced her to build the place after her violent workout sessions kept waking me up in the middle of the night. The joys of living with a retired Gatekeeper with a shit-ton of pent-up rage.

I pushed open the shed door and stepped in, careful to stay out of striking range. Gatekeeper powers or none, Mum could still kick the crap out of me with little effort. Her blond-tinted hair was twisted into a topknot to keep it out her face, her forehead slick with sweat. We shared the same figure—strong and curvy, not skinny or fragile—and expressive eyes. Mine had turned bright green when I'd got my magic, while hers had reverted to their original brown colour after her retirement. Her fists struck the punching bag again and again, as though she was imagining pounding a Sidhe's pretty face to a pulp.

"I thought you were in Edinburgh," she said, without turning around.

"A fae was bewitching humans at a nightclub and I had to haul him over to the Court," I said. "Also, the Sidhe's messenger showed up in our kitchen. The Trials start tomorrow."

She dropped her hands. "They came inside the house?"

"Didn't even knock." I walked to the punching bag next to hers and gave it a whack with my knuckles. "Guess this is it."

"I should have checked the date." She picked up a discarded towel and wiped the sweat from her forehead—unmarked, though she'd once worn the same silver symbol as I did. "I assumed they'd wait until the solstice, but tomorrow's May the first. Beltane."

"It is?" I hit the punching bag again, imagining it resembled the face of the half-Sidhe who'd ambushed me in the kitchen. "They couldn't just show up on a regular Tuesday or whatever, huh."

The Lynn house sat in a liminal space between the two worlds, but time here matched Earth, not Faerie. Beltane was the first day of summer, though most mortals thought summer began on the solstice in June—a fitting day for the Seelie Court to formalise their claim on me.

"Are you prepared?" Mum said. "You know what this means."

Did I ever. Once I was Gatekeeper, anonymity would be a thing of the past. No more sneaking around arresting fae criminals without causing a scene. "Sure. I know what to expect from them."

Her expression softened a little. "I know you do."

Mum had kept a deliberate emotional distance from myself and my siblings for most of my life. She could never guarantee that she wouldn't die on the job, or that the Sidhe wouldn't break their own rules and order us all to be slaughtered. For that reason, we'd never been close, but she and I had bonded over fighting classes and weaponry even before I'd developed my Gatekeeper powers at twelve. Ilsa preferred to bury her head in a book, while Morgan had wanted to spend as little time in the Lynn House as possible. Considering I'd grown up more or less alone with a mother who spent half her life in Faerie, you might be surprised I hadn't turned out more dysfunctional than I had.

"Guess I should text Ilsa. I just had to wreck her big day."

"I'll tell her," said Mum. "You get some sleep."

What she wanted to say was *I'll keep you safe.* But just because the Sidhe were honour-bound not to harm the Gatekeeper didn't mean the rest of the Faerie would do the same. Once I stepped foot in the Summer Court, it was on me to stay alive by any means necessary. Mum had told me the initiation tests for new Gatekeepers were different for each of us, just to keep us on our toes. It wasn't in their interest to fail us, but if we couldn't cut it in the Trials, we'd never survive out there in Faerie.

My hands curled into fists. By taking on the Gatekeeper's Trials, I'd ensure the faeries left the rest of my family alone, and I'd protect the humans in my life from being a part of their twisted games. As long as I lived, I would honour that promise.

Whatever I had to do to keep it.

2

The Summer gate loomed before me, its sharpened points gleaming. An otherworldly humming noise rang in the air, while a dark void loomed beyond the thin thread of magic holding the gates together.

The Seelie Queen stood beside the gate—tall, beautiful, flaxen-haired, and with a smile that could topple empires. But she wasn't smiling now. Her eyes were fixed on the human figure chained in front of the gates. Mum struggled against her bonds, and behind her, dark shapes stirred, yearning to break out of the gates.

I'd watched this scene a thousand times over the last few months, but I still flinched inside whenever the Seelie Queen pulled out the knife. With a cry, I slammed into her from the side, knocking off her aim before she could carve out my mother's heart. The Seelie Queen's mouth twisted into a snarl, transforming her beautiful features into grotesque rage. "You pathetic mortals."

The gate rattled in its frame, a nightmarish shape

appearing etched against the darkness of the void, drawing closer by the second. Mum's Gatekeeper powers weren't enough to restrain it. The Seelie Queen had taken too much.

Mum looked directly at me. "Hazel," she said. "Are you ready to take on the position as Gatekeeper?"

"Don't you dare!" I screamed.

"The only way to close the gate is to surrender its magic to the next Gatekeeper." Her mouth pressed together, her face set in the stubborn manner I knew well. "It's the only way to end this."

The Seelie Queen lunged at Mum, only to crash into the Erlking's staff. He caught her by the throat, magic coiling from his fingertips and wrapping around her. While his elegant face was as stunning as his wife's, cold shadows twisted around his fingertips as the magic radiating off his staff ate away at her defences.

Beside the bitterly struggling couple, Mum dropped to her knees. When she looked up, the Gatekeeper's symbol had vanished from her forehead, and the green light in her eyes had dimmed.

"There must be a Gatekeeper," intoned the Erlking. "If nobody steps up to take this power, the gate will be the enemy's to take."

"I'll take it!" I shouted. "I'm the next in line. I accept the position."

Green light flared across my vision, then a burning pain tore into my forehead, the sensation of the Gatekeeper's mark carving its way deep into my skin…

The trill of an alarm cut through the dream and I woke up, drenched in cold sweat. Fumbling for my alarm, I turned it off, shielding my eyes against the light piercing through the curtains. I flopped back on my pillows, my heart thudding against my ribcage, my breaths quick, urgent. Across from me, the Summer Gatekeeper's circlet sat beside the mirror, edged in silver and green. Waiting for me.

I might have no regrets about stepping up to take on the position as Gatekeeper, but I'd be lying if I didn't say I dreaded seeing the Erlking's face again. While he wasn't the person who'd tricked my ancestor into binding his entire family to Faerie, I suspected he was at least culpable in ensuring my family served the Sidhe forever. Compared to his wife, though, the guy was a saint.

After a quick shower, I dressed in my faerie-made clothing, a plain shirt and trousers made of a soft, flexible material. On one wrist, I wore an iron band engraved with my family name, a present from Ilsa that would be my sole anchor to humanity once I stepped into the realm of the fae. My glamour snapped into place, turning into a knee-length coat embossed in green and gold and concealing the band from sight. I carried a single iron blade, while my other weapons were forged from bone and bark. That might sound odd by human standards, but trust me, being impaled by a sharpened branch is bloody painful.

Finally, I could delay no longer. Picking up the circlet, I turned it over in my hands. I'd been stealing Mum's spare one to play dress-up since I could walk, yet this felt more of a façade than any of those childhood games. In the mirror, I spotted Mum's reflection over my shoulder. She took one step towards me, then two, closing the distance until she stood close enough to touch the circlet herself.

I gave a nod, a small gesture that served as permission, and she lifted the circlet to my brow. At once, it melded to my scalp like a second skin. My reflection stood taller, her bearing more regal. Like a Sidhe, or a human masquerading as one of them.

I tore my gaze away and checked my phone. A message from Ilsa; *good luck.* And another from Morgan: *don't die.*

Encouraging.

I left the phone in my bedroom—technology didn't work in Faerie—and went downstairs to grab breakfast before the Sidhe came to call.

The house hummed with a quiet background noise that followed me through the hall as I munched on an apple. Someone—probably Morgan—had stuck fake moustaches on all the portraits of our ancestors. I pulled a face at the oldest portrait, which showed a handsome dark-haired man, the likeness of Thomas Lynn himself. Nobody knew for definite what he'd looked like, since he'd vanished shortly after his two daughters had been hauled off into Faerie and nobody had seen him since. One day, my own portrait would join the line, but for now, a crayoned of me riding a unicorn in a field of wild-flowers occupied the blank stretch of wall where the portraits ended. Ilsa had drawn it when we were kids, back when Faerie hadn't seemed to truly exist outside of our imaginations. Personally, I thought the lack of unicorns was one of the biggest disappointments of the reality.

When the clock struck five to nine, I tossed my apple core into the bin and let myself out of the house. Mum didn't come to see me off, but saying goodbyes wasn't our strong suit. I reached the gate at dead on nine, yet no Sidhe appeared to spirit me away. Looked like last night's visitor's warnings about punctuality were all talk.

I pushed open the gates, revealing the path into the Summer Court. A wide track bathed in sunlight gleamed invitingly between tall oak trees older than anything on Earth. A group of tall, lean figures stood waiting a short distance away. *A welcoming committee. How nice.*

The Sidhe turned on me, and the clamour of a dozen swords withdrawing from their sheaths crackled in the air like fireworks.

"Whoa." I halted, inches away from the gleaming points of their blades. "I'm Hazel Lynn, the Summer Gatekeeper. I know I was supposed to wait to be called, but I thought you liked punctuality…" I trailed off. I'd expected to see disgust on their faces at the sight of me, or boredom, or simple annoyance. Not pure unadulterated rage. A half-dozen pairs of vivid green eyes shone with enough magic to render a regular human catatonic. I took a step back, my heartbeat accelerating.

"Stay there," ordered one of the Sidhe. Tall and dark-haired, he wore a long black coat edged in green and enough layers of glamour that he could have resembled a baboon underneath and I wouldn't have been able to tell.

His companion was a female Sidhe with olive skin and luscious curling dark hair. We'd met before, but Lady Aiten's gaze held no signs of recognition, and from the expression on her face, you'd think I'd mortally insulted her entire family. *What happened? Did DJ Thorntooth escape and get into Lord Niall's stash of elf wine?*

For all the rumours that the Sidhe had little understanding of human emotions, I'd witnessed more temper tantrums from faeries than I had humans, and most humans didn't have enough power in their fingertips to level a building. As Mum said: "It's not that the Sidhe don't have feelings. It's that they're convinced that their feelings are the only ones that matter."

In other words, hell hath no fury like a faerie slightly inconvenienced.

"Can someone please tell me what's going on here?" I kept my voice calm, as though there weren't a dozen sharpened blades pointing at my exposed throat.

Another Sidhe stepped forward. In daylight, the man who'd broken into my house yesterday looked even more eerily beautiful. Curtains of shoulder-length silver hair framed startling aquamarine eyes, which I'd never seen on any Sidhe from either Summer or Winter. His human parent must have been a serious looker. Pity they'd probably died for it.

Faeries liked collecting pretty things. They didn't necessarily let them *stay* that way. The few humans who survived Faerie returned as husks of their former selves, doomed to wither away to nothing.

"The Erlking," he said, "is dead."

The words took a moment to connect in my mind. The Sidhe didn't lie, or joke, though I was pretty sure they were allergic to humour—or at least the type of humour that humans understood.

"How?" I swallowed hard, my throat dry. *It's not possible.*

"Iron poisoning," said Lady Aiten.

Iron in Faerie? In the Erlking's territory? Nobody was supposed to be able to get near him. His talisman ensured it, and I'd never forget the shadowy magic swirling around his staff, draining the essence from every living thing it came into contact with.

"How did iron get into Faerie?" said the dark-haired Sidhe. "Perhaps a *human* brought it with them?"

"A human who's accessed his territory before?" added Lady Aiten.

I held up my hands. "Look, I appreciate that you're under a lot of stress right now, but I just got here. I swear I didn't lay a finger on the king. I didn't know he was dead. I'm here for my Gatekeeper's Trials—"

"You killed him and stole his talisman," said Lady Aiten. "Do you deny it?"

"I didn't kill him, and nobody can touch his talisman." Not without turning to dust, anyway. While regular Summer magic originated from nature and existed in balance with it, the Erlking's talisman contained a dark reversal of that power, a rare type of magic that drained the life force from anyone who got too close. As far as I knew, the one exception to the rule was the Seelie Queen, whose healing magic allowed her to touch the staff without crumbling to ashes. *The one thing I cannot destroy,* he'd called her. Not a happy marriage, that one.

The dark-haired Sidhe's spear brushed my throat. "I'd say we kill her as a deterrent to any others who may cross us."

"We cannot kill her yet," said Lady Aiten. "Not until she hands over the crown."

"The... crown?" I leaned out of range of the spear's sharp point. "You mean someone stole that, too?"

Without the crown, the Sidhe couldn't elect a new monarch. No wonder they'd lost their minds. Mortality was a sensitive issue here in Faerie at the best of times, given their longevity, but the Erlking had ruled over the Court for hundreds of years. There'd never been another monarch as long as the Gatekeepers had existed. Now he'd departed, sending them spiralling into an existential crisis which might drag everyone in all the realms into its orbit.

"Yes," said Lady Aiten. "No doubt so we would be unable to crown a replacement until we caught the murderer. How fortunate that she delivered herself into our hands."

I looked between the Sidhe. "I'm bound by a vow to serve the Summer Court on pain of death. I wouldn't risk that by murdering the guy in charge. Besides, the Erlking's wife was jailed last year for an attempted coup. This is her handiwork, I guarantee it."

"The Seelie Queen remains behind bars, mortal," said the dark-haired Sidhe. "She has had no contact with the outside world."

Yeah, but she's also the one person in Faerie who can't be affected by the Erlking's talisman. Not that it made a difference to the Sidhe. They'd labelled me as guilty, and humans, unlike the Sidhe, could lie.

"She's perfectly capable of getting someone else to do her dirty work for her," I said, undeterred. "She also hates my family, since we got her jailed in the first place, so she'd have an incentive to make us look guilty."

Mutters broke out among the Sidhe. Then the dude who'd broken into my house stepped forwards. "I will handle the interrogation, as the Gatekeeper is my charge. Come with me."

Say what?

The Sidhe lowered their weapons to allow the two of

us to walk into the woods, and I quickened my pace to keep up with my rescuer. "Charge? What do you mean by that?"

Instead of answering, he said, "Do you know what the Erlking's talisman can do?"

Nice try. "If I had that talisman," I said, "you'd know about it."

"You didn't answer my question."

"I don't know if the Erlking would have trusted you with that information," I said bluntly.

His jaw locked. Oh, he didn't like that I'd implied the Sidhe had entrusted me with more information than him. But what was I supposed to do, go blabbing the Erlking's secrets to every stranger I ran into? Someone in the Court had been involved in his death, and for all I knew, they were still here. While the Erlking had placed Ilsa and me under a spell so that we could never speak a word of the talisman to anyone who didn't already know, I suspected the vow had unravelled now he was dead.

The half-Sidhe halted at a clearing edged in thick oak trees and regarded me with those startling aquamarine eyes. "I could torture the information out of you."

"You could try." I held my fists clenched at my sides and met his stare. "I am no thief, nor a murderer. Believe it or not, I have no desire to see the Courts fall into chaos. Nobody in my family killed the king."

The half-Sidhe gestured towards a tangle of bushes marking the side of the clearing. A hunched shape pushed through the trees, towering two feet or more above me. Tusks sprouted from its jaws, while its leathery skin looked as tough as concrete.

"What is this, a test?" I looked the beast up and down.

A common garden-variety troll—not that you'd want to find one in your garden—with meaty fists, flat feet the size of sledges, and a dopey expression that indicated it had no idea how it'd got here.

"We found this troll roaming around a human village, attacking its inhabitants," he informed me. "If you fail to kill it, I will allow it to finish the job."

Oh, you complete dickhead.

The troll locked eyes with me. Then it charged. I lunged to the side, throwing myself flat to avoid its swinging fists. Rolling to my feet, I unsheathed my iron blade. The knife's point glanced off its leathery knuckles, and the half-Sidhe glared at me.

"What?" I backed up a step. "If you were human, you'd carry iron, too. Otherwise, I might as well walk into a lion's den with a slab of raw meat strapped to my chest."

The troll swung a meaty fist. I caught the blow with my knife, tearing a chunk of flesh from its knuckles. Its nails were long and filthy, and smelled as bad as they looked. I whirled, dealing a vicious slice to its ankle, but the beast didn't get the message that it'd messed with the wrong human.

I pivoted, slicing into its upper thigh in search of an artery. Dark blood splattered the earth, and the beast's leg gave way. I darted backwards, avoiding the solid thump as its knees slammed into the ground.

"See you in hell." I raised the blade over its head.

Before the blow could make contact, the beast disintegrated beneath me, my blade connecting with empty air and sending me sprawling flat on my face. The scent of earth filled my nostrils, and even the blood had vanished.

The whole thing was a glamour. A three-dimensional, breathing glamour. *Holy fuck. Who is this guy?*

The half-Sidhe was breathing heavily as though he'd run a great distance, but he straightened upright when he caught me looking. I climbed to my feet, sheathing my knife. Not a droplet of blood speckled the knife's edges. He had some serious skills for a half-blood.

"You're not the killer," he said.

I brushed dirt from my knees. "Huh?"

"The murderer also took down the Erlking's security troll," he went on. "They left distinctive marks from their weapons, and their fighting style doesn't match yours."

"Wait, *that's* what the test was for? It wasn't part of my Gatekeeper's Trials?"

"You passed, regardless," he said. "Your family will be sent home until further notice."

"You mean you aren't arresting me?" What the hell was the point in all the deception, then? "Okay, then. Show's over. Take me home."

"You'll be staying here," he said. "With me."

"I'm sorry, what?" I said. "Who even are you?"

"My name is Darrow," he said. "And I am in charge of the Gatekeeper's Trials."

3

"*Y*ou're in charge of the Trials?" I said to the half-Sidhe—Darrow.

"Yes," he said. "The circumstances are less than ideal, but the Gatekeeper will play a key role in crowning a new monarch."

Might be hard without a crown. His sharp gaze told me he knew exactly what I was thinking, and I scowled right back at him. Not only had he accused me of murder and manipulated me, the stunt he'd pulled with the illusory troll told me he wasn't interested in playing fair. He'd let the Sidhe throw me into a pit of redcaps if he liked.

I left the clearing and retraced my steps to the main path by the gate. The Sidhe's group had scattered, but I spotted Lady Aiten and her dark-haired friend walking away in the direction of the main Court.

"Excuse me," I said.

The dark-haired Sidhe turned on me, his glamour hitting me smack in the face like the faerie equivalent of someone wearing overpowering aftershave. The sharp point of a spear brushed my breastbone. "Leave, Gatekeeper."

"Hey," I said. "Stop pointing that thing at me. I'm not the killer. Your guy here tested me and proved it. I'd like to request another mentor, because I don't trust someone who accused me of murder to uphold the Gatekeeper's vows."

Not that I'd expected any of the Sidhe to think I was worthy of being treated as an equal, but this Darrow guy was the lowest possible authority.

"Get back here." Darrow's voice carried a dangerous edge. "You must accept me as your tutor or else forfeit the position as Gatekeeper."

"At least prove that my family is safe from further accusations." If I'd been Sidhe, they'd have been tripping over themselves to apologise, but they'd never have accused me in the first place had I been one of them.

Lady Aiten turned to her fellow Sidhe. "I see nothing wrong in allowing her to see her family leaving the Court."

"I suppose not," said Lord Pointy Spear. "But if the Gatekeeper refuses to take on the Trials, her family will be staying with us for much longer."

My hands fisted and I suppressed the impulse to flatten his glamour-perfect nose. "I never said I wouldn't take on the Trials."

"Then there shouldn't be a problem," said Lady Aiten.

Not for you, maybe.

A flash of light bathed the path in bright green, and Mum appeared in front of the two Sidhe, her eyes shining with emotion she couldn't voice in front of her cold-eyed audience. "Hazel."

"Glad you're okay." I gave Darrow a sideways glance, sure he'd be scanning me for weaknesses, but his gaze was on his fellow Sidhe. "What about Ilsa and Morgan?"

"They're at home," she said. "They weren't accused."

She means they're still in Edinburgh. "I'll come home as soon as I can."

In other words, whenever Darrow decided to let me go, which might be days or weeks in human time.

Lady Aiten walked behind Mum to escort her through the gate. Lord Pointy Spear remained on the path, while Darrow kept an eye on him. From their body language, the Sidhe didn't like him and the feeling was mutual. Small wonder, because on a surface level, it looked as though he'd inherited the lion's share of his Sidhe parent's magic.

I'll have to duel this guy at some point in our training. That means I should probably figure out how to get the best of him.

Aside from iron, faeries were vulnerable to brute force. They relied on their speed and graceful balance to dodge attacks, but when they got hit, they went down hard. They also lacked physical strength and leaned heavily on their magic to deal damage. I hadn't seen Darrow fight yet, but given his proficiency with glamour, I'd bet it played a major part in his fighting style. A half-faerie mentor was closer to my equal than a Sidhe would be, so at least I had that going for me.

The Summer gate closed behind Mum, and without another word, Lady Aiten and her companion retreated down the path, leaving me alone with Darrow.

All right. My family was safe, out of reach of the Sidhe. Now the rest was up to me.

"All right, Darrow," I said. "I can call you that, right?"

From his silence, I guessed that was a 'yes'.

"I think we got off on the wrong foot," I went on. "So, let's start over. Do you have a family name?"

"I do." He didn't elaborate.

This was going well. "My name is Hazel. Just in case you wanted a change from 'Gatekeeper'."

He indicated the path to the clearing. "We will walk this way, Gatekeeper."

Well. If *that* didn't tell me where I stood. "Okay, whatever you say."

The forest rustled around us, ancient oaks older than human history reaching finger-like branches to the vibrant blue sky. As a creation of magic, the realm existed in a state of eternal summer, the flowers never wilting, the trees evergreen, the skies unmarked by a single cloud. Fragrant smells of jasmine and honeysuckle drifted on the breeze, mingling with the earthy scents of the under-growth as Darrow's faerie-swift steps led the way down the well-trodden path to the clearing. I kept an eye out for any more glamoured trolls, but it seemed I'd have to wait to see which trick he planned to pull out of his hat next.

"You will face a number of Trials," he said, without turning around. "They'll test your ability to handle all that Faerie might send your way, from glamours to the elements, beasts and natural forces. You also won't be permitted to use iron."

"Iron is as much of an advantage as magic." I folded my arms, feeling the outline of the engraved wristband under my glamoured clothes. No way was I removing *that*. "You'd use it if our positions were reversed."

"Yes," he said. "I would. But those are the rules. No iron. You'll fight as what you are—an inferior mortal."

"You're such a charmer, do you know that?" I halted behind him as we reached the clearing. "What's on the agenda today, then?"

"Today, I will test your limits." He turned around and extended a hand. "Give me the iron."

I unsheathed the blade and held it out handle-first, and he took it without so much as flinching. Oddly, he didn't wear gloves. No half-faerie could stand the touch of iron for long, but he tossed the knife aside as though it were nothing more than a branch.

I checked my other weapons remained within easy reach. "Who will I be duelling? You?"

"Yes." He drew a sharpened blade. "Show me what you've got."

"Was the troll not enough?" I whipped out one of my carved wooden blades. "Hand to hand, weapons, or anything goes?"

He stabbed at me in answer. I dodged, whirling, and our blades clashed. He was as fast as I'd expected—more so, if anything—and a flicker of panic stirred within me. The earlier fight and my near-arrest had sapped more of my energy than I'd have liked. I pushed the raw, fragile human part of me aside and drew on my years of training.

I knew what to expect from Faerie by now. No mercy.

Our blades collided, neither of us giving ground to the other. He moved too fast for me to pinpoint any weak angles, and he fought equally well with both hands. It was standard training in Faerie, and my education had mirrored theirs in some ways. While I'd never fought a Sidhe, I'd spent half my school days sitting in detention for starting fights with the local half-faeries for picking on my siblings. I found myself grateful for those indelicate brawls now, yet no matter how many dirty tricks I tried, Darrow's composure never wavered.

Despite his skill, he never used magic, though he hadn't said it wasn't allowed. Fending him off with my blade, I called the Gatekeeper's power to my free hand and sent a ball of green energy at him. The bolt of green light struck the earth, coalescing into a thorny mass that forced him to step out of range.

Bolstered, I followed up with two more short bursts of green energy. Thorny bushes boxed him in on either side, yet he didn't slow, nor did he show any visible alarm. Our blades clashed, over and over. Sweat drenched my back and plastered my hair to my forehead. *He's going to fight until one of us collapses.*

I directed my magic at the thorny plants, and their stems twisted around his ankles, climbing to his weapon hand. Then my blade found his throat. "Surrender."

Blue light suffused his eyes, and the thorns shattered into fragments as though they were made of glass.

In my split second of shock, he raised his sword and knocked the blade from my hand, sending me flying off my feet. I landed on my back, finding the point of a sword at my own throat. Shards of broken thorn dug into my spine. They'd frozen solid. *No way.*

"Bloody hell," I said. "You're a hybrid."

He could use Winter *and* Summer magic. Both his parents must be half-blood—one Seelie, one Unseelie—which also explained his oddly coloured eyes. Few half-Sidhe of his ancestry had abilities in both types of magic, since one tended to win out over the other.

He lifted his blade from my neck. "Get up."

I pushed myself onto my elbows. "I'm impressed."

It wouldn't kill him to be a little less frosty with me, even if he did have Unseelie ancestry. Okay, he was probably discouraged from making friends with the Gatekeeper, but it'd been a genuinely fun sparring contest, and I'd gone into it expecting to lose. After all, it'd be a short partnership if I kicked his arse before the Trials even started.

He waited for me to stand, then said, "If you choose to proceed with your Gatekeeper's Trials, there's a compulsory binding ceremony you must attend. Since the investigation into the Erlking's murder is taking much of the Court's attention, we will be completing the ceremony alone."

"Sure." Since he didn't oblige, I fetched my iron knife from where he'd thrown it. His gaze cut to me, sharp as the blade point. "What? I'm not going to use the knife on you. I'm taking it home."

The knife had been a present from my siblings, and I wouldn't leave it behind in Faerie.

"Keep it sheathed," he said. "And don't show it to anyone if you desire to walk out of Faerie with your life."

"All right, keep your hair on." I returned the knife to its former place, my hands still shaking a little from the exertion of our battle. "That was a good match. I enjoyed it."

He made no response. Instead, he led the way out of the clearing and walked a short distance through the woods until we came to a meadow of knee-deep grass. The air was thick with heat yet somehow not stifling, while magic's vibrant scent mingled with the fragrant scents of flowers that never ceased to bloom. The sound of a nearby river flowing formed a soothing backdrop, yet otherwise, the Court seemed oddly quiet. No Sidhe riding along the paths on their immortal steeds, no chattering nereids bathing in the streams, no dryads' trees rustling with gossip. Had the Sidhe told everyone of the Erlking's passing yet? Had Winter found out? Questions buzzed in my ears like a swarm of bees, urging me to break the silence.

"Why do I need to do this binding ceremony?" I asked. "I thought I was already bound to serve your Court." It wasn't like I could ever forget it. If I tried to walk too far away from the Ley Line dividing earth from Faerie, the magic of the family curse would kick in and more or less drag me back there. Should I ignore it… well, I had no desire for my dismembered body to end up scattered all over the Scottish Highlands, so I hadn't tested the limits to that extent.

"Before you take the Gatekeeper's Trials, you will be required to swear that you will accept the position of Gatekeeper, should you pass."

"I thought that was in the job description." When his expression went blank, I added, "The second I was chosen as Gatekeeper, I was entered to take the Trials by default. I'm not all that keen on the alternative."

Namely, being torn to pieces by the backlash of a broken vow.

"I suppose you wouldn't be," said Darrow. "However, the binding has another requirement."

"Like what?" Nobody had mentioned a binding. Was it a new thing, or had Mum been ordered not to speak of it to me?

"The binding will make me aware of your movements at any given time," he said. "And if, say, you were to trespass out of bounds, I would know."

"Where would I possibly go?" *That's not good. I don't want to literally be tied to him, thanks.* "I can't say I'm all that keen to pay a visit to Winter."

"I'm told you and the Winter heir are friends."

"I wouldn't go that far," I said. "Have you met Holly yet? Did you train her?"

"I'm not at liberty to discuss my previous assignments."

Right, right. The Sidhe held both of us on a tight leash. He was probably vow-bound not to spread intel gained from the Summer Court with Winter, and vice versa.

Though come to think of it, did that mean the Winter Court employed him, too? I hadn't thought Summer invited people onto their territory who held divided loyalties. Half-bloods weren't born as part of a Court and bound to serve from birth as the Sidhe were, so it was possible he hadn't told them, but deceiving the Sidhe was riskier than prodding a sleeping ogre with a stick.

Our route took us past villages and large estates, yet we never encountered a soul. My skin prickled with unease, and it was almost a relief when a group of chittering piskies flew overhead, tugging at my hair. I swatted them away and carried on walking down the path flanked by leafy plants which led to the ambassadors' palace.

"I know the circumstances are less than ideal," I said to Darrow. "But you could stand to be a little friendlier."

"The Summer Court is in turmoil the likes of which hasn't been seen in generations." His tone was even, his words precise. "It will be your role to see the Court into a new age and either steer it on the right path or watch it crumble."

"Oh, no." I raised my hands. "I'm not obligated to do

anything but stop the Sidhe from letting their warriors wreak havoc on earth." *Again.* "Besides, they don't *want* me to help them. They were five seconds from executing me earlier."

"The Sidhe's behaviour is the result of fear. Not only have they faced death, they've also lost their leader, who they thought to be eternal."

"You don't seem scared." Then again, he was half-blood. He'd live a human lifespan, same as me. While the Sidhe's glamour hid their real ages, he likely wasn't much older than I was, either.

"Your point?" The elaborately carved gate that marked the entrance to the ambassadors' palace opened at his touch. Anyone who didn't know the Erlking's circumstances might assume the impressive palace was the monarch's home, but the opulent building was nothing more than a meeting point for Sidhe ambassadors.

I walked behind him to the oak doors. "Just making an observation."

He'd spoken in a calm, dispassionate tone, not at all like someone who faced the potential destruction of their home. *He can't be that attached to Summer, then.* Most half-bloods idolised the Courts to an unhealthy degree, even those who grew up in the mortal realm. They placed the Sidhe—and the Erlking above all—on a pedestal.

The oak doors creaked inward, inviting us into the cavernous hall. Inside, nature warred with extravagance, as though the Sidhe who'd built it hadn't been able to decide whether they wanted it to look like a greenhouse or a palace. Golden flowers grew up the walls and all over the ceiling, gleaming like jewels, while birds and piskies flew around unchecked. Tall glass windows invited sunlight into the hall, and I shielded my eyes from the glare. "Why did the Sidhe select you to oversee my training if you're not from the Court?"

"Who told you I wasn't?" A glint appeared in his eyes, and magic whispered over my skin, setting my heart racing. Maybe picking a fight with the guy the Sidhe had chosen to oversee my training wasn't a spectacular idea, but neither was binding myself to him without knowing who the hell he was.

"If you were from the Court, you'd be with the Sidhe, running around panicking about the Erlking's death." I couldn't seem to stop digging myself into a hole. When I was nervous or stressed, my mouth ran away with me without consulting my brain first.

"You're certainly judgemental, even by human standards."

"I made the judgement when two of them tried to skewer me for a murder I can't possibly have committed."

"Anything is possible here." His tone carried a hint of warning, and my reply died in my throat. Did he have an idea who the killer might be? In my inexpert judgement, I'd pin the blame on someone from Winter or the jailed Seelie Queen. Or most likely, someone acting on her behalf. Someone with uncanny fighting abilities and access to iron.

Darrow has extraordinary magic... and he handled the iron without any obvious pain.

A chill raced down my spine. I had no power to make accusations, but what better way to hide from suspicion than to volunteer to train the Gatekeeper? If I were the killer, I might have made a similar choice. On the other hand, if I started channelling the Sidhe's paranoia, it'd make the whole experience even more unpleasant for both of us.

Darrow led me through a side door into a room decorated with tapestries depicting scenes of bloodshed and battle, revelry and laughter. A set of concentric circles marked the room's centre, formed from glowing runes in the language of the ancient fae. Darrow halted at the circle's edge. "We will do the binding here."

Apprehension dug its heels in. Despite my wayward thoughts, I didn't really think he was the Erlking's murderer, but his unfriendly behaviour did nothing to quell my apprehension about the binding. "You're saying the bond will only last until I pass the Gatekeeper's Trials, right?"

"Correct," he said. "It gives me no pleasure to be tethered to you for longer than that."

"You're such a heart-breaker." I clutched a hand to my chest over my genuinely thumping heart. I did *not* want to entwine myself in yet another bloody faerie vow. Everyone knew not to make a promise to a faerie if they could avoid it, and the eternal promise my ancestor had made cemented that rule in my mind. *Mum must have done something like this, too, surely. It's not permanent.*

"Step into the circle and extend your right hand." He did so himself, pushing up his sleeve to expose his tanned forearm. Magic hummed to the surface, and while he must possess two currents of magic running below the surface, I only felt the buzz of Summer magic against my palm as I held out my own wrist until our hands were almost touching.

Below our feet, the circles glowed. Thorny vines shot

up from the centre, entwining around our hands, and it took all my willpower not to wrench my arm away.

"Will you take on the Gatekeeper's Trials?" Darrow's aquamarine eyes bored into mine.

"I will take on the Gatekeeper's Trials." The vines wrapped around both of our arms, tightly enough that they should have drawn blood—yet when they let me go, the skin was unbroken. Only a faint mark in the shape of the faeries' rune for 'Gatekeeper' on my wrist indicated the vow existed at all.

"It is done," said Darrow.

"That was intimate." I rolled my eyes at the icy expression on his face. "Relax. I've no intention of failing, and to be honest, I didn't want a permanent bond to a guy who looks at me like I just trod mud on his best carpet."

Instead of answering, he pointed to one of the tapestries. The edges peeled back, revealing the forest path leading up to the Summer gate.

"Go home," he said. "You will have the rest of the day to get used to the bond before you will be called back to begin your training."

"Wow, that's generous of you."

"It isn't a favour."

As though on cue, the mark on my wrist stung. Ow. Maybe it wasn't harmless after all.

"It's been great to meet you, Darrow," I said brightly. "I'm looking forward to our next sparring contest."

I strode through the tapestry and down the forest path towards home. My wrist throbbed again, the mark growing darker around the edges. *Ow.* I wondered if it was hurting Darrow the same way. Why couldn't he just take my word for it rather than forcing me to swear a vow? The Court already had me on as tight a leash as possible.

As I reached the gate, a winged shape flew over my shoulder. I raised a hand to swat at it, and a piece of paper appeared in my hand. The small winged creature gave a short bow before vanishing into thin air. Someone had sent their sprite to deliver me a message.

I turned the paper over and damn near dropped it. I knew that signature. It belonged to the Erlking.

I turned to the main text, and one line leapt out like a brand.

Do not show your mentor this note.

4

I faltered, one step from the gate, and scanned the path. The tapestry had gone, as had Darrow himself. He hadn't seen the note. Good job, considering it implied he was untrustworthy.

And I'd just bound myself to him. Fan-bloody-tastic.

Opening the gates, I stepped through into my own garden. Nobody waited for me, while I couldn't tell from the sky how much time had passed in this realm. Knowing my luck, I wouldn't get a full twenty-four hours before Darrow called me back.

I held the Erlking's note gingerly in my hand. He must have sent it to me before he died. *Me.* Why the hell had he chosen me above all the other Sidhe?

The back door opened, and Ilsa emerged. "Hazel?"

"What're you doing here?" I hurried over to my twin sister and hugged her. "The Sidhe didn't drag you in for questioning, did they?"

"No, but I came home as soon as Mum let me know she was safe." Ilsa released me, her brown eyes wide with concern. "Morgan's not here at the moment, but he knows."

We entered the house through the kitchen and found Mum standing there in the dark. She embraced both of us, not speaking. Then she walked out of the room, and I heard the sound of her study door closing.

"She's taking it well, then," I murmured to Ilsa as we made our way to the living room.

She grunted an agreement, taking a seat on the sofa. The living room looked the same as always—impeccably tidy, with crooked old furniture that Mum was attached to for some bizarre reason, and unflattering baby photos of us on every visible surface.

I sat on the other end of the sofa, moving the cushions around to form a comfy seat. My whole body ached after my sparring contest with Darrow, and I didn't know whether I wanted to hit something, scream, or take a four-hour nap. As per usual, the house picked up on my mood, and a plate of cookies appeared on the coffee table. I picked one up, biting into it. Cookies first, questions later.

Ilsa had other ideas. "Have the Sidhe arrested anyone else?"

"They practically bit my head off for suggesting it was the Seelie Queen," I said through a mouthful of chocolate chips. "Or someone acting on her behalf. She might have hired a human to do it."

Or a half-faerie with loyalties to both Courts.

"I guess." Ilsa fiddled with the hand-knitted throw on her side of the sofa. "Or someone from Winter might have. Have you seen the crime scene?"

I choked on my cookie. "The Sidhe would hire a troll

before they let *me* play detective. They haven't even told me the details of how he died."

They'd never in a million years believe the Erlking had sent me a personalised note, that was for sure.

Ilsa looked disappointed. "Then I assume they're following all the leads they have. Have they asked Holly?"

"You tell me. I haven't been here." I ate the rest of the cookie and picked up another. "My mentor might have gone to hassle her now, for all I know."

Assuming he wasn't guilty himself. I glanced down at the note folded in my free hand, dread rising in my chest.

"What's that?" asked Ilsa. Then she spotted the elaborate seal and her jaw dropped. "No way. The Erlking gave you that? When?"

"He sent a sprite to deliver it to me right as I was leaving. I haven't read it yet." I didn't *want* to. I hadn't asked to have the Erlking's murder added to my teetering pile of responsibilities. But Ilsa's curiosity was not to be assuaged. She leaned in as I unfolded the paper, and read:

One lives without breath

One breathes without life

The third line was a meaningless string of symbols, which I couldn't read.

Then: *do not show your mentor this note.*

Ilsa's brow furrowed. "Is he trying to tell you who the murderer is?"

"Who the hell knows?" I let the note slide to the carpeted floor, a sudden current of anger rushing through my blood. "He couldn't have left me simpler directions if he was going to leave me to deal with the chaos he left behind?"

"Are you sure he meant for you to have the note?"

"Nobody else in Faerie has a mentor." At least, I didn't think so. And I did have the dubious honour of being one of the few humans who'd set my eyes on his face—and his talisman.

I scooped up the note, a vice clamping around my chest. "All I know is that the staff and the crown are both missing."

Horror flashed across Ilsa's face. "You mean even if they find the heir, they can't crown another monarch?"

"I assume not." My hands twisted together, a nervous habit I'd never quite managed to shake. "I also assume he didn't know the killer was going to swipe the crown and the staff when he wrote this note. Since he wasn't dead yet. It'd help if he named an heir, too."

Unless he'd sent messages to more than one person. For all our sakes, I bloody hoped so.

"He knew someone was plotting to murder him," Ilsa said.

"That, or he spent his last few seconds of life writing me this note." I shook my head. "The note implies there was more than one killer, which seems plausible. No way was this a one-person job."

Faerie riddles were not my strong point, and if I guessed wrong, the consequences of making a false accusation would rebound on my family. Besides, the Sidhe wouldn't take my word for it alone even if I figured out the culprit, not without more proof.

I held out the paper to Ilsa and she leaned over it. "Breathes without life," she muttered. "And lives without breath. As for that language... I bet we have a translation in our library."

"I'll leave that part to you." Reading ancient faerie texts

wasn't a strength of mine, but Ilsa had a natural inclination for academics. As a bonus, she wasn't bound as tightly to the Court as I was, so the Sidhe were less likely to spy on her. "I hope sharing the note with you doesn't come back to bite me."

"Better than the Erlking's talisman," she said.

An image filled my mind, unbidden. *The Erlking sat in a throne formed of intertwining roots, surrounded by the rotting husks of dead trees, in the one part of Summer's territory where nothing grew. Tendrils of magic curled around the base of his staff, seeking life to feed on, eating away at it until there was nothing left.*

Now someone was running around with that power, unchecked. Did I know why the Sidhe were so freaked out? Hell, yes. Would I tell my mentor that? Until I knew he wasn't guilty... no. *Sorry to disappoint you, Darrow, but you have to earn my trust.*

And if he was the killer? Who was I even supposed to report him to when the Erlking was dead?

Ilsa pushed to her feet. "I'll have a look in the library."

A sudden twinge of pain spiked up my wrist. Ow. That bloody mark was at it again. "I'll speak to Mum."

"I'm here." Mum walked into the living room. "Hazel, I should have asked how your first day in Faerie went."

"Fine, except for the murder accusations." My wrist stung again. "I could have done without this binding nonsense, too. Anyway, you might want to look at the Erlking's note."

Mum was at my side in an instant. "The Erlking sent you a message?"

"Yeah." I passed her the scrap of paper. "I hope one of you can make sense of it, because I'm clueless."

While Mum read the note, Ilsa returned with a stack of books and dumped them on the coffee table. "I can start by translating that text. Then I'll look through the archives. The person who killed the Erlking might have wanted to take his place, so it might even have been one of the potential heirs who did it."

I scratched the mark on my wrist, which didn't help the stinging sensation. "Who's the heir? I didn't know there was one. The Sidhe are all related to one another anyway. And they're immortal."

Correction: they *had* been immortal. Until two years ago, when their immortality source had gone up in smoke. Now they were long-lived, but no longer immune to death, so perhaps the Erlking had personally selected a successor. He must have left some clue behind as to who it was.

Ilsa picked out a textbook which looked heavy enough to use as a battering ram. "In Winter, they elect the most powerful Sidhe as their monarch rather than following one bloodline. After their leader's time expires, they arrange a contest and everyone who wants to claim the throne is tested by the Winter Court's talisman. The one who claims it first wins the throne, and the others..."

I drew my finger across my throat, and my wrist gave another twinge. Ow. "If Summer tried that, they might lose half their Court. Bet the Unseelie will have to reconsider their methods now death is final, not temporary."

"It's not Summer's style, anyway," said Ilsa. "But if they're hunting down the Erlking's relatives, it'll take them an eternity to find the heir."

"At this rate, it won't be resolved during our lifetimes,

then," I said. "Didn't it once take them twenty years to negotiate a peace contract?"

"Yes," said Mum. "But it takes them rather less time to declare war than to negotiate peace. And in times like this…"

My chest knotted. No Lynn in living memory had ever witnessed the death of a monarch, but the Gatekeepers weren't supposed to get involved in disputes over thrones. Besides, I knew how to pick my battles. As far as I was concerned, my job was to make sure my family—and humanity as a whole—didn't pay the price for the Erlking's death.

"There must be a plan." I looked at Mum. "Please tell me the Erlking at least left a will or some kind of document naming his heir. He must have known he wouldn't stay on the throne forever."

That he'd sent me his sprite with a message was proof enough.

Mum pressed her lips together. "This is unprecedented. The Erlking was over a thousand years old and was married to the Seelie Queen before I was born, so it's unsurprising that he didn't foresee this eventuality."

"Yeah, his children will have been scattered for centuries, I imagine," I said. "As for *her,* the Sidhe blew up at me when I suggested his ex-wife might have bumped him off. Does she have a claim to any of the Erlking's property?"

"No," said Mum. "If he'd taken her on as an equal partner, it would be a different story, but she didn't share his power."

"That's why everyone thinks they married for love." How the two had agreed to their union was a total mystery to me. The Erlking's destructive magic and his wife's super-charged healing abilities were a match made in hell. Not that she wasn't a dangerous force in her own right, and if she hadn't been behind bars, she'd be sitting in the Erlking's place.

Ilsa turned the page of her book. "It'll be one of his children. Legitimacy doesn't matter to the Sidhe."

"Assuming he *had* kids," I added. "For all I know, that talisman of his made copulating difficult. I wonder how he even got married. Did he and the Seelie Queen stand on opposite sides of the room and yell the vows at one another?"

"Faerie weddings aren't—"

"I know they aren't like human ones. I was joking. Anyway, imagine how awkward the funeral will be. Everyone there will be related and will have murdered their own cousins at least once, back when death was temporary."

Ilsa winced. "Or everyone will claim to be the heir and get into a punch-up over his coffin."

"I hope I don't get an invitation, then." There hadn't been a funeral in Faerie… ever, as far as I knew. "I wonder who will get all his money. He must be loaded."

Inheritance customs among Sidhe were almost non-existent, thanks to their long-lived nature and proclivity for centuries-long family feuds. As for marriage, most Sidhe didn't practise monogamy, or at the very least, didn't select a single life partner. Eternity was a long time, and the shifting alliances, betrayals and general backstabbing didn't make for happy partnerships. Just look at the Erlking and his wife.

Half-faeries, with a shorter lifespan, were a little easier

to understand. They had no reason to crave and steal power as the Sidhe did. But that didn't mean one of them couldn't be heir, in name at least. *No way. They wouldn't let a mortal take the throne.*

"I imagine the heir will inherit everything he owned," said Mum. "Anyone might claim to be his relation, but it's a matter of whether they can wield his power."

"You mean the staff."

The staff, with its destructive magic, capable of destroying anything it touched. Whoever next wielded it would hold the fate of the Courts in their hands.

"The staff." Ilsa reached into the pocket of her grey hoody and pulled out a small, square book with a picture of a large black raven on the cover. "Maybe my talisman knows more about it."

"I thought your talisman was supposed to be an expert on the realm of Death, not Faerie." For most people, speaking about an object as though it was an intelligent being would draw raised eyebrows, but most people didn't live in a house fuelled by faerie magic straight from the Summer Court. All talismans contained a certain amount of power, but the more powerful ones attained a certain level of consciousness and influence over their owner. In Ilsa's case, the book changed its contents depending on what Ilsa wanted to know, but when it didn't feel like sharing, the pages turned blank. Like now, for instance.

Ilsa gave the book a shake, but the pages remained empty. "Don't give me that crap. I know you know more than you let on."

"And you wonder why people think we're weird." I

reached out and gave the book a prod. "I don't think it knows anything about the Erlking's talisman, Ilsa."

The book itself was supposed to be a repository of knowledge on all things related to necromancy and the afterlife, but its magic was from a source similar to the Erlking's talisman. Not Faerie, but the magic that had ruled before the Sidhe.

"That, or it's terrified of being turned to dust, too." She turned the pages. "If nothing else, it might tell me more about Death in Faerie."

My mouth parted. The Sidhe alone knew what awaited them after death, and they guarded that information fiercely. Back when their immortality source had remained intact, their souls had passed through the Death Kingdom on the edge of the Winter Court before returning to life… and that was as much as I knew.

"Anything?" I leaned over her shoulder. "Hey, you're a necromancer. There's another way to speak to the man himself."

"Oh, boy." She turned the blank page. "Please don't. Morgan already tried to talk me into asking the Sidhe to let us into the Court to summon the Erlking's ghost. You know they'd never let me, not in a million years."

"Maybe after a million years, they'll have run out of other ideas." In the human realm, hiring a necromancer to investigate a suspicious death was a common enough practice for those who could afford it. On the other hand, raising the dead in the Courts was risky for everyone, including the necromancer in question. I wouldn't ask her to do it if there were any other way to learn the Erlking's last wishes.

"Maybe." Ilsa sighed. "But he must have thought you

could solve the riddle. Besides, finding out *who* the killer is won't tell us where the staff and the crown are."

"True," I relented. "Only one person can hold the staff at any given time, and I can't imagine it's fun to carry around a talisman that kills everything it touches. There must be more than one conspirator."

Her lips pursed. "You'd think the staff would be easier to track. Someone would have noticed if it was still in the Court."

My hands twisted together. "I don't think it is."

Which left two options: the lands of the Grey Vale, where the Sidhe banished their outcasts, or in the mortal realm. The thief would have had to move fast to get it out of the Court, which at least alleviated the possibility that it was anywhere near our house. The whole place would collapse without the magic fuelling it. If it was loose in the mortal realm... well, the upside was that we'd hear about it pretty quickly.

The downside was that it might be the last time we heard anything at all. My Gatekeeper's magic only protected me against faerie magic, not the dark power of the Sidhe's terrifying predecessors. The Erlking must have hoped his immortality would shield anyone else from having to bear the burden of carrying that staff. He'd implied as much the last time we'd spoken.

For all our sakes, I hoped that wouldn't be my last interaction with a monarch of Faerie.

5

D arrow didn't call me back to the Court that evening, but the mark on my wrist kept me up all night, throbbing and twinging like a wild piskie was gnawing on my arm. I got up early and took out my anger on the punching bag, hammering it until the pain grew too intense. Showering and dressing proved difficult, too, and by the time I gave in and went through the gates, I was tempted to punch Darrow in the nose when I found him waiting on the other side. He looked irritatingly fresh-faced, his silver hair gleaming and his lean body clothed in plain black. He shouldn't look as striking as he did, but then again, faeries could make rags look like a monarch's garb.

I gave him a scowl. "I hope you had as rough a night as I did."

"I am not the person who started the binding ceremony," he said. "I believe it was set up after a past Gatekeeper tried to flee their responsibilities."

"Don't look at me." Who might that have been? Mum's

lessons had taught me some past Gatekeepers' tenures had been awfully short-lived, but I'd been more focused on emulating the ones who'd survived.

"You kept me waiting some time."

"You try showering with only one hand working." To my irritation, the pain had faded now we stood beside one another. "I'm not going to attach myself to you like a limpet until the Trials are over."

"The pain should go away after the first day or two," he said. "I've considered your proposal."

"Huh?"

"You said you preferred a different style of tutelage," he said. "And you prefer me to call you by your name… Hazel."

I frowned. "What brought this on?"

A knife flew into his hand, inches from my throat. My hand snapped up and caught his wrist, driving the blade away from my neck. With my free hand, I hammered a blow into his sternum, except he wasn't there anymore, and my hand passed through empty air.

A sweeping kick knocked my legs out from underneath me. I came upright in time for my chin to collide with Darrow's fist. I bit my tongue and tasted blood, my eyes watering with pain. He'd moved too fast even for a Sidhe—and where in hell had his knife disappeared to?

The truth hit me: he hadn't really been there. I'd been talking to an illusion while the real Darrow shadowed me, waiting to strike. The underhanded snake.

I spat out blood. "That was a low blow."

"It's the least of what you can expect in the Trials, mortal."

"Thought you were calling me Hazel now." I lunged for

his arm, trying for a lock, but he twisted free with an elegance that a lifetime of martial arts training would never accomplish.

A muscle twitched in his jaw. "You need to learn not to let your guard down."

"You need to learn not to look away from your weapons." I yanked his knife out of the sheath on his thigh and hooked my legs around his, bringing both of us crashing to the ground. Pinning him between my knees, I pressed the tip of the blade to his throat. "If you want to use cheap trickery, I'll return the favour."

His eyes narrowed, his chest rising and falling. Magic brushed against me, its sharp scent infiltrating my senses. It smelled of oak and ash, tinged with frost. The mark on my wrist tingled. "Don't push your luck, mortal."

"It's Hazel." I returned his glare with a smile and pushed to my feet, ignoring the lingering caress of magic as potent as a Sidhe's. How far did his magical talents go? He could create illusions that breathed as though they were alive and could carry on a conversation with a real person without being detected.

One breathes without life...

A sudden rush of fear chased down my spine. He couldn't have used an illusion to infiltrate the Erlking's home, could he? No... the Erlking's talisman destroyed any magic it made contact with. It wasn't possible for even him to evade its insidious touch.

Darrow held out a hand for his blade. "What is it?"

"Nothing." I gave him his knife back, keeping my smile in place. The Sidhe could smell prey a mile off, and I'd spent too long learning to mask my fear to be cowed by the likes of him.

He sheathed the blade. "We've wasted enough time. Come with me."

As if I'd started the whole thing. "You haven't said where we're going."

"The base for the Gatekeeper's training grounds." He looked me up and down. "Take off your glamour. You'll be wearing a different one for the duration of your Trials."

That's presumptuous. For all he knew, I'd thrown on the glamour immediately after waking up and was stark naked underneath, which I *may* have done once or twice when I'd overslept before classes as a kid. After all, glamour took less than a second to apply, and I'd often suspected that the only reason the Sidhe bothered with clothing at all was because it provided some protection if someone started throwing spears around. Which, to be fair, was a high possibility here in the Courts.

I let the glamour fall away, revealing my plain clothes. Darrow's hands glowed, and I glanced down to find that I now wore black attire edged in green, like his own outfit.

"Nice," I commented. "Bit plain, though."

Without a word, Darrow walked down a short path towards an expanse of grass and halted beside the opening to a tunnel.

"This," he said, "is the entrance to the Gatekeeper's training grounds."

I peered inside, seeing earthen walls and a surprisingly large space underneath the hill. "I didn't know it was underground."

Mum hadn't been allowed to tell me about her own Trials, so I knew nothing of the specifics, only what I'd managed to glean from reading old Gatekeeper's reports. I did know that there was no point in trying to guess our location, because in Faerie, nothing was constant.

"You won't tell a soul about this place," he added. "The binding will ensure it."

I bet it will. Swallowing my renewed annoyance at the mark on my wrist, I followed him through the entryway into an open space with a high, domed ceiling and passages branching off in all directions. The earthen floor was smoothed from the impact of a thousand footprints, while shimmering lights hung at intervals on the wall. To my surprise, several other faeries gathered in small groups, and turned my way when I entered.

"These are my assistants," said Darrow. "They will guard you while the Trials are in progress."

He's not training me alone? What was the deal with the binding, then?

"Coral will show you around." He beckoned one of the faeries over. "She'll tell you the basics, and then I'll introduce you to the training grounds."

Before I could ask another question, he was already walking away, leaving me alone with a roomful of strangers.

"Hey," said the young woman he'd called over. "I'm Coral."

Her generous curves and wavy white-blond hair indicated her human heritage, but her pointed ears were definitely fae. She didn't wear typical court attire. Over a plain black outfit similar to mine, a shimmering white cape hung off her shoulders.

"You're half… selkie." I noted the cape.

She smiled. "I am. And you're human. Hazel, right?"

"That's me." She was the first person who'd smiled at

me since I'd set foot in Faerie, and the first selkie I'd spoken to at all. They tended to keep to themselves. Her Scottish accent indicated she must be part of Scotland's selkie colony who lived in the ocean off the coast.

Coral led me down a passage and through a door on the right. To my surprise, it contained a fair-sized set of living quarters, including a bedroom, kitchen and bathroom. While it didn't have any of the modern conveniences like a microwave or electric lighting, it beat sleeping under the stars, which I'd assumed most Gatekeepers did during the Trials.

"This is all yours for the duration of your training," she said. "The Trials have been known to take place over a number of days, so we wanted to make things comfortable in case you have to spend the night here."

"By 'we', I take it you don't mean Darrow."

Her brows rose. "Made an impression, did he?"

I held up my arm to show the mark on my wrist. "Let's just say I'm a little sleep deprived."

She winced. "I can brew a tonic for that. I don't know if he told you the effects fade after a day, and when you're in this realm, you won't notice them at all."

"That's… not ideal," I said. "But I appreciate the offer."

Selkies weren't given to deceit or trickery, so her offer was likely genuine. The only magic they possessed was the ability to transform into a seal. Unless their skin was stolen, that is—which explained why she wore it as a cape.

She twitched her shoulders under the cape, seeing me looking. "You should know, I'll be testing your knowledge on poisons at some point during your Trials, but I won't do anything underhanded like slip poison into your food or water."

"Now you've told me that, I'm going to be doubly suspicious," I said, in light tones.

She grinned. "Good. It'll keep you alive. I take it you've spent a lot of time in the Court?"

"As much as a human is allowed to," I said. "You're from the Sea Kingdom, right? Does your Queen know you're here?"

"Of course she does," she said. "I'll brew the potion to stop the mark from bothering you. Darrow wants me to show you the whole place, but between you and me, there's not much worth seeing in here, and he'll show you the weapons room himself."

She walked into the kitchen area and began opening cupboards. Someone had fully stocked the kitchen with packaged meals that looked like they'd come from a human supermarket.

"So that's your speciality," I observed. "Didn't know you went in for poisons in the Sea Kingdom."

"Oh, we don't," she said. "We're not fighters by nature, especially not outside of the water. Being employed as food-tasters or bodyguards is actually one of the least hazardous positions one can take in the Court."

"Huh." My knowledge of the Sidhe eclipsed my education on the rest of Faerie—for obvious reasons—but everyone knew selkies were better equipped for life in the water than on land. "What're you, then? Darrow's assistant?"

She snorted, almost dropping the bag of herbs she was holding. "No. Darrow meant we're here to assist with protecting you."

"You mean, stopping the Sidhe from murdering me

because they suspect I killed their king," I surmised. "Is that the reason for the lessons on poisons?"

"You've got it," she said. "It's useful to know, since the Sidhe use poison when they don't want to make an open challenge."

"They don't tend to be that subtle when it comes to me." I'd never heard of the Gatekeeper having extra body-guards before. They must be really worried one of the Sidhe would slit my throat in my sleep. Not a cheery thought. I fidgeted, watching her add herbs to a bowl and stir with practised hands. "Does Darrow hate half-bloods as much as he hates humans?"

"Hates humans?" she echoed. "He doesn't hate humans."

Right. So he has a personal issue with me, then. I didn't get why, considering he at least had volunteered for this, but perhaps he'd gone in expecting someone like Mum, not someone who smiled and chatted and turned his own weapon on him when he wasn't looking.

Coral tipped some of the concoction into a bottle and held it out to me. "You can test it for poison first."

"Nah, I watched you make it." I downed the potion, grimacing at the bitter taste. "Ugh. Tastes like espresso mixed with nettles."

"I could have added something sweeter," she said. "But I thought you might get suspicious."

I held up my wrist and pressed my fingertip to the swirling symbol, which no longer stung. "I appreciate it."

Half-faeries who didn't belong to the Courts didn't often go in for the same vow-type nonsense as the Sidhe did, but it was best not to thank them or imply any obligation. At least until I knew who could be trusted.

"It's my job to keep you alive, remember?"

"Not just yours," I said. "I should introduce myself to the others. It seems in poor taste to let them risk their lives for me without knowing their names."

"You'll have time to get to know one another after today's lessons are over," she said. "I think Darrow wants to get started right away."

"Punctual, is he?"

"To a fault." Coral led me back into the main tunnel, where the other bodyguards gathered in groups. Up close, it became clear they were all half-faeries, and were dressed in the same dark clothing as Coral and Darrow. Of course the Sidhe wouldn't order any of their own people to bodyguard a human.

As I approached, a young half-Sidhe detached herself from the group and sauntered over to me. She had long silky dark hair and full lips that formed a pout as she looked me up and down. "*You're* the Gatekeeper?"

"Yes." I gave her a fake smile. "Is there a problem?"

"I thought you'd be taller."

"Really." My smile turned into a grin. I'd been dealing with faeries commenting on how *human* I looked since I was a teenager. Half-Sidhe seemed genetically inclined to end up at least six feet tall, though at five-nine, I was tall for a woman. While I wasn't exactly built like a stick insect and would never be as lithe as one of the fae, I could arm-wrestle one of them into submission with zero effort.

"Don't want to glamour that?" She made a sweeping gesture at, well, me. "You're meant to be representing humanity, and if you were the first impression I got, then I'd assume all mortals were slovenly and plain."

I stepped around her, deliberately treading on her foot. "Oh, sorry. It's my clumsy human feet. I'll be more careful next time."

None of the other half-Sidhe stepped in to defend me, but if I didn't know better, Darrow looked almost approving when he caught my eye. Whatever. I wasn't here to make friends.

I halted next to him. "I was under the impression I was here to learn how to fight."

"You are." He gave me an appraising look. "What did Coral give you? I smell herbs on you."

"A tonic to stop this bothering me." I held up my wrist.

"If you'd asked, I would have found a way to alleviate the pain."

"You didn't seem that bothered when I mentioned it earlier." Perhaps he was trying to appear fair in front of his fellow half-Sidhe.

"I'll show you the training room." He swept down a short tunnel and through a door into a room filled with makeshift targets. I glimpsed a weapons room next door and took a mental note of the location. "The number of Trials you might face varies. They've been different for every Gatekeeper."

"I know."

"From this point on, any of your actions may count in your favour or against it," he went on. "That means my goal is to target your weaker areas."

"Surely it makes more sense to play to my strengths." I'd always accepted I would never match one of the Sidhe for speed or grace or magical prowess, but I'd learned to harness my own advantages. Now, Darrow seemed deter-mined to strip them away from me, one by one.

"From what I've observed, there's nothing more I can teach you about fighting," he said. "As for defending yourself against magic, you have something of an advantage with your natural deflecting abilities. No weaker magic can touch you, while you can learn to undo much of the rest."

I blinked. "I'm sensing there's a 'but' coming."

He raised his hands. "Let's see how good you are with glamour."

Oh boy. I had an inkling I was about to get schooled. Big time. *Using* glamour wasn't an issue for me. As my siblings delighted in telling anyone who asked, I'd once conjured an illusion of a fancy car as a teenager that was solid and real enough to drive. It had handled like a dream... right up until I drove too far from the Ley Line, at which point it had vanished, leaving me stranded in a muddy trench.

I wouldn't have that problem in Faerie, which had no spirit lines to limit the strength of magic, but Darrow's skill was on another level entirely. The troll had *felt* real, and as for his doppelganger...

I pushed the thought aside and conjured up a quick glamour of a red squirrel. The squirrel gambolled around us, chasing its fluffy tail. "There you go."

Darrow snapped his fingers and the glamour collapsed, winking out of existence.

"Hey!" I said. "You can't do that to my squirrel."

"I just did."

"It's a figure of speech. Since when could you break another person's glamour without touching them?"

I could see through others' glamour, up to a point, but

I couldn't break it. Especially not a Sidhe's glamour. To them, illusions were as real as reality itself.

"Show me another one."

I spun a glamour of a horse, which appeared next to me and gave a realistic whinny.

Darrow scanned it from nose to tail. "Climb onto it."

"Uh, no," I said. "You'll just snap it out of existence and let me fall on my arse."

"I want you to fight me."

"Fight…" I trailed off. "You mean I can stop you from breaking my glamour?"

It sure would have been nice to cover that in my earlier training, but then again, only a Sidhe could truly break glamour, and they were too busy to be bothered with training me before now.

This might hurt a little.

I swung up onto the horse. It felt solid, but only if I didn't think too hard about the empty air beneath the illusion. Grabbing the reins, I steered the horse around to face Darrow. "You might wanna tell me *how* to fight you."

"You know how."

He rested his hand on the horse's head, which flickered in and out of existence, threatening to send me pitching forwards. I shuffled backwards, conjuring up the glamour again, but no sooner had it formed than he broke it. I slid off the horse's back, and I'd have hit the floor if he hadn't moved blindingly fast, catching me in his arms.

Well, this is awkward. He was stronger than he looked, but I was solid and heavy and didn't *like* being carried.

Darrow laid me on my feet. "You need to learn faster if you want to master glamour in time to make use of it in the Trials."

"You need to work on your pep talks," I said. "Look, I didn't grow up in Faerie. In the mortal realm, if I use a glamour, it falls apart the instant I walk away from the Ley Line."

He stepped back. "Then I hope you're ready to learn fast. We'll try again."

We did. Multiple times. After the first couple of attempts, he stopped bothering to catch me when I fell, so I had a nice collection of bruises by the time he called the lesson to an end.

"You have ten minutes to change and make yourself presentable before the Sidhe arrive," he told me.

"Wait, the Sidhe are coming *here?*"

"That was implied, yes."

Faeries. At this rate, I'd strangle him before my Trials were over.

6

I hurried back to my suite to shower and wash off the sweat and dirt I'd accumulated from being thrown to the ground. then I spun a fresh glamour to change my clothes into a green-and-gold dress worthy of a Sidhe ceremony and make my hair look elaborately styled and not damp and tangled. *It'd have been nice if he'd warned me the Sidhe were coming beforehand.* Hopefully, they wouldn't try to arrest me this time.

Coral knocked on my door. "Are you ready?"

"Just about." I checked my reflection one last time. "As long as Darrow doesn't undo my glamour again, anyway. Why are the Sidhe coming here?"

"To formally recognise the Gatekeeper." When I opened the door, her gaze went to my arms. Even my glamour hadn't covered all the bruises from today's session. "I can brew you a tonic for the bruises later, but the Sidhe will be here any second now."

"Maybe it'll make them be a little nicer to me." I smoothed down my dress and walked with her to the main cave. The bodyguards wore a more formal version of their uniform, while Darrow had changed—or re-glamoured himself—into a green and gold ensemble that fitted his slim form and brought out the aquamarine colour of his eyes. His hair glittered like a waterfall of silver. He sure was stunning to look at. Too bad his personality left much to be desired.

The other half-Sidhe didn't seem to think so. They clustered around him like seagulls around someone holding a tasty snack. Maybe they thought if they played their cards right, they'd get a promotion. I rolled my eyes when the half-Sidhe who'd bitched at me earlier attached herself to his arm. *He should have put the binding on her, not me.* She didn't look like she minded being forced to hover over his shoulder. I just hoped the tonic Coral had given me would help with the pain from the binding, because I really needed a decent night's sleep after today.

A dazzling flash of light engulfed the room, heralding the arrival of a group of Sidhe. Among them were Lady Aiten and her dark-haired friend, Lord Pointy Spear. His glamour wasn't quite as dazzling as the last time I'd seen him, and he seemed a little worn at the edges. Perhaps the stress of looking for the Erlking's murderer was getting to him.

"The Gatekeeper will take to the stage now," said Lady Aiten. "And formally introduce herself."

Stage? I scanned the hall and spotted a clear spot that was more of a raised platform than a stage, but one did not argue with people who came to parties armed to the teeth. Making my way over there, I called Mum's lessons to mind. *Hold your head high, so they can see the circlet. Never flinch, and never let them see your fear.*

As I climbed onto the platform, the Sidhe carried on with their conversations as though I wasn't even here. All right, then.

"I am Hazel Lynn, Gatekeeper of the Summer Court," I said. "I'm honoured to serve the realm and to maintain the peace between humans and faeries."

Assuming they don't go to war first.

I glanced across the crowd at Darrow, whose eyes were on me instead of the half-Sidhe attached to his arm, and hid a smile. "I've had a wonderful welcome to the Court, and I look forward to filling my mother's shoes as Summer Gatekeeper."

The Sidhe's expressions didn't change. Sarcasm wasn't their forte. Lucky for all of us, really.

"And you will be welcomed," said the Summer ambassador, Lord Raivan, in tones that implied he'd rather be cleaning a public toilet than celebrating my status as Gatekeeper. Blond and perpetually miserable-looking, Lord Raivan wore a coat with gold cuffs and a vibrant new hat that made him look like an angry tropical bird. "Let us toast the Gatekeeper."

The Sidhe's conversations rose in volume, and they moved away from the 'stage'. While I'd been speaking, banquet tables had sprung up from nowhere, along with vats of wine and even a band. Assuming I'd been dismissed, I left the stage. Lord Raivan gave me a scowl on the way, and I returned it with a smile. He was supposed to be the ambassador for half-bloods and humans, yet he'd been notably absent when the Sidhe had accused me of murder and it did not look like he had any intention of offering an apology.

I walked over to the buffet table to join Coral, since

she was the only person in the room who hadn't treated me like dirt. The Sidhe didn't skimp on parties even for lowly Gatekeepers, and the tables were piled high with fruits and bread, cheese and meats. I hadn't eaten a proper meal all day, and I was bloody starving, so I loaded my plate. "This has all been checked for poison, right?"

"It has." Coral picked up a plate of her own. "You're just the right level of paranoid. Good job."

"The ceremony is normally held in the ambassador's palace, isn't it?" I said in an undertone. "I'm pretty sure my mother didn't have an underground revel on her first night in Faerie."

"It's better this way." She picked out a few grapes and set them on her plate. "At the last initiation party, two half-faeries disappeared into one of the portraits and never came out. Anyway, it's easier if you stay here tonight. Darrow's planning a test for tomorrow morning."

"He might have told me that himself." My gaze flickered over to him. He'd shaken off the clinging half-Sidhe and was now talking to Lord Kerien, the other ambassador for human-Sidhe relations. No doubt they were deep in a discussion of how much of a disappointment I was. "Has a half-faerie always been in charge of running the Trials?"

"I don't know," she replied. "I've only worked here for a year or so. I assume there's always been someone without ties to either Court selected, in the interests of fairness."

"You grew up human," I observed. "You talk like one. Plus you move like someone who learned to walk before learning to swim. Most selkies I've met aren't anywhere near as steady on their feet."

She smiled. "I went to school in Aberdeen. My dad was human, and he had custody of my brother and me until we were old enough for the Sea Court to come knocking."

"So the Sea Court claims half-faeries, too?" I asked. "Summer and Winter only started recently."

"I know," she said. "We were luckier than some, but I'm still in touch with my human family."

Reading between the lines, I figured that meant I could trust her. I was all in, considering it was a welcome relief from the backstabbing and betrayal I'd come to expect from the Sidhe. Feeling slightly better, I dug into my food. "I have two siblings, both in the human realm. And a cousin, but she's... you know. Winter's."

Her mouth formed an O. "I didn't know the Gatekeepers were that closely interrelated."

"There aren't many of us left," I said. "I guarantee there are a lot more people in line for the Erlking's replacement than the Gatekeepers."

I was the last of the line, in fact, and so was Holly. Which meant if we didn't have kids, the Sidhe might well target someone else's children and haul them into Faerie instead. The vow was eternal. We weren't.

Ilsa and I had once made a promise to break the curse, back when we'd been twelve years old and brimming with overconfidence. I wouldn't lie, I sometimes missed those days.

"I hope they find the killer soon," she said. "Darrow wasn't happy that he had to go out there into the Court when the Sidhe were on the warpath."

"Oh?" I said. "Why?"

"Because he's not from Summer," she said. "I assumed you'd guessed."

"He hasn't been forthcoming with sharing information." My heart began to beat faster. "Is it because he's a hybrid with ties to both Courts?"

"No," she said. "I *think* he's from an independent Court, like I am, but not the Sea Kingdom."

No wonder he'd been annoyed at my earlier questions. Maybe it was a requirement that all the people involved in the Trials weren't beholden to either Summer or Winter, so neither Court would be able to accuse the other of giving their Gatekeeper an advantage. It also prevented them from giving away anything the Sidhe didn't want them to, because non-Court members couldn't access any confidential information. Including the Gatekeepers, in most cases.

"So did he think they might accuse *him*?" I kept my tone casual.

"Maybe," she said. "I doubt it. No half-Sidhe would dare touch the Erlking."

I heaped cheese on my bread and took a bite. "You know the others quite well, then?"

"I do," she said. "Aila hates all non-Sidhe, including her own family. Sorry I had to leave you to deal with her, but Darrow ordered us not to intervene if anyone challenged you."

"Of course he did." That figured. While half-faeries were a little easier to understand than the Sidhe, those who lived in the Courts shared their belief that humans were inferior. They spurned their human heritage and spent their time hoping that if they spent enough time with the Sidhe, some of their longevity might rub off on them. Nonsense, but there you have it.

"Those are Laurel and Clove. They're half-dryads." She

pointed to two fae clad in gowns made entirely of leaves, their skin the colour of bark and their vine-like hair pleated with flowers. "And that's Willow." She indicated a pretty female half-Sidhe dressed in a magnificent silver gown, and her cheeks went pink when head tilted in our direction. "She's the daughter of a noble, I think, but I've never managed to find out who."

She went on, pointing out all the main players in the room. I generally had a good memory for names and faces, but I couldn't help wondering if any of the people here fit the descriptions in the note the Erlking had sent me. Perhaps he intended me to do some sleuthing of my own. Not that I really felt like questioning the Sidhe, but maybe more of the elf wine would get me in the mood to mingle.

"That Sidhe is staring at you," Coral commented. "I think he wants to talk to you."

I looked to see who she meant and recognised Lord Kerien. Like most of the Summer Sidhe, he was eerily stunning, with bright green eyes and tanned skin. Gold jewels studded his deep green coat.

"Oh, him," I said. "He used to be the Gatekeeper's ambassador, but he quit for some reason. Bet he's glad of it, now Darrow's dished the dirt on me."

"Excuse me?" The female half-Sidhe noble in the white dress walked past us. "I was just admiring your cape."

Coral choked on her wine. "Thank you."

With a smile on her face, Willow walked away. A grin swept my mouth. I might not know many selkies, but I *did* know that handing over their skin was an act selkies only did to express romantic interest. In selkie terms, she'd blatantly been flirting with Coral.

I nudged her. "I'm taking a wild guess that she wants to talk to you alone."

She looked down at her wine glass. "I'm not supposed to slack off on bodyguard duty."

"Aren't both of you supposed to be my bodyguards? Tell her I'm giving you both a break. For as long as you want." Coral went brick red, and I gave her another nudge. "Go on. I'm off to mingle."

I left Coral spluttering and headed across the room to refill my wine glass. Lord Kerien stepped in to waylay me. "Hazel Lynn."

"Lord Kerien." I gave him a smile and walked past. "Excuse me."

He snagged my arm with his fingertips, just enough to give me a warning bite of his magic. His melodic voice dropped to a whisper. "What do you know of the circumstances of the Erlking's death?"

He seriously wanted to do this now? "Probably a lot less than you do. Darrow already questioned me."

"I'm aware of that," he said. "However, there are gaps in our knowledge of the events that led to his death."

My mouth parted. "Wait, you're not accusing me?"

"No." He took a step closer. "We know the Erlking was shot with an iron-tipped arrow, but not who fired it."

Holy shit. That was practically a declaration of war. The Erlking's defences should have kept a simple bow and arrow out. "Darrow said he had a security beast."

"Also shot, multiple times. Each arrow was a perfect shot."

Damn. I scrambled to get a grip on my thoughts. "I don't understand why you're telling me this."

"We have reason to believe the truth lies in the mortal realm," he said.

Did he know the Erlking had sent me a message after his death? Maybe. I'd have thought he'd come out and said it if he had.

"You're saying…" I hesitated. "You need someone to take another look at the crime scene?"

My pulse accelerated. I hadn't wanted to get involved, not a bit, but that note had been for me alone. If I went to the scene of the crime, I might stand a chance of figuring out who'd killed him. This was an opening I'd be a fool to miss out on.

Lord Kerien's gaze travelled around the room, lingering on Darrow. "Ask Darrow to bring you to the clearing north of the Blood River after tomorrow's lesson. I will be able to get you inside the Erlking's territory, but I cannot guarantee your safety."

The implication was clear. If the Sidhe found out the truth lay in the mortal realm, they might well haul my family in for questioning again. "Okay. I'll do it."

In the blink of an eye, Lord Kerien was gone. Around me, the Sidhe continued with their conversations. As for Coral and her new friend, their conversation was more of the non-verbal variety. I gave her a wink when we locked eyes, my mood lightening despite the bombshell Lord Kerien had dropped.

Spotting Darrow, I made a beeline for him. "I didn't know I was getting my own party. I'm honoured."

"It's custom."

"Uh-huh." I tilted my head. "You aren't drinking the faerie wine. Not going to spring a surprise training session on me, are you?"

I bloody hoped not. Faerie wine wasn't as effective on half-faeries as humans, so he'd have an unfair advantage, considering I was so exhausted that a single glass had turned my knees to jelly.

"No," he said. "Why were you talking to Lord Kerien?"

"He wants to see me after tomorrow's training session," I said. "Said he wanted to meet me by the Blood River. You'd know where that is."

I'd heard the river ran red with the blood of the Erlking's enemies, which was creepy as hell, but that didn't worry me nearly as much as the notion of getting close to the place where the Erlking had breathed his last.

A moment passed. "Yes, I do."

He'd been there before. Had he spoken to the Erlking himself? Surely not, yet Darrow had more clout with the Sidhe than I'd thought, if Lord Kerien trusted him to bring me near the Erlking's territory.

Could I get him drunk enough to start spilling his secrets? I'd seen Sidhe far more stoic than him turn into party animals at Lord Niall's infamous revels. It was worth a shot.

I reached for a spare glass from the table and pressed it into his hand. "It's not poisoned."

"Coral prepared you well." He lifted the glass but didn't drink. "It's unwise to let go of your senses even here, Gatekeeper."

He was *still* calling me 'Gatekeeper'? I'd need him to drink a lot more of that wine if I wanted to win him over.

"I figured it'd be rude to ignore the refreshments the Sidhe prepared for me," I said. "And even ruder to lurk in the corner glowering at everyone. Unless it's just me you have a problem with. If so, please come out and say it."

"I don't have a problem with you," he said, "but you do have a certain reputation among the other fae."

And just what was *that* supposed to mean? "Says who, exactly?"

"The master of revels brought up your name."

A smile touched my lips. Lord Niall had been spreading tales, had he? Admittedly, I *had* once tried to seduce him for information on how to find my mother when the Seelie Queen had taken her captive—unsuccessfully, I might add. Never mind that Lord Niall would flirt with his own reflection if the mood took him. "I'm surprised he remembers me."

"I heard your family was at the centre of an incident in his house."

Aha. So he hadn't been there. The 'incident' in question had involved the Seelie Queen sending a horde of wraiths to attack the Sidhe's revel, and only my siblings' quick actions had stopped them from causing a massacre. And Lord Niall, in typical Sidhe fashion, had blamed us for causing the trouble ourselves.

"Maybe." I sipped my wine. "But I'm not drunk enough to start talking about horrifying nightmare creatures, and you're stone cold sober."

He picked up the glass and took a sip. Finally. Hiding a smile, I pretended to be interested in refilling my own, though I'd need to get Coral to give me a recipe for an anti-hangover tonic if I wanted to be in top shape for tomorrow's test. Still, I'd got him intrigued enough to play along. Even if it did involve revisiting unpleasant memories.

"Tell me, then." His eyes glittered more than usual, or maybe it was the lighting. "Tell me about these monsters."

I finished refilling my wine glass. "Ever seen a wraith?"

"I can't say I have. Care to elaborate?"

His words were carefully chosen, and even in my tipsy state, caution reared its head. Playing games with him wasn't like playing with a Court member. He could lie if he wanted to, same as me.

"Wraiths are the ghosts of Sidhe who died without being able to move on," I said. "They're like poltergeists jacked up to a thousand, and also have all the powers they had when they were still alive. That's how they trashed Lord Niall's house. He, in his infinite wisdom, decided to pin the blame on the only humans present."

"He also mentioned you weren't on the guest list." He tipped back his glass. "You're known for flaunting the rules."

"Which rules are you talking about?" I had a nice buzz going by now, and with it came a rush of reckless daring. How far could I push him with the mask off and the trainer persona firmly put away? "There's a long list."

"The rule stating that the Gatekeeper is to remain impartial, of course."

"The rule says no dating faeries," I corrected. "It says nothing about doing anything else with them."

Let him fill in the gaps there. If he wasn't so uptight, I'd be tempted to see how soft that silky hair really was close up. On the other hand, I knew precisely how soft, because I'd felt it when he'd caught me in his arms after throwing me off an illusory horse.

He arched a brow. He couldn't have guessed my thoughts, could he? "I would expect the Gatekeeper to practise caution at all times around the fae. They aren't like humans."

"Could you be any more patronising?" I sipped my wine, not that it helped me think any straighter. "I don't know how much time you've spent in the mortal realm, but most humans don't know more about Court law than popular culture. I've spent more hours learning how to kill things than I have watching Disney movies. I don't care what issue you have with me, but if you imply my mother wasted her time training me and she hears about it, you might as well dig your own grave here and now."

Murder accusations aside, I was in no more danger in Faerie than he was. He, unlike me, didn't have the advantage of a magic-proof shield and a curse tied into my very name.

"I didn't mean to imply you haven't dedicated yourself to your studies."

I dipped my head in acknowledgement of the implied apology. *Okay. Let's try again.* "Not that it's any of your business, but I was at that party to gain intel on how to find my mother when the Seelie Queen kidnapped her. So you can say caution was first on my mind, and Lord Niall is a prejudiced twat."

His eyes widened a fraction. "The Seelie Queen kidnapped her?"

"Lord Niall didn't tell you that part, huh." It was no big secret, but from the sound of things, Darrow hadn't arrived in the Court until after she'd been jailed. "She also tried to murder her husband. Unsuccessfully, that time."

"You might want to reconsider your statement about caution." He gave me a pointed look. Oh. Right. There were Sidhe everywhere, within hearing distance. Thanks for that one, elf wine.

"I need a massage," I said. "You bruised me from head

to toe today. I'm starting to think you get a kick out of throwing me around."

"It's my job. Besides, you can hold your own."

"Yes, I know. I've been training for half my life." Was I slurring my words? Yes, I was. "So what do they do where you come from? I mean, did you get chosen to come to Summer, or did you volunteer?"

"What makes you think I'm not from Faerie?"

Was Coral not supposed to tell me? "You're way more self-confident than most half-faeries and you aren't scared of the Sidhe."

His expression turned frosty. Perhaps I should have thought before I spoke. Or stopped drinking two glasses ago.

"I think you've had enough wine." He plucked the glass from my hand.

"Hey." I folded my arms. "We're off duty. No giving me orders."

"And were you off duty at Lord Niall's?"

I pressed my lips together. "Why not ask Lord Niall yourself, since you two are such good friends?"

I turned and walked back to Coral before I made a bigger fool of myself. *That went well.* Maybe I'd get another shot at learning his secrets tomorrow, assuming he didn't try to tag along to the Erlking's territory with Lord Kerien and me. And assuming he didn't tell on us, because I was starting to suspect that Lord Kerien was working behind his fellow Sidhe's backs by involving me in the investigation at all.

I needed to tread carefully, or else I'd be dead before the Trials even started.

7

I woke up on a bed of leaves under a patch of trees. Sunlight streamed through the branches, while birds trilled and cawed in the background.

"Oh, you bastard," I muttered.

The Trials had officially begun. I lay in the middle of a clearing, wearing only the thin shirt and loose cotton trousers I'd gone to sleep in. No weapons. At least I had my circlet, while Coral had helped me brew up a tonic to prevent hangovers last night and left me some salve to put on the bruises from yesterday. If she hadn't, I'd be sore as well as groggy and pissed off.

I pushed to my feet in a rustle of leaves and picked out a fallen branch that looked sharp enough to use as a weapon. Then I spun a glamour to turn my clothes into Court attire and the branch into an iron blade. Anyone who touched it would know the truth, and Darrow himself could unravel the whole thing in a snap of his fingers, but my guess was that he wasn't here. He'd be watching from a safe distance to see how I performed.

A cry drifted from the nearby path, and I walked that way. A cage hung suspended between two trees, containing what appeared to be a human male.

Oh, for god's sake.

It didn't take a genius to know this was a trap. The cage was made of interlocking branches, just high enough that a fall would break bones. A scrap of paper fluttered down from above.

I picked it up and read, *"To pass this test, free the human and escape the forest."*

"Dammit." Real or not, the human was part of the test. The trees appeared to be plain old oaks, not dryads, so they wouldn't try to gouge my eyes out if I climbed them. I rested my foot on the nearest trunk, and a deafening roar sounded from behind me.

A beast exploded out of the trees, horns curled against its head and tombstone-like teeth dripping with drool. A wild ogre. Cursing, I spun away from the tree and held up the glamoured blade. As I'd hoped, the beast veered to the side to avoid being impaled, its horns tangling among the low-hanging branches.

The green glow of Summer magic brightened my hands, and I directed it into the tree itself. At once, the branches grew, pushing the ogre back and away from the captive human. Secure that it wouldn't try to eat either of us, I hauled myself onto a low branch and began to climb until I reached the thick branch supporting the dangling cage. Shimmying across the branch, I pushed more magic into the tree. The cage trembled as the branch lowered, bringing it closer to the earth.

The beast's roars grew louder, and splintered branches flew everywhere as it broke free of my trap.

Shit.

I blasted the side of the cage with magic, and the human screamed. Extending both hands through the newly created gap in the branches, I urged him to climb out. "Come on!"

The dazed-looking human caught my hand, and I helped him climb onto the branch. Luckily, his common sense kicked in immediately and he hurried along behind me, jumping for the neighbouring tree. I hadn't the faintest clue how to get him back to the mortal realm from here, but I'd bully Darrow into showing me later. For now, it was time to get the hell out of this forest.

"Do you remember how you got in here?" I asked him. "Or the way out?"

He shook his head. "No."

"All right. Follow me."

I hadn't done much tree-climbing since I'd grown too tall to scale our family's ancient oak, but the trees in Faerie dwarfed those in the mortal realm. The beast's thundering footsteps filled the background, interspersed with snapping branches. I threw a glamour over my shoulder, turning the nearest tree into a barrier of branches. The monster would figure out it wasn't real soon, but it won us some time.

The trees halted at an expanse of muddy swamp, spreading to either side. "Oh, come on."

The swampy water looked like it'd come up to my waist, but who knew what might be lurking underneath. No other way out presented itself, and the human whimpered as the beast's growls grew louder. *Fine, then.*

I shimmied down the tree, then tested the depth of the water with my glamoured stick. Solid enough to walk on.

Beckoning to the human, I stepped into the murky water. "Get on my back."

He did so, awkwardly clambering onto my shoulders. Moving with a person on my shoulders would hamper my speed even more than usual, but at least he was less likely to fall into the water and drown. As a bonus, I was fairly sure ogres couldn't swim.

Using the stick to feel my way forward, I waded through the murky grey-brown water, which soon rose to my waist. *Ugh.* I was a competent enough swimmer, but I wasn't the biggest fan of the water, especially muddy ponds where merrows and grindylows hunted for flesh-and-blood prey.

The ogre steamrollered into the swamp with a sound like a plunger being yanked from a sink. The bloody thing had a one-track mind. I quickened my pace, but without warning, the sturdy ground beneath my feet came to an end, and the stick plunged through emptiness.

The ogre growled, wading through the currents. The water barely reached its ankles. Lucky bastard.

"Hold your breath," I told the human.

I kicked off and swam into the deeper water, barely able to keep my own head above the surface with the added weight of the human on my back. The ogre plunged after me, and then recoiled, its arms flailing for the surface. *Now you remember you can't swim, huh?*

My gaze fixed on the solid mass of trees and earth on the other side of the swamp. Almost there.

Then the human's legs locked around my throat, driving me headfirst into the depths.

Filthy water filled my eyes and mouth, and I choked, writhing and kicking. I broke the surface, gasping for breath, cursing myself for not seeing such an obvious trap. Of *course* Darrow wouldn't give me a meek and obedient human to rescue.

I won't fail this. I won't.

Green light surged to my palms, and I blasted the water with all the power I had. A wave of filthy mud swept forward, propelling the flailing human to the surface and pushing both of us towards the bank at the far end.

Crashing onto my knees, I skidded to a halt in the mud. Pushing a handful of filthy hair from my eyes, I looked for the human, who'd curled up in a ball. He also didn't look much like a human any longer. His skin was scaly, his ears pointed, and his eyes were small and beady. A goblin. Thanks for that one, Darrow.

Grabbing the scruff of his neck, I marched away from the swamp and found myself surrounded by gawking faeries, each of them covered in muddy water. Even Darrow. I wasn't the slightest bit sorry.

I threw the goblin at him. "You can fetch the ogre yourself, assuming it's real."

"It isn't."

Aila broke into gales of laughter. Had she had a say in this task? I had an inkling she might have. Worse, I was supposed to be meeting with Lord Kerien to examine the scene of the Erlking's death, and for all I knew, I was already running late.

Darrow gestured through the tress behind him. "There's a river this way where you can clean yourself up."

Translation: I wouldn't have time to go back to the training base to change into more sensible attire before my meeting with Lord Kerien. Great.

Coral caught up with me as I made for the river. "I'm sorry, Hazel. I didn't know what the task involved."

"I'm supposed to be meeting with one of the Sidhe after this and I'm not even wearing shoes." I didn't have any of my weapons either, so I'd better hope the Erlking's killer didn't revisit the crime scene while I was snooping around. Assuming Lord Kerien didn't mistake me for a swamp monster and try to slay me. "Everyone knows not to go into the water in Faerie, so I'm not all that keen on bathing in a river, either, to be honest."

"It's perfectly safe." She reached the riverbank and dove into the clear waters, her cape shimmering behind her. I watched from the bank, curious to see her shift. Selkies could only speak in their human forms, as far as I knew, but could otherwise live in and out of the water.

"Hazel," Darrow said from behind me. "I need to talk to you."

I wheeled around and was greeted with the view of a half-naked Darrow removing his trousers. *Oh... my. Don't look any further south, Hazel... too late.* "Jesus. Warn me next time you start stripping in front of me."

His brow wrinkled. "You humans have odd ideas about modesty."

"I'm from Scotland," I told him. "You're welcome to try walking around the Highlands in the nude if you want to see why we don't do that sort of thing over there. Even wearing a kilt would run the risk of your balls turning blue and dropping off."

Actually, I thought he'd look damned good in a kilt, but you couldn't pay me to say *that* aloud. He looked smoking hot out of one, for that matter, if you liked pretty silver-haired faeries with lean muscles and striking-coloured eyes. I could admit that and still keep my eyes on his face and not on his sculpted chest.

"You passed the test," he said, entirely ignoring my comment. "I'll escort you to meet Lord Kerien in ten minutes."

Was that an attempt at an apology? To be honest, his comment about my so-called reputation still rankled me more than today's task did. I wouldn't trust Lord Niall's opinion on anything except the finest brand of elf wine.

"Fine." I waited for him to leave before removing my muddy clothes. He might find my reluctance to bear my naked skin in front of an audience weird, but if Aila made another comment about my plain human appearance, I'd punch her in the nose.

The clean water came as an immense relief after my unintended swim, and I fully submerged my head to remove the clumps of mud from my circlet.

When I emerged, I found Coral treading water nearby, her cape billowing around her. "Do you wear that circlet all the time?"

"It's more or less magically attached to my skull." I usually removed it when I slept, but not here in Faerie. Certainly not after the Erlking's murderer had stolen his crown. "Even a Sidhe would be hard-pressed to knock it off."

"Nice." She pulled at the edges of her cape. "Same with this. Okay, not *quite* the same, but male selkies think it's funny to run contests where the first to steal another selkie's skin gets to give them a kiss. It's supposed to be a game." She pulled a face. "Selkie males are so immature."

I snorted. "And Willow? You two seemed to be having a good time at the party."

She flushed bright red. "I was trying to find out which noble Sidhe was her parent, but we got distracted…"

"Distracted." I made quote marks with my fingers, and her flush deepened. "It doesn't matter who, right?"

"She's from the Court, so possibly, yes," she said. "I'm only in Summer for as long as this job lasts, and then I'll have to find another one or go back home."

"The Sea Kingdom's off the coast of Scotland, right? Near Skye."

"Yep." Her cape swirled. "Okay, I'll shift. I can tell you're curious."

"I'm not—" But before I could finish my sentence, she wrapped the skin-cape around her body and shifted into a seal. Her selkie form was grey-white and spotted, and her dark eyes twinkled with mischief as she splashed me with a flipper.

With a flourish, Coral turned back into her human form. "You did a great job passing the test, despite Aila and her sick sense of humour."

"I *knew* the goblin was her idea." I ran my fingers through my hair to untangle my matted curls.

"Yeah, that wasn't supposed to happen," she said. "The Trials are intended to test your skills, not your morals. That's what Darrow said, anyway."

I made a sceptical noise. "He doesn't like me much. How long have you worked with him?"

"Since he took over as head of Gatekeeper training," she said. "He's not much of a talker, but don't forget most people who work in the Courts have to hide their true motives. He can't show favouritism, especially towards you."

No kidding. Most people in the Courts wore masks,

but I'd never been a fan of duplicity. I was usually good at making judgements, too, but Darrow was hard to figure out.

"I tried to get him drunk last night," I said. "Get him to loosen up. He told me I have a *reputation.* Any idea why he'd care?"

Her brow crinkled. "No. Says who?"

"Lord Niall, apparently."

"Oh, *him.*" She snorted. "Reputation? He's the guy who threw a party in which three people drowned in a single barrel of wine."

"I take it that wasn't the permanent kind of death?"

"Keep it down," she said in an undertone. "The Sidhe still don't like people talking about… you know."

"Death." Up until the Sidhe's immortality had come crashing to an end, they'd been free to risk life and limb without any fear of repercussions. Yet for many, their first impression of what awaited after death had come during the wraith attack at Lord Niall's revel. Hell of a wakeup call.

"Yeah. That." Coral swam to the bank. "I'm heading back to the training grounds. Darrow's just over there, waiting for you."

Of course he is. I checked the last of the mud was gone, then swam to the spot where I'd left my clothes.

The problem was, they were no longer there.

Great. Normally, I'd draw the line at walking into the scene of the Erlking's death with no clothes as well as no weapons, but it was typical of the way my luck was going today. I raised a hand, conjuring a glamour that covered me from head to toe in a mirror of the outfit Darrow had put on me before my arrival at the training grounds. As long as he didn't try any of his glamour-breaking tricks, I'd be fine, but Darrow didn't seem to care about my dignity.

He waited for me a short distance away in his black-and-green ensemble, which might be glamour for all I knew, and frowned when he caught sight of me.

"What?" I said. "Some dickhead stole my clothes. I didn't leave a gap in the glamour, did I?"

"No, but I think these would work better." He handed me a pile of clothes, and I blinked, startled. He'd even included shoes. That was unexpectedly kind. And suspicious. Maybe he thought the Sidhe would be annoyed at him if I flashed the entire Seelie Court.

Ducking behind the bushes, I examined the plain trousers and shirt. They weren't Darrow's, but they were designed for someone three inches taller than me and considerably smaller in the chest. I'd have to go through the forest wearing what amounted to a corset and hope that my boobs wouldn't pop out in the middle of the site of the Erlking's murder. Oh, and in front of Darrow, whose brows rose when I stepped out from behind the bushes.

"What is it this time?" It wasn't like I had anything he'd never seen before. Frequently, if he'd lived in Faerie a while. It seemed I'd been wasting my time trying to get him drunk last night when I should have worn a corset instead.

"Nothing," he said, several seconds too late.

"Uh-huh." I grinned. "C'mon. Lord Kerien will be waiting."

8

Lord Kerien waited for me at the border north of the Blood River. Despite the name, the waters shone like liquid crystal, without so much as a drop of blood in sight. He wore plain dark clothing rather than his usual green and gold armour, his glamour toned down so thoroughly that my gaze passed over him twice before I spotted him among the trees.

He dipped his head in acknowledgement. "I'll take her from here."

"Are you certain?" Darrow said. "The Gatekeeper is my charge. I'll be displeased if anything happens to her."

Yeah, right. More like he wanted to know what our secret meeting was about.

"I will keep her safe," said Lord Kerien. Since he couldn't lie, it seemed he meant it.

"Very well." Darrow turned to me. "You may go home after your task is complete. I will call you back when it's time for your next training session."

Hmm. He didn't sound like he resented me going to

the crime scene. Maybe I'd guessed wrong about him after all. He hadn't alluded to knowing what the Erlking's talisman was capable of, but then again, I hadn't known Lord Kerien had seen it, either, much less that he was involved in the murder investigation. Like most Sidhe, he hadn't set eyes on the Erlking in decades.

I turned to the Sidhe lord as we walked. "I didn't know you were a detective. Or that you knew the Erlking personally. What brought this on?"

His lips compressed. "After his wife's attempted coup, the Erlking fired his entire team of advisors."

Whoa. "Seriously?"

"Yes, of course, mortal," said Lord Kerien. "He jailed anyone who conspired with the Seelie Queen. Those who were left, he dismissed on the grounds that they could no longer be trusted, and started afresh."

"And hired you," I surmised. "Before then, you didn't know why he kept everyone in the Court at a distance. Everyone thought he was sick. That's why some of them aren't surprised he died."

I'd worked that much out. Only the people who'd been closest to the Erlking knew the truth about why he'd isolated himself, but I hadn't realised the Erlking had hand-picked a new security team prior to his death.

"Correct," he said. "He chose a small number of us to confide in about his situation. Perhaps he saw an attempt on his life coming."

It wouldn't surprise me if he had. It *did* surprise me that he'd readily shared the details of the talisman's power with anyone at all.

"So do you think one of the other new advisors might have been the one who betrayed him?" I asked.

"Perhaps," he said, "but we have searched the whole of Summer for any traces of his talisman and found no traces of it. Nor the crown."

"What about the heir?" I said in a low voice. "I know you can't choose his successor without the Erlking's crown, but perhaps it'd stop the general panic if you nominated someone as a temporary replacement."

"The Erlking was clear that he alone would choose the heir," said Lord Kerien. "We have searched his territory extensively, and evidence of the Erlking's choice has yet to be found."

You might know it. Then again, if he'd sent anyone else a personalised note, they'd probably be compelled not to speak to anyone else about it. The bloody Sidhe just couldn't make anything simple.

"All right," I said. "Forget the heir, then. Was anyone else known to be near the Erlking when he was murdered?"

"No," he said. "He used trolls to guard his territory, due to their resilience. That… staff of his caused adverse side effects in anyone who went close to him. His personal sprite delivered messages to his advisors."

That sounded like an impractical way to do business. Granted, he'd once trusted the Seelie Queen to take messages for him and she'd responded by conspiring with Lord Daival behind his back. As she was the only person in the Court unaffected by the talisman, she could stand at his side without being harmed, so perhaps he'd felt he had no choice but to trust her. They must have had had one hell of a weird relationship. Trapped alone in a forest with someone you hated made my family's curse look like a relaxing weekend at the beach.

"Can you tell me who the other advisors were?" I asked. "I know he fired Lord Daival, since he helped the Seelie Queen with her attempted coup."

"He didn't tell any of us the identities of his other advisors. I have my suspicions, but we're vow-bound not to share that information even with the other Sidhe."

Figures. The Erlking hadn't trusted a soul after his wife's betrayal. "You used to handle petitions from mortals. It's quite a step up from that to working with the King of Faerie himself."

"Yes, it is," he said. "I confess, it seems unclear to all of us what his motives were. It may be that he was losing his grip on his sanity, which is what most of us once believed to be the reason he kept his distance."

I was more inclined to think of his actions as the result of understandable paranoia, but he'd seemed intelligent and calculating when we'd met. And it wasn't necessarily strange that he'd want every trace of his wife wiped out of his Court after her attempt to take his throne.

"In any case," he went on, "I do not believe a Sidhe committed the murder."

"What, you don't?" I blinked. "You think it's more likely that a human or half-faerie got in?"

"Not alone," he said. "But I have seen things, mortal, in recent times, which show that nothing is as immutable as we once believed. I have seen humans wielding our talismans. I have seen half-bloods enter our territory and trick their way into power. I have watched our eternity cast in doubt, and our allies' minds poisoned. And I have no doubt that what stole our king's life was as a force as unnatural as any of those."

Unnatural force? The Erlking's staff was pretty

damned unnatural in its own right, but the guy must have fielded hundreds of assassination attempts in his time on the throne. Why had this been the one to kill him?

Lord Kerien turned a corner and halted in front of a set of gates. A staff appeared in his hand, and he pressed its glowing tip to the spot where the two gates touched. The glow spread through the gates, to its edges, and they opened without so much as a whisper.

"That's not your talisman," I observed, eyeing the staff.

"No," he said, tucking it into his belt. "It's a security talisman which only opens this gate and is the sole method of gaining access to the Erlking's territory. There are a small number of them dispersed among the Sidhe by the Erlking himself."

"How could they have accused me of committing the murder?" I asked. "I didn't even know to steal one of those, let alone how."

Lord Kerien flashed me a sharp look. "You met the Erlking once before."

"I used the Gatekeeper's vow to transport myself directly in front of him to warn him of an impending coup. Why would I then turn around and use the same magic to take his life?" It had been the only way to warn the Court of the Seelie Queen's betrayal, since the Erlking held the highest authority and none of the other Sidhe had believed me. I never would have guessed that decision would implicate me in his murder.

To my surprise, lush forests greeted us on the inside of the Erlking's territory. A short distance in, we passed by the wide grounds of an elegant estate.

"That's not the Erlking's home." It couldn't be. I'd seen

the clearing where he spent his time, and not a living thing had survived the staff's touch.

"This is the house where the Seelie Queen lived."

That explains it. "I know she hardly saw her husband. Didn't she get lonely?"

"She brought her lovers through the gate, but she required no talisman to get in."

Oh. That meant if she'd sent someone to kill her ex-husband, they couldn't have broken in without assistance. "Are you absolutely certain she hasn't left the jail?"

In my view, prison was too good for her, but the usual punishment for betrayal was exile. Since the exiled faeries were the ones who'd attacked Earth just over two decades ago, there'd been little doubt exile would allow her to continue her scheming in the realm of the outcasts, and the Sidhe had agreed.

"She has not left the jail," said Lord Kerien. "She may have had a hand in this, but not in person."

The forest grew more tangled the further we walked. Sidestepping a husk of a dead oak, we came to a mass of fallen trees. Blood spattered the wooden trunks. Not human blood. "Is that where…?"

"That's where the Erlking's security beast was killed." Lord Kerien led me around the wreckage to a spot where the living trees turned to dead ones, forming a clearing as stark as a vicious scar on the otherwise living forest. The Erlking's throne sat in the centre, formed of entangled tree roots. Grey and lifeless, they sat frozen in time, surrounded by decay.

An image burst into my mind—a man wearing a golden crown decorated with thorns, holding a carved staff which brimmed with power. He'd sat on that throne for centuries, yet no traces remained of his legacy but the trail of lifeless trees his talisman had left behind.

I stopped inches from the throne, taking in the faint traces of drying blood. "And he died… here?"

Lord Kerien had halted at the edge of the clearing, as though he didn't want to tread too close to the place where his king had perished. "Yes, he died inches from his throne. A single arrow to the forehead killed him instantly. By the time anyone reached the scene of his death, the staff and crown were gone."

I turned the information over in my mind. One shot meant an uncommon skill with a bow and arrow, for sure. The killer would have needed to stand far enough away not to be affected by the staff's magic—not to mention spotted by the Erlking himself. I took a step back, mentally calculating the distance across the clearing. This couldn't be the extent of his territory, surely. He didn't sleep in his throne, right? Okay, I wasn't sure the Sidhe actually needed to sleep. Not like humans did. If they wanted to, they could party for days at a time or go for months without rest.

I paced to the edge of the clearing and damn near tripped over a raised section of tree root concealing the entrance to a tunnel. Catching my balance, I crouched down and peered inside. Since when were there underground tunnels in Summer?

I lifted my head. *Oh.* From this angle, the clearing rested on top of a mound not unlike the one that contained the Gatekeeper's training rooms, so the Erlking's living quarters must be underground.

If there were other tunnels beneath his territory, perhaps the killer had sneaked up on him via some subterranean route. I stood beside the tunnel entrance, measuring the distance to the throne. If the killer had popped out of the entrance and fired an arrow off immediately, that would have done it, but it didn't explain how they'd got *into* the tunnels. The other entrance must be elsewhere in the forest, beyond the reach of the Erlking's talisman.

I ducked through the entrance and climbed into a narrow passage which opened into a wide hall like the one leading to the Gatekeeper's training grounds. More tunnels branched off, presumably into the Erlking's living quarters. In some places, plants and fungi had begun to grow, roots sprouting beneath the earth and moss coating the walls. Summer thrived on life, and even a talisman that killed anything living couldn't keep it out forever.

The first tunnel halted at a dead end. When I backed out, my gaze snagged on a faint light and a flutter of wings. A pair of eyes shone from a semi-transparent humanoid form with delicate wings like a butterfly's. The small creature flew backwards with a faint cry of alarm.

I crouched down and beckoned to the sprite. "Hey. It's only me. Can you lead me to the other entrance? In the forest?"

The sprite flew closer, wings beating like a humming-bird's, and beckoned me into a tunnel. Its transparent body was barely visible in the gloom, and I hurried after it, using my hands to feel my way between the narrow walls. The roots of dead plants broke away at my touch, and my feet crunched on the decaying remains of insects. From the musty smell of earth and rot, they were newly dead. The talisman's magic had touched this place recently.

The killer walked out this way.

I quickened my pace. Light streamed in ahead of me, and I came to a halt at an opening that led out into the forest. I reached through and caught a handful of branches. Trees lay across the entrance in a trampled mass, forcing me to crawl out through the spiky remains. *I know where this is.*

The murderer had deliberately chosen this spot to kill the security beast, so the trampled trees and crushed roots would conceal both the tunnel entrance and the damage done by the staff. Few would know the Erlking's quarters were underground, but the killer must surely have known it wouldn't be long before someone figured out how they'd sneaked up on their target.

Maybe they were buying time. So the Sidhe would bicker among themselves instead of guessing the truth.

My feet caught on an arrow, discarded among the branches. *Hello, a clue.* The arrow was rough, misshapen, and tipped in silver-grey metal. I slipped it into my pocket and threw a glamour on top, silently thanking Darrow for loaning me trousers with actual pockets.

"Mortal?" Lord Kerien's voice came from the clearing.

She has a name, you know. "Coming."

I scanned the undergrowth to see if there were any other secret passageways under the earth. The forest near the gates had been undisturbed, suggesting the killer had found some other way to smuggle the staff beyond the boundaries of the Erlking's territory.

"Gatekeeper," Lord Kerien said, louder. "Where are you?"

"Here." I marched back to the clearing. "Keep your hair on. Also, you might want to have a closer look near where that beast was killed. There's an underground passageway that goes into the Erlking's home."

His brows rose. "Underground passages?"

"Look over there." I jabbed a finger at the mass of fallen trees. "There's an entrance hidden under those trees. I'm sure that's how the killer got into the clearing without being detected. It goes a long way to explaining how they got out of the forest without damaging it with the staff, too."

Lord Kerien's piercing eyes pinned me to the spot. "You are correct. Now, you must leave before you're found here. Go. The gate is open."

Damn. I *knew* there must be more evidence here in the forest. Who had even known about those tunnels? Except for—

The Seelie Queen. I'd bet there was another tunnel entrance on *her* territory, too, on the off-chance that she wanted to pay a visit to her husband. She'd lived there for centuries, and even if she'd only taken one lover every few years, that would add up to an awful lot of Sidhe who knew the tunnels existed. I'd been fairly sure she and Lord Daival had had a thing going when they'd been arrested, though he was in jail, too. But that left a lot of other possibilities. And had the Erlking himself had lovers, for that matter? Had he had children, and where had they grown up?

So many questions. No wonder they hadn't found the heir yet, if they weren't too preoccupied with the Erlking's death to start looking. That was out of my area, but I was one step closer to finding the killer. And my next move would be to come back for a look around the Seelie Queen's home.

9

I'd forgotten my uncomfortable attire until I walked through the Summer gate into the heat of my family's back garden. As I'd suspected, more than a day or two had passed, judging by the position of the sun, and I was sweating buckets by the time I reached the house.

The instant I unlocked the door, a ball of fluff collided with my legs, nearly bowling me over. "Whoa."

"Down, Pepper." Morgan, my older brother, beckoned to the ball of fluff, otherwise known as a cu sidhe or faerie dog. I gave the puppy a stroke on the head, and he gambolled around my feet, yapping excitedly. "He likes you."

"He likes anyone who pets him." I crouched down to give the puppy some attention. "I probably smell of dirt, too. Took an unexpected bath in a swamp."

"What the bloody hell are you wearing?" Ilsa entered the kitchen, a huge textbook balanced on her arm.

"Is that a *corset?*" Morgan cracked up laughing.

I rose to my feet and gave him the finger. "The faeries

stole my clothes. This was all I could get. Besides, I'd rather wear a corset than a cloak that makes me look like the Grim Reaper."

Aka, the standard necromancer uniform. Morgan and Ilsa were off duty today, so they wore plain T-shirts and jeans. Morgan's looked a little worse for wear, and his shoes were falling apart at the seams.

"How many pairs of shoes has he chewed through now?" I asked.

"He's teething," said Morgan, giving the puppy a stroke.

"Or he's developed a taste for Converse." Ilsa's dark brown curls were tied back and her eyes were shadowed, suggesting she'd been pulling all-nighters in the library since I'd last seen her.

"What does Mum think of you letting him run amok around the house?" I rolled my eyes at my older brother.

"She's too busy to notice," Morgan said confidently. "C'mon, give us the gossip on Faerie."

I extracted the arrow from my pocket and held it out to Ilsa. "Entertain yourself with that. Got it from the scene of the crime."

Ilsa dropped the textbook, catching it between her fingertips before it hit the floor. "You went back?"

"With permission, don't worry." I handed her the arrow. "Be careful. I don't know if it's deadly to humans, too."

I left the room and went upstairs to change into my own clothes. I'd have preferred to take a proper shower, but from the excited barking noises downstairs, the puppy was as fascinated by the arrow as Ilsa was.

Sure enough, when I came down to the living room, I

found Ilsa examining the arrow, while Morgan restrained the puppy from jumping at her. At only a few months old, he was already up to my knee, and cu sidhe could grow to the size of a small car after a year or two.

I flung myself on the sofa. "What're you two doing here, anyway? Did you know I was coming home today?"

"Lucky guess," said Ilsa. "Mum's into one of her projects again and she wanted me to help out."

"So she dragged me along as well, since River made excuses," said Morgan.

"He wasn't making excuses," said Ilsa. "He's busy at the necromancer guild."

"I'm surprised his dad hasn't got in touch from the Court," I commented. "How's he taking the news?"

As a half-faerie who'd chosen the human realm over Faerie, Ilsa's boyfriend River would be a little behind on Court gossip, but I'd bet even the half-bloods in the mortal realm with no links to Faerie knew of the Erlking's passing by now.

"He's worried, of course," said Ilsa. "How can he not be? That's Mum's new project, by the way."

Ilsa jerked her head towards the coffee table, where a large spread of paper covered all the available space, featuring the sprawling lines of a family tree. Not our family tree, but the Erlking's. "She's trying to figure out who the heir is?"

It must have taken hours to sift through history books spanning thousands of years and pull out all those names, but Mum had nothing but time on her hands now.

"Don't ask me why." Ilsa turned the arrow over in her hands. "It gives her something to do. I can't figure out where this arrow came from, by the way. It isn't marked."

"Pretty sure the killer wouldn't have signed it," said Morgan.

"That's not what she meant." I looked closer at the arrow, which was shorter at one end and unevenly carved. "It looks manmade. Not fae."

"It's dipped in iron poison, all right," Ilsa said. "But to tell you the truth, I don't think it's magical at all."

"What is that?" Mum stood in the doorway, her eyes red-rimmed and her a pen tucked behind her ear. "Please tell me you didn't get that from the crime scene."

"Lord Kerien invited me to look around," I explained. "He thinks the Sidhe might be missing a clue only a human could spot. I found this arrow left behind."

"Did anyone see you take it?" Her voice was quiet yet sharp as a whip, and when she used that tone, part of me wanted to curl up in a ball, remembering the time she'd temporarily turned me into a tree to startle me into stopping a particularly extensive temper tantrum when I was a toddler. Unconventional parenting, maybe, but it'd worked.

"No," I said. "The only other person who knew Lord Kerien and I met today was Darrow, my mentor."

"Is this Darrow person trustworthy?"

"Are any of the Sidhe?" He'd thrown me around during training, let Aila try to drown me in a swamp, and then given me some clothes out of the apparent goodness of his heart. Who the hell knew? "I did make a friend, Coral. She's half-selkie."

"Oh?" She arched a brow. "Is she a spy for the Sea Queen?"

"A spy?" Damn. I hadn't even thought of that, but it

was a logical reason for a non-Summer faerie to be in the Court. "I don't know."

It was a risky move if she was. On the other hand, what better place to gather intel than the place where the Sidhe trained their human ambassadors? Nobody would question the presence of someone not from the Courts if they'd been told to hire people who fit that criteria. And it'd be just my luck if the one friend I'd made turned out to be a spy for another Court.

"Never mind her," said Mum. "Why did Lord Kerien let you look at the crime scene? He was disdainful at best towards humans when I worked with him as an ambassador."

"He's not anymore," I said. "I mean, he was promoted from being ambassador to being one of the Erlking's hand-picked personal advisors. The Erlking fired all his staff after the Seelie Queen was jailed."

"That makes sense," Ilsa put in. "Hazel's impartial. Plus she's actually been there."

"Which is why we were accused to begin with," I reminded her. "Anyway, he confirmed that the killer stole a security talisman to get into the Erlking's place, and then shot his personal troll guard dead. I also found some tunnels underneath his territory, which answers the question as to how the killer sneaked up on the Erlking and smuggled the talisman out. The surrounding forest wasn't damaged at all."

Mum's brows shot up. "Did you tell the Sidhe?"

"I told Lord Kerien. It's up to him if he wants to pass it on to his fellow Sidhe or not," I said. "Not sure what it all means. Perhaps the killer wanted to avoid leaving an obvious trail, so they used the tunnels to avoid destroying the entire forest on the way out."

"Why would they care if they killed the forest on the way out?" Morgan wanted to know. "If they were that fussed about killing things, they wouldn't have shot the Erlking."

"Thanks for that contribution, Morgan," said Ilsa. "Perhaps they wanted to make sure they didn't accidentally hit one of their allies."

"Which backs up the theory that there was more than one person involved," I added. "I doubt they could control the talisman right off, either. Imagine carrying that thing around and vaporising any living thing within range? There'd be no do-overs if they killed someone without meaning to."

"The real question is whether they claimed it," Mum said. "If they did, it'll be that much harder to get it back."

My throat went dry. If you tried to win over a talisman, you either claimed its magic or died. Nothing in between. That particular talisman was dangerous whether it had a wielder or not, but if another person took that insidious magic into themselves, they'd become its official owner, as powerful as the Erlking himself.

"We can't know for sure if they did," said Ilsa. "The killer must have been confident the arrow would reach its mark before the talisman's magic got within range. Really, it was a smart choice of weapon. The arrow is already dead and isn't magical at all."

"Smart?" Morgan said. "Hardly. Anyone can pick up an arrow like that at the market."

"The bow they used might have been enchanted, though." My hands twisted together. "If it was faerie-made, it must have been. And this scheme was well-planned enough that they must have at least seen a map of the territory to know which areas to avoid."

That, or they had personal experience with it.

Mum's grim expression told me she'd guessed my thoughts. "How many people set foot in the Erlking's territory?"

"Aside from his advisors?" I said. "Lord Kerien said the Seelie Queen used to bring her lovers through the gate herself. They'd have known how to get back in, and probably how to navigate the tunnels too. She might have told anyone else before she was jailed. Even Lord Kerien admitted that."

"I'm glad they're considering the possibility," said Mum. "I was starting to worry they'd let their focus on outsiders make them forget the enemies within their own Court."

"He still thinks a human or half-faerie did it," I added. "I'm not so sure on that one, but as long as we're not accused again, I'll take it."

"Have you not considered summoning up the Erlking's ghost and asking who shot him?" Morgan said.

"Don't even think about it," said Ilsa. "If you walk into the Court and announce that you raise the dead for a living, the Sidhe will turn you into an antelope. Besides, I nearly ripped a hole in the universe the last time I tried using necromancy in Faerie."

"Yeah, we want to avoid that," I said. "For all we know, he'd come back as a wraith."

Darrow's mention of the incident at Lord Niall's party was a reminder that to most Sidhe, their only experience of the dead were the dark spirits from the realm of the outcasts.

"You *haven't* seen any wraiths, have you?" Ilsa said. "Because… well. I'm pretty sure even the Sidhe know where the murderer must be hiding."

I know. There was no way the Sidhe, even divided and bickering, wouldn't have noticed the talisman's presence on their territory by now, and even Winter wasn't immune to its destructive power. I'd heard no word of it in the mortal realm yet, which left one place… the Grey Vale.

"No, I haven't, but the murderer doesn't need to set a wraith loose in the Court to spark panic. That talisman is more than enough."

Most spirits were harmless, and since the Erlking had died in the Court, he'd have moved on without a fuss. Wraiths, on the other hand, formed when Sidhe died in a place even death didn't dare to touch. A fitting place for a talisman which turned the living to dust.

"You have a message from your father, by the way," said Mum, handing me my phone. "Wanting to know how your training is going. I told him you were going to take some tests to become Gatekeeper."

"Oh." As a human with zero connections to Faerie, Dad knew the bare minimum without the gory details. It was easier that way. He didn't need to know about murdered monarchs or talismans or crime scenes. I typed a reply—*training was fine*—and hit send.

"*Is* everything going fine?" Mum enquired.

I put the phone down. "Pretty sure my mentor's trying to kill me, but it could be worse."

"Not in a literal sense, right?" said Ilsa.

"I hope not." Maybe I shouldn't tempt fate. "I still don't know why the Erlking's note insisted I didn't show it to him. Have you figured out that riddle yet?"

"I've been trying to make sense of it," Ilsa said. "One breathes without life, and one lives without breath. I guess the first one might refer to some kind of spirit."

"Or a zombie," said Morgan.

"Zombies don't breathe," said Ilsa. "And don't exist in Faerie, either."

"And the other lives without breath," I said. "What about the arrow? It used to be alive, once, technically."

"It's a piece of wood covered in poison, Hazel," said Morgan. "Maybe the Erlking was trolling you from beyond the grave."

"Don't talk to me about trolls." I shuddered. "Or ogres."

Ilsa pressed her mouth together. "Whoever did it, they picked a weapon so bland, nobody would be able to trace the source. I bet the bow itself was magical... so maybe make a list of all the Sidhe who are good at archery?"

"All of them." I slumped against the cushions. "Because there's nothing the Sidhe can't do."

Except solve their leader's murder, since Lord Kerien had even been desperate enough to ask *me* to help him out. It wasn't flattering. It was worrying.

10

I made my way to the gate alone the following morning, half-expecting to find Darrow waiting on the other side to demand I tell him what Lord Kerien and I had been meeting about yesterday. Instead, I found myself on the path fringed with long-leafed plants leading to the ambassadors' palace.

Strange. Perhaps Lord Kerien had moved the gate during the night to invite me to discuss our discoveries in the Erlking's territory yesterday. He owned the palace, though nobody lived here, and it was one of the few parts of the Court which wasn't dangerous to humans. I scanned the grounds as I entered, spotting a familiar silver-haired faerie disappearing around the corner of the palace.

What was Darrow doing in there? Something about the furtive way he moved made suspicion rear its head, and I trod after him, ducking behind a leafy plant. He leaned over the flowerbed, muttering under his breath.

No—talking to someone. Someone small and semi-transparent with pointed ears and glittering wings.

A sprite. He was sending a message. To whom?

I held my breath and inched closer. I wasn't *bad* at stealth when it was necessary, but I just… wasn't Sidhe. They could casually stride down a path littered with landmines and somehow not tread on any of them without even looking where they were going. No human would ever be able to compete.

Sure enough, when the sprite vanished, Darrow straightened upright and turned my way. "What are you doing here?"

"Someone moved my family's gate." I stepped out from behind the plant as though I'd concealed myself by complete accident. "Was it you?"

"No." He gave me an appraising look. "But since you're here, we'll conduct this morning's lesson in the grounds. We'll need an open outdoor space."

"For what?"

"Today," he said, "I'll see how you handle Summer magic."

I should have seen that one coming. While magic came easier to me here in the Court than it did in the mortal realm, he had an unfair advantage on me with both types of magic at his fingertips, and he knew it.

We walked around the palace to a wide lawn of vibrant grass. Bright flowers bloomed in the flowerbeds, while thick hedges surrounded the lawn on all sides. My Gatekeeper's magic did give me some degree of immunity to the overwhelming assault on the senses in the Summer Court, but everything was so much more *intense* here, from the verdant gleam of the grass to the perfumed scent of the flowers.

I let the slightest stream of magic pour from my hands, and the grass grew an inch or two. "Will that do?"

Darrow glanced at my handiwork. "I didn't think you were capable of such subtle magic."

"Your compliments could use some fine-tuning." I gave him an eye-roll. "I can be subtle when the occasion calls for it, but don't forget the Sidhe have been known to declare war on one another over the wrong kind of elf wine."

Green light sprang to his palms. "Let's check your shielding."

I barely raised my hands in time to deflect the blast of energy. A rippling shield pulsed in front of me, but I didn't give it my all. "You know I have a natural shielding ability, don't you?"

It was part of the same vow that bound me to the Summer Court: no faerie magic could harm me. Not even his, though the gleam in his aquamarine eyes told me he was going to do his best to get around those restrictions.

"Drop your shield, then."

He couldn't seriously be saying he could circumvent my family's protective magic, could he? Breaking my glamour was one thing, but the vow binding my family to Faerie was as solid as iron.

I fed more magic into the glowing shield in my palms, then turned it into a frontal assault. Our attacks hit one another and fizzled out in a shower of sparks.

A second Darrow entered my peripheral vision, and a sudden blast of magic smacked me in the face and sent me flying back onto the lawn. Bloody Darrow and his illusions.

I lay there, winded, my mind reeling. "It's that binding spell, isn't it? You included some kind of small print that lets you hit me with magic without my shield getting in the way."

"I wouldn't be able to train you if all my attacks bounced off you."

Like that bond he'd forced me into didn't have enough downsides already. If he *was* the killer, I might be in a world of trouble. Granted, my shield only deflected offensive magic—not physical assaults, glamours, or sense-altering magic—but it was one fewer advantage at my disposal.

I sat up. "And you just lectured *me* for not being subtle."

"Maybe," he said, "but that's the longest you've been quiet since you got here."

Was that supposed to be funny? Who even knew at this point. I pushed to my feet. "I'd be able to deflect your attacks if didn't throw me off with decoys."

"It sounds like we ought to work on your skills at breaking glamours," he said. "Have you been practising?"

Well, no. Mostly because I had nobody to practise with who had skills on his level. Not that I'd tell him *that*. "Try to land a hit on me, then. I'll see if I can break the decoy first."

Another Darrow appeared at my side. Then a third.

"Are you sure?" said all three Darrows at once.

"I said *one* decoy, not two."

"I don't remember you specifying." One of the clones

blasted me with magical energy. I flung up a shield, but the attack winked out of existence before it touched me.

A spark grew, and I threw myself onto the lawn as a bolt of magic whistled over my shoulder.

"You're supposed to be shielding, not diving onto the grass."

I flipped off one of the Darrows, hoping it was the real guy. "The only rule here is to survive by however means necessary."

"So be it."

Five more Darrows appeared. *Oh, come on.*

Three attacks flew at me from different directions. I threw a shield around myself, scanning the Darrows for any clues about which was the real one. Even he couldn't direct multiple clones without taking at least some of his attention off me, which meant he was more likely to be near the back, out of the line of fire.

Three Darrows were on the back row, so I had a one in three chance of guessing right. He was directing the clones like a necromancer directed a swarm of zombies: his attention was split. If I timed this right...

I reached out, feeling for the humming threads of magic keeping his illusion active. With a yank of my hand, one of the Darrows vanished. My other hand conjured a ball of green energy, directing it at the Darrow on the back right.

The illusion vanished, and a bolt of green light hit me from the side. The clones must have switched places in the seconds it'd taken me to reach the back.

"Dammit!" I sighed. "Almost got it."

"If that were a Trial, you'd have won," he said. "Few

others in the Court can manipulate multiple illusions. It's a rare skill."

Like shooting a bow and arrow across the Erlking's clearing? Without the effects of an excessive amount of elf wine, I managed to refrain from asking that question. "Shouldn't you be testing me on skills the other Sidhe *would* use against me?"

He tilted his head. "All right. You head into that maze —" He pointed to the hedges bordering the lawn—"and I'll try to hit you with magic from behind. I'll give you a head start. If you make it to the forest on the other side, you win."

I'd walked headfirst into that one. "Fine."

"Also," he added, "you're not to use your own magic to make the hedges grow. I'll know if you do."

"If you insist." How could he possibly tell? That was a question for another day, because I wouldn't let him beat me twice in a row.

I stepped into the hedge maze. The floor was littered with leaves but not the sort that crunched when you trod on them. Birdsong sounded above, while rustling noises came from the hedges. The smell of fresh earth drifted from the forest ahead. Darrow would expect me to go charging straight through the maze, so I veered to the side, behind a taller section of hedge. If I deliberately went in the wrong direction, he'd be less likely to assume I was nearby.

The faint scent of oak and ash tickled my nostrils. Close—and too close to be part of the forest.

Darrow. He must have guessed my plan. He'd said he'd know if I used magic… and now I understood how that was possible. The Sidhe possessed heightened senses, including the ability to sense magic itself. While I didn't have a Sidhe's enhanced sense of smell, Darrow's scent of Summer and Winter magic was unique enough even for my human senses to pick up on.

I veered away from the scent and headed in the opposite direction, towards the branches of a drooping willow tree marking the end of the maze.

The sting of magic brushed past my shoulder, sending a branch thumping down in front of me. I broke into a sprint, and the second blast of magic hit me square in the back, sending me stumbling.

Darrow stepped out behind me. "Good effort. You almost made it."

I poked the ground with my foot. "I was out of the maze when you hit me."

"So you were." His brow furrowed. "How did you know to change directions back then? I didn't make a sound."

"I have my ways." Catch me letting on that I'd sniffed him out. Okay, he'd planned to catch me in the same way, but it was easier to sniff out a human than another faerie… unless they were half Winter and half Summer. "I should get to hit you at some point, you know. It's only fair."

"Then we'll try that next."

My plan didn't quite work out. While my Gatekeeper's power would never hold a candle to a Sidhe's talisman, Darrow was just plain impossible to hit. He moved too fast, conjuring illusions as easily as flicking a switch, and saw no issue with striking me while my back was turned.

In the brief seconds between assaults, I pondered how he'd honed his talent. Aside from their talismans, Sidhe often possessed abilities such as shapeshifting, healing powers, and communicating with animals. Glamour was second nature to all of them, but his unique level of skill must have come from a master's coaching.

Not that I had much time to dwell on it. My body was one giant bruise by the time he called the lesson to an end and let me head to the stream on the east side of the garden to wash the sweat from my face and quench my thirst. One point in Faerie's favour was that the water was clean and pure, free of pollutants. Shaking water droplets off my circlet, I looked up and saw that two Sidhe had entered the garden. Lady Aiten and her dark-haired companion, Lord Pointy Spear. The male Sidhe looked bored, while Lady Aiten's smile when she saw me was as false as the glamour on her curled hair and glowing features.

"Gatekeeper." Lady Aiten's gaze lingered on my damp hair. "Is Lord Kerien here?"

"No," I said. "Any reason?"

Might she be one of the Erlking's trusted advisors, too? I doubted it, given how swiftly she'd come to accuse my family, yet her involvement in the investigation implied she'd been in on at least some of his secrets.

"That's no concern of yours, mortal," she said.

I arched a brow. "All right. I was looking for him, too. If you see him, can you let me know?"

Understanding flared in her gaze, and a scowl marred her pretty features. *Aha. So she* does *know.* I half-expected her to level another accusation at me, but Darrow stepped in. "Lady Aiten, is there something I can help you with?"

"I'm looking for Lord Kerien," she said. "So, apparently, is the Gatekeeper."

Thanks a bunch. "He's not here."

"I'm aware." She beckoned to her companion. "Come, Lord Veren."

The two of them walked away. Darrow, meanwhile, turned to me. "Why were you hoping to speak with him?"

"I wanted to know who moved the gate over here," I said. "I assumed he did, since he owns the palace, but I'd prefer my family not to have any more unexpected visits from the Sidhe."

Did Darrow suspect what we'd really been doing yesterday? Perhaps he did, but he couldn't possibly know I'd removed evidence from the crime scene. Besides, it was none of his damn business.

"Really," he said. "And why did you meet yesterday, precisely?"

What's it to you? "Secret Gatekeeper matters."

"Like this?" He held up the Erlking's note. I'd put it back in my pocket when I'd been at home, and it must have fallen out during our training session. Shit, shit, *shit.*

11

D arrow held the note inches from my fingers, his gaze roving over the page. "This parchment has the Erlking's official seal on it. Where did you get this?"

There was no point in lying. He clearly thought I'd stolen it, and if he reported me to the Sidhe, I could say goodbye to any more clandestine visits to the Erlking's territory.

"He sent it to me," I told him. "His sprite visited me after his death."

"This would have cleared your name," he said. "Why not tell the Sidhe?"

"I don't trust them." I raised my chin. "I think the killer is still among them, and clearly, so did the Erlking."

But is it you? His expression betrayed nothing, his gaze skimming the note. "One who breathes..."

"I can't make any sense of it," I added. "Unless you have an idea about who he's referring to?"

"No." He handed me the note back. "I'd advise you not to leave that lying around again."

"I didn't intend to." For all I knew, he'd sneaked it out of my pocket himself when my attention had been occupied with his clones. I wouldn't put anything past him, after the number of underhanded stunts he'd pulled during today's training. "Only two living people in this realm know about that note, and we're both standing right here."

"Why you?" he said. "Why would he pick a human?"

"Beats me." I folded the note and stuck it deep in my pocket.

"You must have some idea." He wasn't going to let this drop, damn him. "Is that why you met with Lord Kerien? The two of you went to the Erlking's territory, didn't you?"

"I'm not at liberty to discuss confidential matters."

"You aren't vow-bound, are you?" he said. "You can speak freely."

"Not everything has to be a vow."

"Perhaps not to you," he said, "but we take our promises seriously."

And just what was that supposed to mean? "I didn't promise to do anything except see to it that my family and I aren't arrested again. That's all I want. May I leave now?"

"No," he said. "You have another task waiting for you at the Gatekeeper's base."

Great.

Even the sight of Coral waiting for me inside the Gatekeeper's training base didn't cheer me up. After Darrow's sleight-of-hand, I wasn't in the mood for any more duplicity.

Coral smiled at me. "You're with me this afternoon. There's food in the kitchen."

"Good. I'm starved." I headed to my quarters and found a plate of food laid out on the table. "What's on the agenda for this afternoon?"

"Poisons," she said. "Come and find me in fifteen minutes. I'll be in the room three doors down on the right."

At least it's not more glamour training. I needed a full bath in healing salve to get rid of all my bruises.

I finished my meal and went to find Coral. She waited in a plainly furnished room containing a large oak table covered in corked bottles.

"What's this about?" I asked.

"Your task is to identify the poisons. The non-poisoned bottles contain nothing harmful, so I'm supposed to order you to drink the ones you don't believe are poisoned."

"Lovely."

"Sorry." She took a seat at the table. "Not my idea. If it helps, we can talk shit about Darrow while you work. I noticed you're limping again."

"I'm now well acquainted with the lawn at the ambassadors' palace." Spy or not, I didn't enjoy being wary of my friends. It was one thing holding myself back from talking about the Erlking's murder, but I wanted someone here I could just *talk* to. Being a spy didn't mean she was an enemy. "You're a spy, aren't you? For the Sea Court."

Her eyes widened. "Please don't tell Darrow."

"Why, would he kick you out?" I glanced down at the bottle in front of me and gave it a sniff. An acidic scent burned my nostrils. Definitely poison.

She bit her lip. "It's complicated. But trust me, the Sea Court is a fraction of the size of Summer, and our Queen wants nothing to do with the Seelie or Unseelie Courts whatsoever. I'm not a warrior. I'm just here to make sure the tension in Summer doesn't lead to war in my own kingdom."

She didn't sound like she was lying. The Sea Court was hardly big enough to pose a threat to Summer, and the sea fae's freedom hinged on the people in charge of the main Courts allowing them to maintain independence. That made it unlikely that the Sea Queen had engineered the Erlking's death, at least, since the new monarch might well decide to conquer the lesser Courts or absorb them into Summer itself. If I belonged to an independent Court, I'd want to keep an eye on the major players, too.

I sniffed at another bottle and moved it to the 'safe' pile. "All right. I just wondered. You know how it is."

"I do," she said. "Anyway… please don't think badly of me for it."

"I don't." Next bottle—poison. "It just took me by surprise that the Sidhe let you work for them. They only started letting half-faeries who were the children of major nobles into the Courts a year or two ago."

"True," she said. "My Queen has had spies here for years, as have the other independent Courts. I expect there'll be more coming to keep an eye on who is chosen as the new monarch."

The image of the family tree on our living room table entered my mind's eye. Mum hadn't even spoken to the Sidhe since she'd been cleared of murdering the Erlking, so the family tree couldn't be anything more than a way of reassuring herself that the situation was fixable.

"At this point, it's anyone's guess," I said. "Half the Court might claim they're distantly descended from the Erlking. Besides, he might have chosen an heir himself and left that information somewhere nobody has checked yet."

Unless the killer had taken the evidence along with the crown and the staff. *Did Lord Kerien consider that?*

"We have a simpler system in the Sea Court," said Coral. "The laws of succession follow through the royal selkie family. Back when the merpeople ruled over our territory, it used to be determined via trial by combat, but that's probably why they ended up halfway to extinction."

"You aren't wrong." The Sidhe could afford to have a cavalier attitude towards bodily harm—at least back when immortality had been taken for granted, anyway—but half-fae had never had that luxury. "I heard they do something similar in Winter. Duel for the crown. I suppose it does force the Sidhe to accept the result, if it's done using a binding contract."

Not that any duel involving the Erlking's talisman would in any way be a fair contest. Being able to disintegrate one's opponent at a touch wasn't exactly good sportsmanship.

"It's easier for us," said Coral. "Most of the Sea Court's population is half-blood or quarter-blood, so we have shorter lifespans than the Sidhe. If we hadn't interbred with humans, we'd have died out."

I looked up from the bottles. "Is that why you grew up with humans?"

"It is," she said. "When I came of age, I was invited to the Sea Court like an equal. It was a bit of a shock to come here and see how they treated half-faeries in Summer and Winter."

"I bet." I moved my current bottle to 'extremely poisonous'. "Dealing with change is not their forte. I kind of feel bad for the next monarch."

They'd never let a half-blood claim the throne, but even a Sidhe who took the Erlking's place would be at risk from assassination, especially if they weren't able to gain power over his talisman.

"Luckily, that isn't your job," she said. "All you have to do is be present for the various ceremonies and try not to get killed."

"Hey, I haven't done a terrible job at staying alive so far." I laid down the last bottle in the 'safe' group. All three safe bottles smelled distinctly of elf wine. "You know, if I have to drink three bottles of elf wine, I'll be too wasted to do any more training exercises today."

"I'll help you." She grinned. "This is your last task of the day, besides. And between you and me, I don't think anyone will notice if we skip over the 'mandatory tasting' part. I doubt anyone's coming to check. Darrow was in a real mood earlier when he left. I think it's because he was arguing with Lord Kerien earlier."

"He was?" I hadn't thought to ask if he'd seen Lord Kerien himself.

"They were arguing about the Sidhe's response to the Erlking's death," she said. "Or lack thereof. It sounded like Darrow was pressuring him about it."

More like pressuring him to explain our secret errand yesterday. "Why? It's not like he's part of the Court. I don't think you were supposed to tell me that, by the way. He gave me this really dirty look when I mentioned it."

"Huh." Her brow crinkled. "Maybe he doesn't want the Gatekeeper to know."

"So you didn't hear which Court he's from. Darrow, I mean."

She shook her head. "Nope. It doesn't matter, in all likelihood. Like I said—we independent Courts have almost no power. And it's not in anyone's interests to start a war with Summer. Even Winter's."

No… the enemy most likely lay within Summer's own borders. And while the Seelie Queen was in jail, she'd been in a position of power for centuries. She'd had enough time to spread her influence among her followers, playing on the rumour that the Erlking was ill and infirm. I needed to speak to Lord Kerien again to learn more of the Sidhe's theories, but not when everyone else was trying to get hold of him at once. Especially Darrow.

I knotted my hands together on the table, tracing the callouses swordplay training had left on my palms. "You know, I might have a glass of wine, after all."

"Knew you'd change your mind." Coral rose to her feet, at the same time as two Sidhe entered the room. Lady Aiten and Lord Pointy Spear. "Is there a problem?"

"Lord Kerien has been found dead," said Lady Aiten. "Come with me, human."

12

Lady Aiten and her companion escorted me out of the Gatekeeper's training grounds and through the forest, which seemed quieter than usual, though my thumping heart drowned out all other sounds. Lord Kerien hadn't been avoiding everyone earlier today after all. Someone had murdered him.

"How?" I spoke through dry lips. "Where?"

Lady Aiten glanced sideways at me. "Lord Kerien was found on the Erlking's territory, killed by a wound that could only have been inflicted by a single weapon."

Chills raced down my spine. "The Erlking's talisman."

"Yes," said Lord Pointy Spear. Lord Veren, she'd called him. "Do you know who might be responsible?"

"No." I was too stunned to think clearly. Had the killer known Lord Kerien and I were investigating the Erlking's death? Nobody else had known of our clandestine trip aside from Darrow, and while Lord Kerien had been alone when they'd ambushed him, for all I knew, I was next on the killer's list.

What did Lord Kerien learn that was worth killing him for?

We reached the gate to the ambassadors' palace, where Lord Raivan stood wearing a furious expression. I braced myself for the hit, but it was Lady Aiten he addressed. "I assure you my skills are better suited elsewhere. I will not waste any more time dealing with mortals—"

"As you told us, and the Sidhe collectively voted otherwise," interjected Lady Aiten. "You *will* take Lord Kerien's place. He named you to inherit this palace, and you will honour his last wishes."

Lord Raivan's pale face flushed with anger. "This is an outrage."

Some people need to get their priorities in order. I gathered Lord Raivan hadn't been in the Erlking's inner circle, given his lowly status in the Court, and Lord Kerien must have believed he wasn't the killer if he'd entrusted him to take on custody of the palace. Which gave me one person to trust—pity he was such a whiner.

Ignoring Lord Raivan, Lady Aiten led me up the stairs and through the oak doors into the palace hall. After exchanging some words with her companion, she gestured through a side door into a tapestried room. The same room where Darrow and I had bound ourselves, mentor to apprentice. Lord Veren walked away, leaving the two of us alone in the room, and with a snap of Lady Aiten's fingers, the door closed.

I cleared my throat. "Is this an interrogation?"

"You were looking for Lord Kerien earlier today, around the time he was killed," said Lady Aiten.

Crap. If the Sidhe used their magic to wring the truth from me, they'd know I'd been on the Erlking's territory. Not only would it land me back on their suspect list, I might well be the next to die if the murderer got wind of my involvement. When the Erlking had foisted this mission on me, he might have considered that it would be a thousand times harder for me to investigate when everyone in the Court wanted me to stay the hell out of their business.

"I wanted to ask him how my family's gate ended up outside the ambassador's palace," I told her. "It's not important now, anyway. Did the killer leave any identifying clues behind?"

"No." Her eyes glittered with green light. "Tell me… what were you doing this morning?"

"Training with Darrow. You *saw* me." I'd had about enough of this crap. "As for my family, they were at home, and the gate was right here. They don't even know the way to the Erlking's territory, and they wouldn't touch that talisman with a ten-foot pole."

"Your sister carries her own talisman, does she not?" said Lady Aiten.

Nice try. "It's a book that can summon the dead, not a staff that destroys everything it touches. Major difference there. She's also living in Edinburgh and can't get here without me to open the gate for her. Why are you so dead set on blaming my family?"

She gave me a long look. "Your family's circumstances make you look guilty by default, and given the method in which the Erlking was killed, I felt it was prudent to step in and question you before the other Sidhe get any ideas. There are many who would not weep to see the Gatekeepers driven out of Faerie."

Wait, she thought someone was trying to frame us? Or was I reading too much into it? "You're not exactly helping that impression, hauling me off into a room to interrogate me."

At least she hadn't made me swear another vow.

"Would you rather face the full council?" she said.

"I've told you everything I know," I said through gritted teeth. "I don't know who killed the Erlking or Lord Kerien, and that's the truth."

Everything else I'd concluded, they could work out on their own. Even the tunnels. It wasn't hard to guess. The question was, why had the killer chosen to use the talisman against Lord Kerien when they might have used any other method to kill him?

To send a message, a warning to every Sidhe in the Courts that none of them was safe from the talisman's magic. A bloody effective one, too.

The door opened with a creaking sound, revealing Lord Raivan, Lord Veren and several other Sidhe.

"Lady Aiten," said Lord Raivan. "Are you still questioning the human?"

She has a name. "I think we're done in here," I said. "I was in the back garden of this palace when Lord Kerien was murdered. Darrow can back me up."

They must know that our bond also told him where I was at any given time, too. Not that I could trust him to have my back when it came to my ill-timed visit to the Erlking's territory.

"No human could have wielded that talisman," said Lord Veren. "The traitor is one of our own."

Mutters broke out among the other Sidhe, but none looked directly at me. Without Lord Kerien, I was back to square one in terms of Sidhe allies, but at least they weren't shouting accusations. I'd take it.

"Sounds like you should be looking for any Sidhe who are currently missing from Court," I told them. "Not someone who has an alibi that can be confirmed by multiple people. Even the person who killed the Erlking probably wasn't human."

"Oh?" Lord Raivan cocked a brow. "What gives you expertise on that matter? He was poisoned with iron."

"Yes, but the killer managed to sneak up on him without being detected," I said. "They also knew the layout of his territory and how to remove his security. Even without the details, I can guess that they must have had inside help from someone who knew his territory well. As for how he died? Even if the killer used iron, they must have had magical advantages at their disposal."

"Lord Kerien did suggest the weapon used to kill the Erlking must have been enchanted," said a silver-haired male Sidhe who wore deep-green armour patterned with holly leaves. "That means the killer was Sidhe. Or half-blood, perhaps."

"Half-bloods wouldn't be familiar with the Erlking's territory," said Lady Aiten. "The Queen would never—" She broke off, with a glance at me.

Aha. So she does agree with my theory.

"The Queen would never what?" I said. "Hook up with a half-faerie? I don't know her well enough to assume anything, but she might have told anyone how to get in. She had no love for her husband."

"She is a known traitor and conspirator," said a blond Sidhe. Lord Torin, River's father. He wouldn't toss my family under the bridge, even if his influence among the higher Sidhe was minimal.

"Leave, human," said Lady Aiten. "We will discuss this further among ourselves."

I left the room, my mind spinning. The Sidhe believed me. The apocalypse was nigh. Not that I was all that keen to usher it in. After all, while the Sidhe and I might be on the same wavelength, it seemed someone was murdering them for it.

In the entrance hall, Darrow stood waiting for me. "Come with me."

So much for being off the hook. "I already answered all Lady Aiten's questions."

"You met with Lord Kerien yesterday for a reason." He walked into step with me as I made for the exit.

"I wasn't the last person to see him alive," I pointed out. "Also, he was killed while we were training, which gives both of us an alibi."

"I know," he said. "So does Lady Aiten. What I would like to know is why he chose to take you with him to the Erlking's territory, especially if you were telling the truth earlier and he didn't know about the note."

"Of course I was telling the truth," I said, irritated that he'd assume otherwise. "I wish you and the Sidhe would put as much effort into catching the culprit as you put into interrogating me. Maybe then Lord Kerien would still be alive."

"You've seen his territory before, so Lord Kerien assumed you might have insight into the Erlking's death," said Darrow, seemingly unconcerned by my comment. "I understand why you would feel reluctant to confide in the other Sidhe, but I'm not your enemy."

Uh-huh. "You report everything I do to the Sidhe yourself. Don't deny it. Even if not, they can wrench the truth from you with a word if they so desire."

He halted in front of the oak doors. "I find it hard to believe that you chose not to confide in me out of concern for my safety."

More like because I don't know if I can trust you. Each clue I unravelled made him less likely to fit the profile of the killer and it was unlikely he'd zipped over to the Erlking's territory to murder Lord Kerien while I'd been with Coral, but that didn't mean he didn't have his own agenda.

"I didn't *ask* to be entrusted with this," I said. "If you must know, there's nothing Lord Kerien didn't tell me that the other Sidhe haven't already concluded. The killer sneaked up on the Erlking through the tunnels under his territory. It sounds like Lord Kerien went back for a closer look and the killer ambushed him."

His brows rose. "Tunnels?"

"Yes, tunnels." I pushed the oak doors open and walked out of the palace. "The Erlking was shot from a distance, which means it was probably a Sidhe or half-blood. No humans are that good at archery."

"Unless the bow they used was enchanted," he said.

"Feel free to hand that theory over to the Sidhe." My heart gave a sudden lurch. A bow that never missed its target might be enchanted... or it might be a talisman. Why hadn't I thought of that?

I turned back to the palace, wondering if the Sidhe had come to the same conclusion. A large proportion of the Sidhe wielded talismans, but most favoured swords or spears, not bows. Add in the murderer's familiarity with the Erlking's territory and the suspect list shrank even further.

"I will," he said. "I hope for your own sake that you leave the investigating to the Sidhe from now on."

"Why?" I tilted my head. "Now you're worried for my safety, are you? Or just your own position?"

He opened his mouth to reply, but whatever he planned to say, I never found out. A furious shout drifted over from outside the gates to the palace. A human voice.

"They went after my family." Anger rose, sharp and potent, and I marched out of the palace's grounds in time to see someone disappear through the Summer gate.

"Hey!" I shouted. "Where do you think you're going?"

A male Sidhe turned and gave me a cold look. His hair was blue-black, pulled into a ponytail, while his gold-plated armour clung to his muscular frame. "The killer is no longer in our realm," he said. "This is the nearest exit."

"Like hell." I marched over to the gate, hearing Mum's raised voice from the other side. "You're trespassing."

"Everything your family owns belongs to the Seelie Court, Gatekeeper." He drew a gleaming sword and pointed it at me. "Do not overstep your boundaries."

"Touch my daughter," said Mum, "and you die."

Mum stood on the gate's threshold, an iron knife in her hand. *Holy crap.*

The Sidhe spun around, blade and all. "Life is fragile. I'd keep it in mind before you threaten me, mortal."

"If life is fragile," said Mum, "perhaps you ought to cherish yours more."

Uh... wow, Mum. Part of me wanted to tell her to calm down before the Sidhe skewered her, but it came as no surprise to see her snap, considering she'd worked for the Sidhe thanklessly for years and they'd repaid her by invading her home and trying to arrest her family.

Clearing my throat, I jabbed a finger at the lawn visible through the gates. "Look at the grass there. It's alive. If you've ever seen the Erlking's territory, you'd know his talisman destroys anything living. Clearly, it's not in my family's garden."

The Sidhe gave me a scowl, but the two other Sidhe walked through the gates and back into Faerie. As soon as they did, I joined Mum on the other side. "Are you okay?"

"Of course." She pushed the gate closed. "I should be asking you the same question."

"I'm fine, despite Lady Aiten's best efforts." I stood stock-still, my body thrumming with tension. When the gate opened again and Darrow stepped through, I made no effort to hide my groan. "If you're here to accuse us, please do us all a favour and throw yourself in the pond so I don't have to do it for you."

"I'm not." His gaze flicked to Mum. "Did they violate the treaty?"

"No." Mum lowered her knife. "Hazel, tell me if you'll be staying here tonight and I'll take precautions."

She turned around and walked back to the Lynn house. Darrow watched her leave, his brow cocked. "She raised you alone?"

"Three of us," I said. "Word of advice: don't fuck with her."

"Three of you," he repeated. "The others aren't bound to serve the Court."

"No, and if the Sidhe go after my siblings, I'll give them the same treatment I gave that troll."

"I'm starting to understand where your attitude came from." His gaze followed Mum as she entered the house through the back door.

"I like to think I have an attitude all of my own." And if the Sidhe were willing to break the rules, then I'd return the favour. I made for the gates again and opened them, entering Summer once again.

Darrow stepped through behind me and caught my sleeve. "That shield of yours won't stop them from running you through with their swords."

"I'm aware of that." His fingers were curled loosely around my wrist, just above the mark of our bond, and tension hummed in the inches between us. I didn't think he was the killer, not anymore, and I wanted to trust his judgement. Pity I knew I was right, and since he'd pressured me to confide in him, his own head might end up on a platter if the killer realised he knew the details of the Erlking's death, too.

I retraced my steps to the ambassadors' palace, strode through the oak doors into the hall, and made straight for the Sidhe's meeting room. After knocking on the door twice, I yanked it open. "I need to speak to you, Lady Aiten."

"I told you to leave, mortal," she said, her voice flinty and sharp.

"That was before several of your fellow Sidhe tried to attack my family." I took in the other Sidhe's shock at my brazenness with some satisfaction. "I want a guarantee that my family members will stay safe from any further unwanted visitors."

Lady Aiten looked me up and down. "I won't be long. Please continue the discussion without me."

I waited until the other Sidhe were out of earshot before I spoke again. "We can do this any way you like, but I don't trust the Sidhe to uphold the treaty with the Gatekeepers for the duration of the investigation."

"Why should I do you a favour?" she said.

"Because I have information that I think you'll want me to keep to myself," I told Lady Aiten. "Lord Kerien worked for the Erlking. The Erlking told me himself, and he told me another of his close advisors was you."

Silence hung between us for an instant. "You lie."

"Prove it." For once, being distrusted by default worked in my favour. "I might add that the killer seems to be targeting the Erlking's former advisors, so the more people who know, the more likely it is that you'll be the next victim."

Her gaze cut into mine. "I give you my word that I will not allow anyone to harm your family for the duration of your time as Gatekeeper, provided you share that information with nobody else."

"Done." Lady Aiten must *really* not want anyone to know she'd worked for the Erlking. And she couldn't lie, so she'd be bound to keep her word. "Pleasure doing business with you."

"I hope you're ready to pay the price for that bargain, mortal," she said softly.

When Lady Aiten walked back to the meeting room, I released a breath, some of the tension leaving my shoulders. Her influence wouldn't keep every Sidhe from harming my family, but it reduced the risk that Mum would be hauled off to jail while my back was turned.

"That was risky," said Darrow.

"So was saying and doing nothing," I said. "The Gatekeeper's treaty isn't enough to guarantee my family's safety at a time like this."

"No, you're right." Surprising hints of respect gleamed in those deep aquamarine eyes. "You handled that admirably."

My mouth fell open. "Praise. I didn't think you had it in you."

He frowned. "I always tell you when you perform well."

"You spend ten times as long pointing out my flaws." I shrugged. "But I like it. Keeps me on my toes."

He shook his head. "Are you always so… direct?"

"Mum says I wear my heart on my sleeve."

His brow wrinkled. "That sounds painful. Unless you're referring to that iron you wear?"

Right… the band on my wrist. Of course he would have noticed it, though it surprised me that he hadn't said anything until now. "It's a figure of speech." I pushed up my sleeve to my elbow. "But I guess it is, technically. This was a gift from my sister."

He read the word engraved into the iron band. "Lynn. Your name."

"*Our* name." A reminder that the Sidhe would never take away our loyalty to one another. Darrow, being as literal as the other fae, probably wouldn't understand the concept.

His gaze clouded, then cleared. "Like partnership bonds."

"I guess." Instead of engagement rings, the Sidhe often exchanged engraved bracelets or other trinkets engraved with the name of their beloved. "Do they do the same where you come from?"

"Yes, but I think it's unwise to make a public declaration of one's weak points," he said.

"You and I have very different ideas about what constitutes weakness, Darrow." I'd almost forgotten his words when we'd first met, when he'd insinuated that having a conscience meant opening oneself up to being stabbed in the back. Being raised by the Sidhe had likely bestowed the message that acting like a human was a sign of weakness, but the slightest edge to his voice spoke of a history even I wasn't nosy enough to go poking into—yet. Maybe I'd save that for the next time we were both in close proximity to a vat of elf wine.

"I suppose we do," he said.

"Maybe it comes with not being immortal, but I figure it's better to risk heartbreak than to spend your life closed off from everyone." I held up my wrist, revealing the band. "Also, there's a reason this is made of iron. As far as I'm concerned, that's no weakness at all."

"I respect your opinion," he said. "Your lessons for the day are over, but Coral asked me to inform you that she has a surprise for you back at the Gatekeeper's base. You're invited to spend the night in Faerie, if you so wish. Extra guards will be posted outside your doors."

"I'm not all that keen on the idea." Then again, given Mum's earlier behaviour, heads would roll if I stayed at the Lynn house and the Sidhe dragged me out of the bed in the middle of the night. "But fine. As long as I get to sleep in."

13

As it turned out, I needn't have worried about my return to the Gatekeeper's training base. Coral had mobilised the other half-Sidhe to prepare for my return, and I entered one of the training rooms to find them seated around a makeshift picnic table laden with the bottles of wine from the earlier training exercise and plates of pizza that looked like they'd been lifted straight from the mortal realm.

"It's not quite the same as a party," she said. "Hope it's okay."

"Are you kidding? It's perfect." I picked up a plate. "I'd take this over a fancy ball. It's just what I need right now."

"Awesome." She beamed, passing plates around. "We're on your side. All of us. What the Sidhe did to you was bullshit."

"It was," agreed one of the half-dryads.

It looked like all the other bodyguards had come to join in. Except for Aila, but that suited me just fine. "I don't want you in trouble for slacking off on duty."

"We're rotating shifts. Anyway, we won't get into trouble for smuggling in pizza and shot glasses." Coral winked, taking a seat at the table.

"I knew you smuggled it in." I grabbed a slice of pepperoni pizza, dripping with mozzarella.

"Faerie doesn't have Dominos," added Willow.

"I like you already." I gave Coral a grin. Willow's olive-tinted skin and thick dark hair put me in mind of Lady Aiten, and I wondered if Coral had seen them side by side and put two and two together.

I'd never been shy about making friends, and I had a great buzz going by the time we'd finished the first round of shots, enough to introduce the others to a few drinking games from the mortal realm and share some of the less scandalous of my stories.

Darrow entered the room in the middle of a long anecdote about the time I'd accepted a dare from a half-Sidhe and ended up chased across the Highlands by a pack of Little People wielding sharp instruments.

I gave him a wave. "Come to join in?"

"No. There are some Sidhe here who want to talk to you?"

"Seriously?"

I dragged myself to my feet and walked into the entrance hall to find three unfamiliar male Sidhe standing side by side.

"What is it now?" I said. "We were playing Never Have I Ever, not plotting murder."

Coral stopped beside me. "Uh, Hazel, they aren't from around here."

Now she mentioned it, the newcomers wore long dark clothes, in total defiance of Summer's usual bright fashions. While their eyes glittered in the same green shade as most Seelie fae, their hoods were up, masking their ethereal beauty. The Sidhe in the centre stood a foot taller than the others, a giant even by faerie standards, which made his two companions look puny in comparison. Unfortunately for all of them, their cloaks looked like they'd been bought by someone who hadn't bothered to check the sizes, because the two shorter Sidhe were surrounded by puddles of spare fabric while the central Sidhe's cloak ended around his knees.

"Who are you?" I said.

"You took our king from us," said the Sidhe on the right-hand side of his giant companion.

"I didn't take anything from anyone," I informed him. "If you aren't part of a Gatekeeper's Trial, please kindly get lost."

"We do not respect the Gatekeeper," added the leftmost Sidhe.

Coral swore under her breath. "You revoked your Court vows."

"They *what?*" I'd thought only exiles were freed from their binding to the Court, at the cost of being stripped of their magic and booted out of Faerie altogether. These guys didn't look like outcasts, but they didn't look like much else either. Except Lord Voldemort's followers, maybe.

The tallest Sidhe lowered his hood, revealing a waterfall of silky dark hair topped with a thorny circlet. "The everlasting king still wears his crown, and we await his return."

"Then go and wait for it," I said. "Are you're implying the Erlking is still alive?"

I should have seen something like this coming. In Faerie, immortality had ruled for countless generations, and the ripple effects of its loss were only just beginning to stir. I hadn't expected some of the Sidhe would flat-out deny the Erlking was dead, though.

"He will live forever," said Right Sidhe. "And you are preventing his return."

"I'm not hiding him under the bed." I folded my arms. "And we're busy, so if you don't mind…"

The *snick* sound of weapons being drawn pulled a sigh from me. I wasn't drunk enough for this, not to mention only armed only with a plastic pizza fork.

Coral raised her fists. "Stop threatening the Gatekeeper and go and talk to the Sidhe if you're concerned about the heir to the crown."

"The other Sidhe have moved beyond their former king already," said the central Sidhe, anger darkening his expression. "They are plotting to drown his loss in revelry."

"They're organising a funeral?" Funerals weren't generally a thing in Faerie—for obvious reasons—but the Sidhe never passed up an opportunity to throw a party. "Look, I'm lost on how this is supposed to be my fault. Do the other Sidhe know you're defying your Court vows?"

Right Sidhe raised his blade. I threw the plastic fork in his face, causing him to stumble onto the end of his over-long cloak, and swept his legs out from underneath him while he was unbalanced. Coral traded punches with the other short guy, who was a surprisingly sloppy fighter for a Sidhe. Maybe they'd been drinking, too. With one well-timed strike, she sent him crashing sideways into a puddle of cloak.

As I'd predicted, the bigger guy was even easier to knock down. I feinted, then punched him hard in the gut, winding him. Then I grabbed one of the Sidhe's discarded blades and thwacked him over the back of the head with it. He went down like a falling pillar, right on top of his two buddies. Two piteous shrieks came from within the tangle of cloaks, and it was at that moment that Darrow entered the main hall again.

"What is going on in here?" He eyed the pile of fallen Sidhe. So much for the extra security guards.

"We were just having a friendly chat." I kicked the big guy when he stirred. "About the Erlking and his death. Seems they're a little confused about his untimely passing."

"I'll take care of them," he said. "You should have called me."

I gave the nearest Sidhe a poke with my foot. "I'd be more concerned about their safety than mine, to be honest."

A grin crept onto Coral's face. Then she broke into laughter, and so did I. Darrow looked at both of us as though he was seriously questioning our sanity, which only made me laugh harder.

As far as assassination attempts went, I'd seen worse.

Raised voices in the corridor outside my room jolted me from sleep. Lifting my head groggily, I distinguished Coral's frantic voice among the clamour.

I got out of bed and pushed the door open. In the main hall, Coral stood with her back to the wall, while several

Sidhe surrounded her with their weapons drawn. Lady Aiten's remorseless gaze pinned my friend to the spot.

"Lady Aiten." I walked over to her side. "What's going on this time?"

"Your friend has committed treason."

I gave Coral an alarmed look, my heart plummeting. "If you mean those fanatics we trounced yesterday, they broke Court law."

"We have spent the last day scouring the Court for a bow that cannot miss its target," said Lady Aiten. "Our records show that the Erlking traded an item that fitted that description to an ally some years ago."

My brain woke up a little. "You mean the weapon that killed the Erlking? There *is* a talisman in the form of a bow that's enchanted never to miss?"

"Yes," said Coral quietly. "It belongs to my own Queen."

Shit. "Really?"

Coral raised her chin. "The Sea Queen has owned the bow since the days of the treaty with Summer and would never turn it on her allies. You're welcome to search my rooms if you want to ensure I don't have any talismans with me."

"You're free to search mine, too," I put in. "I've had as much contact with the Sea Kingdom this week as she has."

Lady Aiten's eyes narrowed. "Coral is the only member of the Sea Court known to be here in Summer, so naturally, she's our first point of contact with the Sea Kingdom."

"If you wish to speak with the Sea Queen, you'll have to go in person," said Coral. "She hasn't set foot on land in decades."

"In that case," said Lady Aiten, "you are to speak to her yourself and confirm her talisman was not involved in this atrocious crime."

Damn her. I'd forced her to swear not to harm my family, so I'd bet she'd gone looking for ways to target my friends herself. Granted, I hadn't known the Sea Queen possessed a talisman which fitted the description of the weapon used to murder the Erlking, but Coral had committed no crimes. I didn't doubt that for an instant.

"Coral is my bodyguard," I said. "She can't do her job if she's away in the Sea Kingdom."

Lady Aiten turned to me. "Then you'll go with her and act as our emissary to speak with the Sea Court."

"Lady Aiten." Darrow entered the main hall. "What is going on?"

"We have found evidence that the weapon used to murder the Erlking matches the exact description of a talisman owned by the Queen of the Sea Kingdom," said Lady Aiten. "As an ambassador for the Sea Kingdom, Coral must return and speak to her Queen to confirm her talisman was not used in the crime. The Gatekeeper will go with her."

"Very well."

"Excuse me?" Whatever happened to his taking my side against the Sidhe? I hadn't signed up for an impromptu trip into the ocean, and if I left, there might not be a Court to come back to at this rate.

On the other hand, what if the talisman the Sea Queen wielded really was responsible for the Erlking's death? Perhaps the truth lay beneath the waters of the Sea Kingdom, not here in the Court.

"Hazel requires testing in diplomacy and negotiation

as part of her Trials," Darrow said. "Provided she comes to no harm, I will allow her to go to the Sea Kingdom and speak with the Queen."

Ordinarily, I'd leap at the chance to go as far away from Summer as possible while the Sidhe argued among themselves, but it couldn't be more obvious they wanted me gone in a more permanent sense. If I perished in the depths of the ocean, my bargain with Lady Aiten would become void.

"It is settled, then," said Lady Aiten. "We shall take our leave."

The group of Sidhe about-turned and vanished in a flash of green light, leaving the three of us alone in the cave.

"Wonderful." I gripped my right wrist with my left hand. "Sorry, Coral. I hoped they'd started to come around and stopped accusing innocent people. I... may have baited Lady Aiten yesterday for letting the other Sidhe go after my family."

"There's a great deal of unrest in the Court at present," said Darrow. "Speaking to the Sea Queen will assuage their fears of an outside threat and will also confirm we still have an ally in the Sea Court."

"That's if their Queen doesn't take offence at being accused of murdering the Erlking," I pointed out. "Besides, the unrest isn't going to go away in a day. Look at what happened last night. I bet those fanatics aren't the only ones out looking for trouble."

"Perhaps, but by the time you return, the Sidhe will have come to a decision on whether to conduct a celebration of the Erlking's life and death," said Darrow. "It has been so long since death has touched the Court, but many believe the Erlking would have wanted it."

"Celebration," I said. "You mean some of them want to throw a funeral party. Let me guess… Lord Niall is one of them."

"Yes." His mouth thinned. "If you go with Coral to the Sea Kingdom, it will count towards your Trials whether you learn anything new or not."

Translation: going into the Sea Kingdom would bring me one step closer to getting rid of the bond. As a bonus, I might find out which Court Darrow really belonged to. I wouldn't lie, I was kind of curious about how things worked in the independent Courts, and with Coral at my side, I'd have at least one ally.

"Fine," I said. "I'll have to drop by the Lynn house first to grab a water-breathing charm. Will I need anything else?"

"I recommend wearing suitable clothing," said Coral.

"Pretty sure Mum has a faerie-proof wet suit somewhere." She'd been on a fair few diplomatic missions herself. "I'm just going to grab some shoes, then we'll leave."

I backed into my room and threw on a fresh outfit, not that it mattered considering I'd need to change into something suitable for swimming in when I got back to the Lynn house. I splashed water onto my face to wake myself up and imagined Mum's expression when I told her about my mission. *I couldn't just have a normal Gatekeeper's induction, could I?*

I re-joined Coral in the main hall. "Let's go and meet the Queen."

"You know, I'd have liked to take you on a tour of the

Sea Kingdom when your Trials are over," Coral admitted as we walked out of the tunnel and into the daylight. "But this is different. The Queen might well lash out at you for accusing her."

"I don't know about you, but I'd like to stay out of the Court until the Sidhe stop arguing about funerals," I said. "You never know—the Sea Queen might have a theory about the Erlking's death that we haven't thought of yet."

It wasn't outside the realm of possibility that the Seelie Queen's conspirators weren't all from this Court, either.

"She might," said Coral, but she sounded doubtful. "That talisman is designed for war. There hasn't been one in our Kingdom for a very long time."

"The person who did this already stole at least one talisman," I reminded her. "They'd need one to get into the Erlking's territory to begin with. Maybe they targeted the bow in an attempt to pin the blame on your Queen."

She shook her head. "I really don't think so, Hazel. The Sea Queen keeps the talisman with her all the time, even when she's sleeping."

"That might not be enough to convince the Court, though." When the Sidhe fixated on a theory, they wouldn't let it drop.

"It won't." She sighed. "The Queen's talisman can't miss. And the Sidhe seem certain an enchanted bow killed the Erlking. If I'd known he was shot with an arrow, I'd have realised she might be accused."

"I should have told you." I lowered my head. "Faerie is rubbing off on me." That, and Darrow's safety lectures.

"About that," she said. "How'd you know a bow killed him before I did? They couldn't have let that much slip at your own interrogation."

"Lord Kerien," I said. "He showed me the crime scene."

She halted mid-step. "Whoa. Is that why Lady Aiten went after your family?"

"She doesn't know," I said, "but she just plain doesn't like me. I managed to force her to promise to leave me and my family alone, but I didn't know she'd go after you next."

"Given the nature of the Erlking's death, it was inevitable," she said. "I don't blame you, Hazel. There are no easy choices here. But my Queen hasn't left the water in years—that is the truth."

"I believe you," I said. "I think the Sidhe are desperate. Not to mention at odds with one another over this supposed funeral. To be honest, I'd rather not stay here and get dragged in as a scapegoat. Darrow says this mission counts towards my Trials, so I'm all for letting the Sidhe fight it out while we're not around."

She smiled. "I appreciate the support, regardless."

I just had to hope my decision wouldn't come back to bite me.

———

The instant I entered the Lynn house, Mum appeared before me wielding a knife in her hand.

I raised my palms. "Whoa. It's only me."

"Hazel." Mum lowered the knife. "I thought you were staying in the faerie realm for the foreseeable future."

"I'm taking a quick detour," I explained. "To the Sea Kingdom. It seems they have a talisman which matches the criteria for the weapon that killed the Erlking."

Her brows rose. "The Sea Queen's bow?"

"Did I learn about it? I forgot." No wonder, since my education had barely skimmed over the Courts outside of Summer and Winter. "Anyway, I need a spell for water-breathing and a wet suit. Preferably one with built-in armour." Grindylows, merrows and other nasties lurked in the deep, keen to ensnare human prey.

"There's a spell in the store cupboard," she said. "And a spare wet suit upstairs. It should fit you."

"Cheers." I gave Coral a thumbs-up out the window, glad I hadn't invited her into the house when Mum was in such a trigger-happy mood. "The Sea Queen's ambassador, Coral, is waiting outside, by the way. Please don't throw any knives at her."

I made for the hall, where the door into Mum's study lay open. So many piles of junk filled the small cupboard-sized room that it was a wonder she could find anything at all in here.

"The Sidhe didn't go after Ilsa and Morgan, did they?" I called over my shoulder.

"No," Mum said from behind me. "Do they suspect the Sea Queen had a hand in the Erlking's death?"

"No idea." I picked up a box of spells, sifting through in search of a water-breathing charm. "The Sea Queen's bow might be powerful, but it sounds like it would have been difficult to smuggle it into the Court. Besides, it's not in the Sea Kingdom's interests to start a war with a Court so much bigger than theirs."

"Perhaps, but it seems a prudent time for the Seelie Court to check up on their allies," she said. "Especially as the murderer may have hidden the Erlking's talisman in a neighbouring kingdom."

Yeah, right. She and I both knew that was bollocks.

There was one place the Erlking's talisman and its thief must be, and she had nightmares about it even more often than I did.

The Grey Vale. The land of the outcasts.

"They're trying to decide whether to hold a funeral for the Erlking." I returned the box to the pile and tried another, finding a water-breathing spell nestled among a collection of other handmade charms. "I also got attacked by a group of fanatics who think the Erlking never died and he's going to be reborn as their messiah or something, but they were about as threatening as a dead slug."

"I'm surprised it didn't start sooner," she said. "Word of his death has spread among the half-blood communities here in the mortal realm, and many are claiming to be the Erlking's relations in the hope of getting an invitation into the Court."

"Already?" I withdrew from the study with the water-breathing spell, which was shaped like a silver bracelet patterned with leaves. "How's the family tree going?"

"I'll show you later," she said. "You'd better go and change. That water-breathing spell lasts three hours, by the way."

"That should be fine." I climbed the stairs to Mum's bedroom and pulled her old wet suit out of the back of the wardrobe. The two of us were the same size, and sure enough, it moulded to my body like a second skin. It wasn't the most flattering garment, but it was custom-made with padded armour to keep me safe from under-water fae and came with a hood to cover my circlet.

Downstairs, I pulled the accompanying flippers onto my feet and hop-shuffled out of the house to find Coral.

"Don't laugh," I said. "I know I look like a penguin."

She snorted. "At least you're well-protected."

I slid the spell onto my wrist. "This lasts three hours. How are we getting there?"

"We need to find somewhere with water," she said. "Anywhere works. I can create a pathway to the Sea Kingdom from there."

"That saves time," I said. "I did wonder how you hoped to fly to the coast from here. We can't use the pond in the grove—the waters in there are magical, they might have side effects. But there's another pond over by the fence."

I shuffle-hopped over to the pond at the garden's edge and gave the bracelet on my wrist a firm twist. Magic rushed up my arm, making my chest flutter. *Hope that means my lungs are ready to be submerged.*

Coral leaned over the pond's murky surface. "Ready?"

Not really. "Sure."

Coral spoke. "We wish to enter the Sea Kingdom, by invitation of the Sea Queen herself."

At once, the pond's surface turned dark and shimmering. My heartbeat kicked into gear.

Coral took my hand and pulled me close to the edge. "Let the current take you. Don't try to fight it."

I sucked in a breath. "You know, Coral, I'm really not that sure about—"

A torrent of salt water rose and crashed over my head, carrying me into its depths.

14

Darkness descended, and despite the water-breathing spell, my lungs constricted, the world shrinking to a bubble. The current continued to tug on me, and I held myself still, letting myself be pulled along. The tight sensation in my chest disappeared, and I blinked to clear my vision as the currents slowed enough for me to look around and see Coral swimming alongside me in the form of a seal. Sleek and graceful, she swam in a circle and waved at me with a flipper, beckoning me to follow her.

"That was rougher than I expected." Hey, at least my voice was still working. Another effect of the water-breathing spell. It wouldn't be easy to negotiate with the Sea Queen if we couldn't communicate with one another.

Coral waved her flipper again, beckoning to follow me. Then she swam down into the deeps, leaving me in the dust—or rather, water.

I was in good shape, but swimming wasn't something I did on a regular basis. Muscles I didn't even know I had burned in protest by the time I caught up to her. She'd turned into her human form, her golden hair streaming behind her in the water and her feet touching the sandy floor. Behind her, I spotted the outlines of several stone buildings etched against the surrounding gloom.

A grey seal waited nearby. He had the same markings as Coral did, white splotches on his grey skin, while his dark eyes regarded me with suspicion.

"This is my brother," she said. "Shift to human form, Cliff, won't you?"

"You can go without breathing even in your human form?" I asked.

"We don't," she said. "Breathe, I mean. Not when we're in the water."

"Guess you learn something new every day. I have a three-hour time limit." The bracelet on my wrist glowed while it was active, but I wished it came with a timer to let me know how long I had until the spell ran out. Three hours should be enough, but in the faerie realms, time had a tendency to disobey the usual rules.

The grey seal shifted into the form of a man with sandy hair grown to his shoulders and knotted with strands of seaweed. "My sister didn't tell me she was bringing visitors."

"I didn't get much warning," I admitted. "The Sidhe ordered me to come here to talk to your Queen."

He scowled at Coral. "Our mother is not having one of her best days."

"Your mother." Wait. "You're the prince? That means Coral…"

"Shh." She pressed a finger to her lips. "He's next in line, not me. The Summer Court doesn't know."

"Really?" That surprised me, but I wouldn't begrudge her right to privacy. "She will speak to us, won't she?"

"Yes," said Coral. "Cliff, can you let her know we're on our way?"

His gaze flicked to the Gatekeeper's mark on my forehead with dislike shimmering in his dark eyes, before he shifted into a seal and swam away towards the stone houses.

Coral frowned. "Sorry about him. I could have sent a warning, but given how the Sidhe were acting earlier, I thought it was better for us to just show up."

"It's okay," I said. "Maybe you should be the one to talk to the Queen, though. I'm not so sure I'm welcome here."

"We just don't get a lot of outsiders. Obvious reasons." She beckoned me to swim after her. The outlines of the houses became more distinct, most of them made of stone and curtained with swaying water plants. Others had been converted from the ruins of capsized boats and decorated with barnacles and kelp.

The further we swam, the more people we saw. At a guess, the Sea Court was about half merfolk, half selkies, with a few nereids gathering in clusters. The merpeople had long tails and blue-green hair and wore thin dress-like garments, pointing up at us and goggling at the mark on my forehead. Selkies were recognisable by their seal skin capes, and while some remained in their seal forms, the majority turned human when they saw us, gathering to whisper among themselves.

We halted in front of the carcass of a sunken ship, covered in barnacles and shells in decorative patterns. *This* is the palace?" I whispered to Coral.

"It is." She swam up to the wooden door placed in

front of a hole in the ship's side, whose faded paint made it look like it'd been snatched from a human establishment. Around us, amphibian-like fae clustered, their webbed fingers reaching to touch me. I pulled my arms closer to myself, suppressing a shudder.

"Don't worry, the grindylows here don't bite," Coral said over her shoulder.

"I'll take your word for it." I swam up behind her, peering into the gloom beyond the door. "Are you sure the Sea Queen is at home?"

Despite the glowing rocks placed at intervals within, the empty vessel had a distinctly abandoned air. I swam close behind Coral, and movement ahead jerked me to a halt. A wild-haired faerie woman lurked in the gloom, pointing her bow at me.

"Uh," I said. "I take it you're the Sea Queen?"

The weapon in her hands could only be the talisman. Elegantly carved and shimmering with green light, the bow was almost too big for the woman holding it. Thin and frail-looking, she stood in stark contrast to the other selkies, barely able to support the bow's weight even in the water.

"Mother, stop that at once!" Cliff called to her. "You're not strong enough to fight."

"I am strong enough to shoot down traitors."

This was going well. I squinted around the gloomy room but saw no signs of the Erlking's crown—or his talisman. "Who am I supposed to be a traitor to, exactly?"

"Not you," said the Sea Queen, aiming an arrow at her daughter.

Coral stiffened. "Mother—you *asked* me to spy on the Summer Court."

"You brought an outsider into my home." The bow sagged in her grip and Coral swam to her side. She caught her mother's shoulders, gently steering her into a throne formed of discarded planks of wood and decorated with rows of glittering jewels. I debated asking if splinters were an issue, but now didn't seem a spectacular time to bring that up.

Cliff, meanwhile, returned the talisman to its place at the Sea Queen's side. Magic rippled around the gleaming bow, stirring the currents in the water and bringing a chill to my skin. Not Summer or Winter magic, but the magic of their predecessors, the beings who'd walked in Faerie before the Courts had ever existed.

The Sea Queen regarded me with bleary eyes. "Get out. Both of you. Leave me and the Gatekeeper alone."

Coral shot me a worried look, but I gave her a reassuring nod in return. She and her brother swam out of the room, while I positioned myself at a safe distance from the throne, keeping one eye on the gleaming talisman.

"I'm grateful for the chance to talk to you, your majesty," I said. "It's an honour to meet you."

"We are not friends of the Gatekeepers," the Sea Queen said.

Thanks for telling me that, Mum. "I'm not Gatekeeper, yet," I said. "And I am not here on my own account. I elected to accompany Coral on a mission from the Sidhe to speak with you about the Erlking's passing."

"I heard." The words rippled through the water, laced with melancholy. "I also heard he was indisposed for years. Then again, they say the same about me."

Tread carefully. I didn't want to give away anything the Sidhe would prefer to stay within Summer, but I didn't fancy being impaled by an arrow, either. Her veiny hands dug into either side of the throne with a wooden creak.

"I'm not sure how much you know about the circumstances of his death, but we still have yet to find the murderer," I went on.

"You think too much of yourself, Gatekeeper. You are not Court, nor will they ever let you forget it. You're a tool, no more."

"Let's say I am, then." Arguing with her would use up my three hours and it couldn't be clearer that she was a card or two short of a full deck, to say the least. "I'm here to find out if anyone in your kingdom knows who shot the Erlking. He died from an arrow wound, fired by a bow that cannot miss."

Her gaze snapped to the bow at her side. "The Sidhe think I would seek to break my promise and undo decades of peace, do they? Or is it a ruse so they can steal my talisman back once again?"

"No," I said. "I came here to aid a friend, nothing more. I was ordered to bring Coral here and speak to you, on pain of punishment from the Sidhe of the Summer Court."

"And who rules your Court now?"

"There is nobody on the throne."

"Nobody." She chuckled. "Finally, a worthy leader. In that case, nobody has authority over you."

I blinked. "You just said I'm a tool of the Court."

"A tool is still a tool, whether anyone wields it or not."

Right... "Are you sure your talisman hasn't been used against the Erlking? Might anyone have taken it without your knowledge?"

"The Sea Kingdom can only be accessed by its own members," she said. "No outsider can have stolen it."

Whether she told the truth or not, I doubted she'd made it all the way to the surface and into the Erlking's territory in her condition without being caught. "What about someone from inside your Court?"

"The outsiders are from no Court," she said. "You've seen the place no light can touch, have you not?"

A deep chill settled within my bones. *Yeah, I've seen the Vale.* "Has anyone removed the weapon from this room in the last few days?"

"No. I have been here the whole time. My servants can verify it." She waved a hand, shifting it to a flipper. "You may leave."

She shifted into seal form, which in selkie speak meant *go away.* I backed towards the door, treading water. I wasn't convinced her word would be enough for the Sidhe, but they wouldn't be able to deny I'd followed their orders to the letter. If they wanted to argue with the Sea Queen, they could send one of their own people instead.

Coral and her brother weren't waiting outside, to my disconcertion. I swam alongside the sunken ruin of the ship, peering through the dull glass windows to see if they were inside.

Out of nowhere, a pair of webbed hands caught my legs, dragging me into the shadows. Another hand clamped over my mouth to muffle my scream. *Merrows.* Grey-skinned humanoid creatures with flat heads and eyes on either side which made them look like angry frogs surrounded me on all sides. Their appetites sought human prey, and they knew I was no sea fae, which made me fair game.

I kicked out, hard. One leg broke free of their webbed fingers. I gave another firm kick and felt something solid crunch beneath my heel, then reached for the nearest strands of sea plant, calling magic to my hands. Green light spread from my palms to the plants, which grew, wrapping around the merrows' ankles and anchoring them to the spot.

Then Coral appeared, a rock in her hands. She hit a merrow on the shoulder from behind, forcing him to let go of me. Gasping a thanks, I reached for a rock of my own and struck the merrow who held my ankle, breaking his grip. A pair of webbed hands reached for me and I hit out, pain splintering my knuckles. *Ow.*

The merrows had had enough. Yanking at the kelp ensnaring them, they swam away into the shadows, leaving us a clear path to escape into the village. I swam with Coral into the blue, above the stone houses and out of the Sea Kingdom.

As we swam, my left ankle burned with pain, while my right hand felt bruised or sprained. A cut on my face stung painfully, made all the worse by the salt water. My lungs seared, my eyes starting to tear up. More time had passed than I'd thought if the spell was running out. *Come on, Hazel. You can do it.*

My head broke the surface of the water, which turned from a glimmering expanse of ocean into the murky pond in my garden. I sucked in air, catching my balance as the torrents of salt water vanished into nothingness. Coral climbed out of the shallow pond, while I stood ankle-deep in pond weed.

I spat out a mouthful of salty water. "Sorry, Coral, but

I don't think I'll be going back to the Sea Kingdom anytime soon."

"I wouldn't in your position either," she said. "I suppose you understand why I didn't stay at home."

I waded out of the pond. "Your brother did."

She pushed her wet hair out of her eyes. "Our mother wants him to take her place when she dies. She won't live as long as a Sidhe since she's half-blood, like us. Which makes us more quarter-blooded, really, but it's pretty much the same to the faeries."

No kidding. One drop of mortal blood was enough to ensure a lifespan as short as a human's. "So she hasn't been Queen that long, in comparison to the Erlking."

She shook her head. "She's been deteriorating for years, too. My brother and I were initially invited underwater to meet her in case she needed to retire early. Then she revealed she was our mother."

"So you didn't know before then."

That must be why she didn't act like the other nobles. She hadn't grown up among them.

"No," she said. "I didn't know about her talisman either, for that matter."

"I didn't know the Erlking traded it to the Sea Queen in person," I said. "I guess that might be why the Sidhe suspected she might have had a role in the Erlking's death. But it's not from Summer. The talisman, I mean. Not originally."

"Really? Where is it from?"

The sincerity in her tone disarmed me. I hadn't known there were still faeries who didn't know about the gods or their magic. The Sea Queen's words resonated in my mind. A place with no natural light, cast in shadow.

"The Grey Vale," I said. "The part of Faerie with no magic, where the Sidhe send their exiles to die. Has your Queen ever been there?"

If she never left the water? Probably not. But she'd known of them, either through rumours or some other means.

"The exiles from the Courts?" Her brow furrowed. "Oh. You mean the ones who attacked Earth. No, of course she hasn't. She hasn't left the water in over two decades. If she was ranting at you, she likely didn't mean anything personally by it."

I was sure the Sea Queen knew more than she let on, but if the Sidhe wanted to accuse her of murder, I'd prefer for Coral and me not to suffer the consequences.

"She seemed insistent that nobody from outside got into the palace and took the talisman, but I'm not sure I trust her judgement." I removed a strand of pond weed from my circlet. "Still, the Sidhe only said we had to talk to her. If they want to question her further, they can bloody well do it themselves."

———

I headed to the ambassadors' palace an hour later, after taking a long hot shower and changing into clean clothes. Lady Aiten waited for me in the tapestried room.

"What is your report?" asked Lady Aiten. The other Sidhe didn't seem to be around, which was one point in my favour.

"The Sea Queen is not capable of having committed the murder," I said. "The talisman is under constant guard in her palace and would be difficult to smuggle out. She herself hasn't left the Sea Kingdom in decades."

"I'm told she's infirm," said Lady Aiten. "Weak. Easy to overpower and manipulate."

"If you want to verify that, feel free." I folded my arms across my chest. "I was only able to stay a short time due to the need to use a water-breathing spell. I did what you asked and confirmed the Sea Queen wasn't responsible for the Erlking's death."

"You did not confirm that her talisman wasn't used to commit the murder," said Lady Aiten.

"If the Sea Queen or one of her people had killed the Erlking, they would have brought his talisman back into their kingdom," I told her. "I saw no evidence of its presence."

"Not if she cast it into the ocean," she said.

Anyone would think she'd drop dead on the spot if she admitted she'd been wrong. "She wouldn't have done the same to the crown. Didn't you put an enchantment on it that stops it from being removed from Faerie? I understand why you wouldn't do that to the staff, but if you need the crown in order to name a new monarch, it seems like common sense." Whatever the case, I was sick to the back teeth of the Sidhe aiming for the easiest target instead of doing their own dirty work.

"That is none of your concern, mortal," she said. "The independent Courts have everything to gain from removing the Erlking."

"Gain?" I said. "More like lose. The Summer Court's army is bigger than any other except Winter's. Besides, if I'd pushed further, she might have turned that talisman on me, and you'd be one Gatekeeper short."

"You overvalue your life," she said coldly.

I stared right back. "I wasn't aware that not wanting to meet an early death was such a foreign concept to you. Your entire society is built on evading death, isn't it?"

Her sharp gaze hit me like a slap to the face, and I found myself deeply glad for the defensive shield preventing her from striking me with magic. "Be careful, Gatekeeper. Not everyone believes you should retain your position. If the new monarch decides to remove your status, you will lose all the protections that come along with it."

She thinks the next King or Queen will try to get rid of the Gatekeepers? Maybe the Sea Queen's comment about me being a tool was the truth, at least in terms of the vow that held my family captive, but I hadn't forgotten my childhood promise to escape the curse. On the other hand, turning my back on the Courts in a time of peril didn't sit right with me. If I walked away, who would stop the Sidhe's wrath from engulfing humanity along with their own realm?

"I'll keep that in mind," I told her. "In the meantime, I'd invite you to reconsider arresting the Sea Queen based on pure conjecture, unless you want to make enemies of all the other independent Courts."

And with that, I left the room, almost walking into Darrow in the lobby.

"Oh, hi," I said without much enthusiasm. "Please tell me I don't have any more ambassadorial missions today. I just got threatened by the Sea Queen for accusing her of murder on behalf of a group of people who can't even decide whether to celebrate their leader's death. I'm not in the mood for diplomacy."

"The Sidhe have come to a decision," he said. "The Erlking's funeral has been scheduled for tonight. They wish to honour his memory before the heir is crowned, and it's their belief that this will settle some of the animosity that has been brewing in the Court."

"Seriously?" I raised an eyebrow. "They want to put a bunch of Sidhe in the same room with a vat of elf wine and expect the hostility to just go away? You know, I take it back. I think the indecisiveness was better."

"There'll be strict rules on who can enter," he said.

"So we're not invited."

"We are," he said. "As security."

Well, shit. "Security? For whom? If the Sidhe get into a brawl, I'm staying out of it, thanks."

"Our task is to watch for outside trouble," he said. "In other words, those rebels who believe the Erlking survived."

Oh. "That, I can do. Those three fought like they'd just crawled out of Lord Niall's wine barrel."

"Good," he said. "I'm more concerned that their message will get through to the other attending Sidhe, but they shouldn't be any trouble to handle."

"They still have their magic, though. Not like the other outcasts." If another king took the throne, they were in the shit, but they could still make our life difficult in the meantime.

"They do," he said, "but there are long-term effects to betraying their Court vows. Besides, as soon as a new monarch is crowned, they'll be forced to either pledge their loyalty to their ruler or to find a new home."

A new home. Aka, the land of the outcasts... and

where the person who'd stolen the Erlking's talisman must be hiding.

I wished I could talk to someone in the know about the Sea Queen's bizarre comments. Coral knew little about the outcasts, and now Lord Kerien was dead, too. Who else could possibly be trustworthy enough not to blab to the Sidhe? Not Darrow. Like hell was I making him my confidant after he'd approved the Sidhe's plan to throw me into the deep end—literally.

And now I was about to go back to the first place I'd witnessed the dead arrive in Faerie from the depths of the outcasts' land and hope it didn't end up being a repeat performance.

15

I was far from in the mood for a party *or* a funeral, but Darrow left me to my own devices when I returned to the Gatekeepers' training grounds. After a meal and a power nap, I felt almost normal again.

Back to her cheery self, Coral bounded into my room with a dress draped over her arm and a bottle of healing salve.

"For your wounds," she added. "Those merrows are nasty."

"They are." I took the dress from her. It wasn't a dress, in fact, but some kind of robe with gold trimmings. "This is my guard uniform?"

"You've got it," she said. "Some of us will be stationed outside the palace to make sure nobody gets close to you."

"You'll be guarding the security guards." I tipped some of the salve into my palm and rubbed it into the marks left by the merrows' fingers on my upper arms. "Do the merrows typically come so close to the palace?"

She moved in to help me reach another cut on my upper back. "They aren't supposed to, but they probably caught your scent."

"Ugh." I massaged the salve into the sharp gouges left by their webbed fingers. "Yeah, I know they don't typically attack sea faeries. Are you sure they weren't sent after me?"

"No." She reached for the salve and helped me massage it into my shoulders. "You might have gathered that the Queen has not been well for a while. I think things will be better when my brother takes her place on the throne."

"As long as Summer doesn't declare war by then," I added. "I hope I did the right thing. Lady Aiten didn't really give me much leeway, and the last thing I wanted was to have to go back down there and threaten someone who owns a bow that can't miss."

"You fulfilled the requirements of the mission, so the Sidhe can't complain," she said. "I think the mission was an excuse to get us out of the Court while they argued over the Erlking's funeral arrangements."

"You aren't wrong." Though the funeral itself would offer ample opportunity for them to make mischief.

Coral left to change into her own uniform, while I slipped on the robe. Green with gold cuffs, it made me look oddly regal for a security guard. I adjusted the circlet above the Gatekeeper's mark. I'd hardly been able to feel it underwater, perhaps due to my distance from the Court. *You had a lucky escape back there, Hazel.*

Someone knocked on my door. "Are you ready?"

"Sure." I walked to the door and found Darrow waiting outside. He wore a mirror of my own outfit, a fitted green-and-gold ensemble that brought out the greener side to his eyes and made his silver hair look even brighter. Damn, his magic was strong today. He must be glamoured like hell to hide any traces of his Winter magic in case any of Summer's fae sniffed it out. "You clean up nicely."

"Likewise." He reached out and I tensed, expecting him to undo my glamour. Instead, he traced the edge of one of the cuts on my collarbone, covered in salve but not quite hidden. "You didn't say you were injured."

"Those merrows hit harder than you do," I said.

"Merrows," he said. "In the Sea Court?"

"They thought I was a free snack," I said. "Lucky me. Please tell me that'll be the last diplomatic mission involved in my Trials."

"I can't promise that, but you did pass," he said. "There won't be an official announcement of your presence at this celebration."

"Don't worry, I'm not offended. I already had my party, remember?" I walked with him into the main cave, where the other half-Sidhe gathered in groups. Their own uniforms were green and black, nowhere near as fancy as Darrow's and mine. "Are they our bodyguards or the guests'?"

"Both," he said. "Since Lord Niall's revels have been attacked twice in the last year."

"Haven't they considered using a different venue?" I said.

"There was a vote, and Lord Niall won."

I'm not surprised. He'd probably bribed the other Sidhe with free elf wine. "This is a Trial, isn't it?"

At a guess… yes, it was. I was starting to think the

Sidhe adapted the term whenever it suited them. Or whenever they wanted to make my life difficult.

Oh, well. At least a party was familiar territory for me, unlike the depths of the ocean, and would help dispel my lingering unease about the Sea Queen and her ominous words.

Lord Niall's estate lay behind a gate made of living thorn bushes. While the half-Sidhe dispersed around the perimeter, we waited outside for our host.

"So you're the Gatekeeper," said a soft, lilting voice.

The master of revels himself stepped into view. His long silver hair was topped with a crown made of golden thorns. Loose green robes flowed to his feet, while vivid magic hummed in the depths of his eyes, making it impossible to look directly at him yet also impossible to look at anything else, either. I blinked hard, keeping my expression blank.

"Yes," I said. "I'm Hazel Lynn."

"And you're here to celebrate the life and death of our king." He chuckled. "I imagine you had *quite* the start to your tenure as Gatekeeper."

"That's one way of putting it."

He was already halfway to wasted, at my estimation, given how his green eyes glittered with magic. I had more immunity than most, but I still found my body swaying towards him. Darrow placed a hand on my arm, and I jerked my gaze away from his impossibly beautiful face.

Lord Niall's attention went to Darrow, and a frown puckered his brow. "Do I know you?"

Darrow dipped his head. "I'm in charge of the Gatekeeper's Trials."

"Half-blood." Lord Niall sniffed, then walked away, swaying with every other step.

"He's been at the elf wine," I murmured to Darrow. "Better hope we're not the only security on duty tonight. I doubt he'll be much help if anyone crashes the party."

He wasn't even carrying a talisman. Annoyance prickled at me. If not for their immortality, half the Sidhe would have perished from sheer recklessness by now. It was just like faeries to put on a magnificent revel when their Court was falling apart around their ears, too. Still, maybe it was better to let them blow off steam, celebrate their leader's long life, and then get on with figuring out the important things. Like the heir, for instance.

Darrow and I took up our positions on either side of the gates, and before long, the first Sidhe began to arrive on horseback. They hadn't taken their cues from funerals in the mortal realm, because everyone dressed in the same bright finery as usual. Some wore coats made of feathers, flowers or leaves, some wore armour, others wore little clothing at all. All were armed with swords and spears, knives and bows. With each new arrival, the current of magic humming around the place built, until Lord Niall's manor house shone with so much glamour that if I was a normal human, I'd have been knocked senseless within five seconds.

Between the royals came their attendant brownies, elves, and hobgoblins, while piskies and sprites flitted above our heads. There were also a surprising number of Unseelie who thought they could get away with pretending to be on the guest list.

"I am from the borderlands!" a goblin insisted. "You can't throw me out."

"You have frost on your ears," I said. "And I can *smell* Unseelie on you. If the Winter Queen wants to meet with the Summer Sidhe, she can send someone at a more appropriate time. I'm not going to be responsible if one of the Seelie knights brains you."

He tried to slip some gold into my pocket, and I trod on his foot. "None of that."

"Cruel, cruel human!"

"Good lord." I rolled my eyes after him as he scuttled away. "I should have seen that one coming."

"He's one of her spies, of course," said Darrow. "The Unseelie Queen is keen to hear the news of the Erlking's successor."

"I bet she is."

Is she your Queen? I still couldn't puzzle out who his loyalties lay with. Definitely not the Sea Queen. I couldn't think of any small independent Courts who employed half-bloods with both Summer and Winter magic and a talent for glamour, but Summer had trusted him enough to stop any riffraff getting into Lord Niall's house.

Once the gates closed to new guests, we moved back into the grounds to keep a closer eye on the festivities. I understood why the others had voted to host the revel here, because Lord Niall's home was magnificent even by Sidhe standards. A maze of cobbled paths wound between elaborately carved statues, glittering fountains, and opulent tables covered with all manner of dishes and wines. The walls and ceiling shone bright with flowers, while vibrant Summer magic surrounded the Sidhe in a green haze.

Thorny plants cloaked arched windows with a clear view of the courtyard on the right-hand side, where a band played a melody that wormed into my head despite my best efforts. Darrow arched a brow at me as my walk turned into a waltz, and I gritted my teeth, managing to steer my limbs under control.

"Perhaps we need to work on training your ability to resist faerie music," he said.

"Don't you even think about it," I muttered under my breath.

Worse than the band was the wooded grove on the left side of the house, accessed through a curtain of ivy. Sensual energy filled the air every time the curtains parted, awakening animal instincts in anyone who went too close. As we passed by, a trickle of magic streamed from the grove and slid down my body like a lover's caress. My hands itched to pull the curtain of ivy aside, but that was a bad idea. Last time I'd taken in one breath of magic inside the grove, I'd ended up with a Sidhe's tongue down my throat while a bunch of wraiths had damn near torn the house to shreds.

Despite that, I couldn't resist stealing a peek at Darrow, whose aquamarine eyes had brightened even more than usual. He absently ran his fingers over the binding mark on his wrist, sparking a tingle of magic in my own mark. *Whoa, there.* I stepped away from the grove, weaving towards the back of the room in the hope of shaking off the irrational urge to press my marked wrist against his.

At the very back of the hall, a large tree had fused with the wall, its roots snaking beneath the marble floor.

"There used to be a secret tunnel there," Darrow said. "But it was recently rebuilt after someone sneaked in and tried to blow up the place."

"Seriously?" I scanned the tree for hidden passages, and a series of soft moans came from behind a tangle of tree roots. "I think we're interrupting something."

Sure enough, two Sidhe lay wrapped around one another, their talismans discarded nearby. Inspiration struck, and a grin sprang to my mouth.

Someone in here had a security talisman which allowed access to the Erlking's territory, and I intended to 'borrow' it.

I stepped away from the tree. "I'm going to get a drink."

I left Darrow to continue circling the room and went to the nearest hobgoblin, taking a wine glass from him. Then I ducked behind a statue and pulled on a glamour, making my ears pointier, my face more angular, my hair darker. Lastly, I conjured up a large flowery wreath to hide the circlet on my head. It didn't make me any less conspicuous, but with any luck, Darrow wouldn't look in my direction while I did what I needed to do.

One of the Sidhe who'd been entangled in the tree roots staggered towards me. "You're human, aren't you? I was looking for a human to join us."

Ew. I took a step back. "Not today, thanks."

"You have unusual skill with glamour for a human," he said in a slurred voice. "Lord Niall says a human got through those tunnels once before."

"Oh, really?" I resisted the impulse to lean back out of reach of his wine-soaked breath. "Isn't someone supposed to be on security tonight? Someone, perhaps, with a special talisman?"

He chuckled. "Lord Farin is supposed to be watching the tunnel, but he's being very bad."

I leaned closer. "Is he? Won't you tell me where he is, so I can tell him how very bad he's being?"

"I'll tell you if I can have a kiss."

Double ew. I pressed my lips to his cheek, fighting a shudder. "Done."

He chuckled. "Clever mortal. Lord Farin is by the wine, sleeping. He'll be punished for this, make no mistake."

"Thank you." I took him by the arm and steered him back to the tree. He tripped over a root, curled up and went to sleep. *Honestly.*

I glanced over at Darrow, who'd continued on his path around the room's edge. Certain he hadn't spotted me, I veered towards the wine barrel, and the guard the Sidhe had pointed out. This Lord Farin appeared to be asleep on his feet, his dagger hanging loosely at his side.

I shuffled in front of his gaze, noting his eyes were half-lidded. Still awake—just.

"Hey, handsome," I purred. "You wouldn't let me get a little peek at your talisman, wouldn't you?"

"Talisman." His hand twitched towards his thigh, and a faint glow came from a sheath strapped beneath his cloak. "No. I'm not allowed to let anyone touch it."

"Pity." I held out my wine glass. "Can you hang onto that for me?"

He snored, his eyes closing, but he gripped the wine glass by his fingertips. My hand brushed the hem of his cloak in search of the sheath. He was also naked underneath, so I'd have to be careful not to grab the wrong— ahem—sword.

Carefully, I slid out the talisman and palmed it, stepping behind a bush to slide it into my cleavage. Then I shook off my glamour and turned human again, stopping by a passing hobgoblin to snag a glass of elf wine before taking a shortcut around a glittering fountain to catch up with Darrow.

He tilted his head as I caught up, his expression tight with disapproval. *What?* Sidhe hooked up at their revels all the time, and I wouldn't judge him if he'd slipped into a corner for a quickie. Okay, maybe a little, because it bothered me to picture him with another Sidhe for reasons I couldn't quite put my finger on.

Whatever. I had the security talisman, and I'd have liked to think I'd do a better job keeping hold of it than the guy who'd fallen asleep on duty. "What's the problem?"

"You're supposed to be watching for trouble," he said. "The Sidhe can see right through your glamour. They know you're human. If you pursue them, they'll think…"

"They'll think what?" I gave him a challenging look. "They'll think I'm easy to manipulate? Inferior? Weak? Name one person in this room who doesn't already think that."

"You aren't weak."

"That's high praise coming from you." I sipped from my wine glass, the tart sweetness of elf wine bursting across my tongue. "What *is* your problem with me? Why do I get under your skin so much?"

Fresh from my victory with the talisman, I was in the mood to try for a second achievement of the night. Namely, figuring out what made my mentor tick. Something about him intrigued the hell out of me, and it went deeper than the mystery of where his loyalties really lay.

When he didn't answer, I said, "Is it because I say what

I mean? You'd think it'd be a change from all the back-stabbing manipulators in here. At least I tell you outright when I don't like you."

"You don't like me."

"I don't *get* you," I said. "Not the same thing. What were you expecting the Gatekeeper to be like, then? Older? More serious? Because Mum is both of those things."

"I know," he said. "Now I've met her. I can tell she would be very different to work with. She taught you how to fight?"

"She did," I said. "As for why her personality didn't brush off on me, my sister always said my grandma's rebelliousness skipped a generation. She gave the Sidhe a fair bit of trouble in her day. More than me, if possible."

"I'm having a little trouble believing that."

"Oi." I'd hoped for him to drop a hint or two about his own family, but he didn't. "She even stuck around as a ghost after she died just to annoy the shit out of our family. That takes dedication."

He blinked. "She was a ghost? Is that… normal, in the human world?"

Aha. I'd piqued his curiosity. "No, but maybe a few resident ghosts would help the Sidhe get used to death being an inevitability. It'll make life so much easier for them. As long as no more monarchs get assassinated, anyway."

He shot an alarmed look across the hall, and I hid a smile. "Chill, Darrow. They can't hear us. I think most of them have forgotten they're at a funeral at all."

One glance told me a Sidhe had already passed out in

the wine barrel, and the others simply moved him out of the way whenever they wanted a drink. It seemed Mum's comment about the Sidhe learning to cherish their lives now they were capable of being cut short was slightly off the mark.

"Who taught you, then?" I asked. "To use glamour, I mean?"

Instead of answering, he continued his circuit of the hall. "You talk a lot, did you know?"

I gave him a mock-wounded look. "No. That really hurt my feelings."

A smile flickered across his mouth, almost too quick to notice. "I doubt you're so easily hurt, Hazel."

"See, you can call me by my name. It's not that hard." I also liked hearing my name from his mouth. Though that might be the effects of the sensual magic whispering from the grove as we drew nearer to the west side of the room. "Better than 'Gatekeeper', 'human' or 'mortal'. Or just 'Lynn'."

"Lynn," he repeated. "You took your mother's surname."

"Of course I did," I said. "Granted, the Sidhe would have been able to track me down even if I didn't. Bloodline curses are fun like that."

"Bloodline curses?" His eyes widened a fraction. "You mean, being Gatekeeper?"

"I thought you knew." I frowned. "Everyone knows the Gatekeeper position runs in the family. We're not immortal, so…"

"So the newest Gatekeeper is chosen from among the children of the previous one."

"Yes," I said. "The vow doesn't discriminate. We all had an equal shot of being chosen. Why?"

Darrow didn't answer. We'd reached the grove, where curtains of ivy separated the forest from the main room, and Sidhe traipsed in and out in various stages of undress. I grinned as Lord Niall staggered past and fell headfirst into a flowerbed.

"Big surprise." I snickered. "The master of revels has lost his clothes again. Better hope there aren't any fire imps in that bush."

Magic trickled out from the grove, sliding across my skin, tightening my core. My breasts peaked under my dress, and I became acutely aware of the stolen security talisman nestled in my cleavage. *Hope it doesn't start glowing. That'd be awkward.*

Music drifted overhead, and I found my legs jerking into motion again. I caught Darrow's arm and tried to get him to spin me into a dance, but instead, he snagged the wine glass by his fingertips. "Watch out, or it'll spill."

"That'd be a shame." I giggled. Fuck, that wine was strong. "You need to loosen up a little, you know."

He frowned. "How much did you drink?"

"Like this much." I measured a small amount between my fingertips. I hadn't tasted anything odd, but the sheer volume of magic in the air was bound to have some other side effects. My body continued to sway in time to the music, and Darrow kept hold of my arm as though worried I'd disappear if he let me go. Magic shone from his gaze, mingling with the spell the grove wove around us, highlighting his silver hair. "Has anyone ever mentioned you look like a god?"

"Hazel."

A thrill went through me. "Say my name again."

Shit. I didn't say that out loud, did I? Darrow was as smoking hot as any of the Sidhe, but he was also my mentor, and… why was this a bad idea again?

He leaned in closer, his eyes brighter, his pupils dilated. "That's not appropriate."

"Says the guy who thinks standing stiffly against a wall at a party is appropriate." I tilted my head, hearing the hitch of his breath as my fingers peeled his hand from my arm. Magic crept down my wrist, igniting the bond that linked us, and my heartbeat quickened. "You aren't worried I'm not taking my position seriously, are you? You're more concerned that I might distract you from yours."

"I'm not as easily as distracted as you think." While I hadn't released his hand, he made no effort to free himself from my grip. His eyes were bright with magic, both Winter and Summer. Magic that hummed along the surface of my skin and through every pulse of blood in my veins. Drawn to him. To his scent of oak and ash, frost and flame.

A deeply buried part of me, somewhere far below the surface, craved this. The part of me who understood how humans could step into a faerie circle, venture into the woods after dark, fall under a spell as easily as slipping under the surface of a lake.

The part of me who wanted to give in, and dance.

I entwined my hands around his neck, and whispered, "Prove it."

He brought his mouth down on mine. Magic sparked and hummed between us, an electric current that blanked my thoughts until I became nothing more than pure, primal need. I wound my body around his, fisting my hand in the soft strands of his hair. He made an inhuman noise deep in his throat, and the part of me that wanted answers threatened to disappear beneath a torrent of desire, the need to take him down in those bushes and show him I'd earned every inch of my so-called reputation.

His lips broke from mine, and an oath escaped, whispered under his breath. "Hazel. Stop."

"What if I don't want to?" A voice screamed in the back of my mind, but our skin was fused, and a potent cocktail of magic and lust ignited every cell in my body. "What if *you* don't want to?"

A voice in the back of my head screamed that hooking up with him was a monumentally *terrible* idea, but along with that jolt of common sense came a whisper of curiosity. I'd come here intending get some answers, after all.

I licked my lips, then leaned forward to murmur in his ear, "So. About your Court—"

A dazzling flash of light engulfed the room, and I caught Darrow's arm for balance, blinking the glare from my eyes. When the light cleared, a group of cloaked faeries gathered in the midst of the guests, and the band's music stuttered to an abrupt halt.

"The king will rise!" cried one of the cloaked newcomers. "While he waits to return, you mock him by celebrating his death!"

Screams drifted over from the courtyard on the east of the room. I gave Darrow a look to tell him to deal with the leftover Sidhe—they were far outnumbered, so he could handle it—and ran for the courtyard. The shouts grew louder, and when I reached the back of the crowd, I saw precisely why they were screaming.

On the stage, the Erlking stood among the ruins of the band's instruments, watching the audience of captive Sidhe.

"You have betrayed my Court," said the Erlking. *"Bow before me."*

Magic rippled out from the words, spoken in a language that wasn't English and wasn't fae either. The Sidhe dropped to their knees, and an unbearable pressure on my upper back forced my own knees to touch the earth, my head bowing. He'd spoken an Invocation, and when the Sidhe used the language that had belonged to their gods, those words took literal form.

"No!" a Sidhe cried out. "Please forgive us."

"Forgive us all!"

Good lord. "It's just a glamour." I forced my head upright, fighting the lingering effects of the magic. "He doesn't even sound like the Erlking, Any Sidhe can speak an Invocation."

But none of the Sidhe here had actually met the Erlking in person, and they were too freaked out by his sudden appearance to care about the details. It was amazing how quickly their impeccable coordination and grace disappeared when they were scared. Some fled, while others threw themselves at the feet of the man pretending to be their king. Snarls and yells mingled together as several Sidhe shapeshifted into animals in their panic.

"That's not your king!" I shouted, but the clamour drowned my voice.

The person who'd conjured the illusion must be among the guests, but the sheer volume of magic in the air made it impossible to track its source. Gritting my teeth, I pushed between two Sidhe, wincing when their thorny coats snagged my bare arms, and scanned the crowd for a face that didn't show panic.

A hooded figure at the side of the stage stood out to me, standing calmly among the chaos. *Aha.*

I let the crowd's momentum carry me around the veranda. The hooded man spotted me, and the sharp point of a sword gleamed in his hands.

I ran at him, jabbing my elbows into anyone in my way. Then in a flying leap, I crashed into the hooded figure and tackled him into the grass. Pinning his weapon hand, I yanked his hood down, revealing an angular face and pointed ears.

"Get rid of that illusion," I commanded. "Or I'll let them trample you."

Tendrils of magic wrapped around my arms, and my gaze jerked to the sword pinned between us. Green light shone from its hilt, and my heart jolted. *Dammit. He has a talisman.*

He was using a talisman's magic to maintain the illusion. No wonder it hadn't broken.

Magic crept over my skin, the glow spreading across

my legs. A tingling sensation ran to my nerve endings, and fur began to sprout from my skin. *Dammit.* If I let go of him, I'd lose him in the crowd, and not even my Gatekeeper powers would save me from being trampled to death.

"Let her go!" Darrow's furious shout cut through the noise. Then he was behind me, his blade skimming past my shoulder and sinking into the hooded Sidhe's chest.

The fur disappeared, the threads of magic retreating, and I stumbled to my feet, watching the Sidhe's body crumple onto the grass.

The false Erlking shouted, "Murder!"

Shit. The illusion still wasn't gone? That must mean there was a real person under there. The hooded Sidhe had been a decoy—and now the crowd was mad instead of scared. Darrow shoved me out of the way as they descended on the pair of us. Alarm blared through my mind when he vanished behind the furious crowd, but the false Erlking was right there. I couldn't miss my chance.

Reaching with both hands, I felt for the magic humming around the stage and pushed at it, demanding the glamour unroll at my touch. *Break, damn you!* Darrow made it look so easy. If I had iron, it'd be over in seconds, but the Sidhe and their bloody rules had made that impossible.

I stopped fighting the glamour and conjured an illusion of my own, throwing it over my shoulder. The huge shape of a giant troll burst through the door, roaring to the heavens. To my relief, I spotted Darrow break away from the Sidhe as they turned to face the new threat.

I'd give it three seconds before they realised the troll wasn't real, but that was more than enough for an opening. I lunged for the stage and grabbed the hem of the false Erlking's cloak, dragging him towards the edge. He snarled, but I latched on with both hands and put all my strength into it, tugging him off the stage and onto the grass.

"My king!" gasped the nearest Sidhe. "The human will pay dearly for her transgression—"

"Oh, for the love of hellhounds." I yanked the false Erlking's head upright. "Look at him. No crown. No staff. No talisman at all."

I tugged on the strings of the illusion. It didn't *quite* shatter as impressively as my glamour had at Darrow's touch, but the Erlking's likeness disappeared, replaced by an unfamiliar face curtained with dark hair.

Rough hands grabbed my shoulders. "Don't you dare lay your hands on our king."

"It's not real!" I squirmed free of his grip, addressing all the Sidhe. "The Erlking has gone. He was a glamour. See for yourselves."

"Deception!"

With cries of loathing, the Sidhe descended on the false Erlking. I ducked out of their midst and scanned the crowd for Darrow. My gaze snagged on his glamoured form standing beside one of the arched windows, where he must have concealed himself after I'd diverted the Sidhe from trampling him. My arms stung with a dozen fresh cuts from being caught in the crowd, but I'd got off easy considering the mess they'd made of Lord Niall's house.

"Let's go," said Darrow. "Lord Niall is dealing with the other intruders."

Inside the main room, Lord Niall stood draped in a

deep green cloak, a gleaming blade in his hand. Threads of magic flowed from his talisman, and one of the cloaked outcasts rose into the air, choking and flailing. A shrill scream escaped the trapped Sidhe, and then thorns sprouted from his skin, blood spraying the floor. The Sidhe stopped struggling, but the thorns continued to rip through his flesh from the inside out.

Holy shit, Lord Niall.

I did *not* want to stick around to see the fallout. Bile burned the back of my throat, and the screams of the Sidhe drifted after me into the night as Darrow and I left the house behind.

"I didn't expect him to do that to another Sidhe." They might treat humans and half-bloods with casual cruelty, but I'd assumed they only slaughtered their fellow Sidhe on the battlefield, or at least gave them the option of a dignified death.

"There is nothing worse to the Sidhe than a traitor," he said. "Especially a traitor who betrays the memory of their king."

"They must have known what would happen," I said. "Nobody's glamour is totally fool-proof."

"Speaking of which, you did an admirable job of unravelling it."

My mouth parted. "Seriously? You don't think I took too long?"

"It was a complex spell."

His praise took on a whole other meaning when I considered the unexpectedly heated moment we'd shared. What the hell had happened back there? Sure, Darrow was attractive—he was half-Sidhe, it came with the territory—but I hadn't wanted to bone him there in the bushes, had I? He was part infuriating trainer, part judgemental prick, part stuck-up arse… and yet for all that, it couldn't be plainer that he was attracted to me.

If I were more like the Sidhe, I'd use it to my advantage, but I'd been as enthralled as he had back then. That was dangerous, and not because of the no-dating-faeries rule. Since I was a teenager, I'd always had an unfortunate tendency to be drawn to trouble-makers. The guy was trouble, all right… but not the good sort.

————

I had to wait until after my lessons the following day to pay a visit to the Erlking's territory with the pilfered security talisman. Darrow let me sleep in, so I hoped to sneak off before lunch, but when I left my room, he accosted me and called me into a training room.

"You still need training to resist sense-altering glamour," he said. "Given the events of last night, I think it's something we need to work on."

"What, you mean the magic the Sidhe use to mess with humans?" I said. "No human can resist it. It's too subtle for my shielding abilities, and it's impossible to cut off my senses entirely unless I got someone to transform me into a troll or something."

"It's subtle, yes, but it's not impossible for you to use your magic to resist," he said. "Put your hand on my arm."

"Excuse me?" I said.

He held out his arm, his sleeve pushed up to show the binding mark on his wrist. "It's easier to demonstrate if you're touching me."

"Sure. No problem." It *shouldn't* be, yet being this close

to him brought reminders of how his mouth had felt on mine yesterday, how his scent had infiltrated my senses alongside the seductive magic of the grove.

I rested my palm over his wrist, and felt his magic tingling below the surface, drawing me in.

"Closer," he said. Was his voice slightly breathier than usual? "We need skin contact for it to work."

I closed the last half-inch between us, holding onto his forearm. At once, magic zipped from my fingertips up my arm, drawing a gasp from my mouth before I could quite get hold of my senses. My pulse thundered in my ears.

"Form a shield with your magic," he said.

Magic? What magic? All I could feel was his, whispering along my skin, alight with unspoken promises.

I held my breath, feeling for my own magic churning under the surface. Green light sprang to my palms, forming a barrier. At once, the tingling effect of his magic faded a little. I released a slow breath, my hand slamming against my ribcage. Was his pulse racing, too, or was it my own? I really couldn't tell.

"Better," he said. "As I said… it's not entirely resistant. But it ought to be enough to break out of a trap, if need be. Like last night."

Trap? He thought the grove's magic had driven us together, not the off-the-charts chemistry surging between us like a storm about to break? *Someone here is in denial, and it's not me.*

"I don't think it could hold off the grove's magic." I looked up at him. "Can I try again? This time, go all-out."

"Are you certain?"

"You didn't have a problem with giving it your all

when it came to throwing me off invisible horses or knocking me onto the grass."

His hand clasped my wrist, his bright eyes suddenly inches from mine. They didn't make faces like his in the mortal realm, yet at least some of the attraction must be my own mind projecting onto him. They said the Sidhe looked different to every person who saw them, depending on what they found appealing. It seemed my subconscious was enticed by silver-haired gods who smelled of oak and ash.

Oh. Right. I was supposed to be resisting his glamour.

Magic sprang to the surface of my skin, mingling with his. His mouth hovered above mine, and my heart skittered fast, too fast. *Focus, Hazel.*

I wet my lips. "Did the same person who taught you to use glamour teach you this, too?"

He didn't answer, but his grip loosened a fraction. Perhaps he assumed I'd intended to finish our conversation from the party that those Sidhe had so rudely interrupted. Which I hadn't, but while the idea of lying beneath a smoking hot half-Sidhe for the afternoon wasn't an unappealing one, the weight of the security talisman in my pocket reminded me I had a job to do.

And what better way to stop him from following me to the Erlking's territory than to convince him to admit his attraction to me?

Magic pulsed at the surface of my skin, pushing him back. "I don't think you're trying hard enough."

The glow in his eyes and around his skin brightened, and suddenly I was floating, beyond the reach of human senses. My mortal form slipped away, leaving me suspended in a realm where nothing existed but my desire for him. To be bound to him. To serve him.

Reality crashed headlong into me, leaving me reeling in a sudden rush of sensation. I blinked the glare from my eyes, startled to find Darrow's hand on the iron band around my wrist. I hadn't been able to feel anything at all back then, but the iron—the iron must have broken his spell. My heart lurched against my ribcage, and he released me so suddenly that my knees hit the ground. I caught my balance, disarmed to spot him several feet away from me. Damn, he moved fast.

His eyes glowed with an eerie light, making him look both sinister and astonishingly beautiful.

"What the fuck was that?" I forced out the words. *Glamour?* To humans, the slightest glimpse of a Sidhe was enough to convince them to pledge their service for life, but I'd never seen that sort of trick get through my Gatekeeper's glamour before. "What *are* you?"

"Someone who shouldn't be teaching you glamour," he answered. "You've got the hang of the basics. Feel free to practise by yourself for the remainder of the day."

How can I practise without someone else? The question drifted through my shock, but I didn't say a word as he left. That power he'd used—*what was it?* I'd entertained thoughts of convincing him his attraction to me was more than just glamour, but he hadn't made me want him. He'd made me worship him.

If I hadn't left the iron band on, what might have happened?

With difficulty, I shoved the thought aside. Unconventional methods aside, I'd succeeded in getting him off my back, and I had somewhere else I needed to be.

Time to pay another visit to the Erlking's territory—and I intended to leave with answers.

17

I walked swiftly through the forest with the security talisman concealed up my sleeve. Risky though it might be, I refused to put anyone else in danger by dragging them along with me. Lord Kerien was already dead, and I intended to find out what he'd discovered before his untimely passing.

The security talisman was warm to the touch, dagger-sized, and didn't seem to object to a human carrying it. Or stowing it in my cleavage, either. Unlike most talismans, it wasn't bound to a specific person, so its magic remained self-contained. Before her betrayal, the Seelie Queen had been in charge of maintaining access to the Erlking's territory, and she'd never have let the guards doze off on duty. The Sidhe really needed to get their shit together if they wanted to survive to see a new monarch take the throne.

I followed the route Lord Kerien and I had walked along last time, hoping Faerie hadn't rearranged things again. Had I been Sidhe, I might have been able to use my magic to shortcut to my destination, but perhaps it was best if I went in the subtle way to avoid being tracked. I kept my weapons close at hand, but I reached the gate without encountering a soul.

Pulling out the security talisman, I used it to open the gate and slipped into the Erlking's territory. At once, the putrid smell of decay slammed into me. Dead trees stood rooted in a bed of shrivelled leaves, their branches bare and lifeless. Decaying moss hung in tatters, and the desiccated carcasses of insects littered the dry soil. The killer had escaped through the gate this time, and they hadn't cared what they'd damaged on the way out.

I veered towards the Seelie Queen's estate, following the path of decay the killer had left behind them. The wooden doors of her manor house hung from their hinges. *Were they like that before?*

I didn't relish the idea of treading in the footsteps of the scheming Queen who'd tried to kill my mother, but I had an inkling where Lord Kerien had been when the killer had found him. Holding my breath, I pushed the remains of the door aside and stepped into the hall.

The manor's interior would have been beautiful, even after nature had reclaimed it, were it not for the shroud of death that lay over the place like a mould-infested blanket. Trees sagged from the walls, pine husks crunched beneath my feet, and the smell of rot tickled the back of my throat. Further back lay a crater in the floor, where earth and dead tree roots were piled atop the collapsed remains of a trapdoor.

I'd bet my circlet that Lord Kerien had come back here to investigate the tunnel that linked the Seelie Queen's house with the Erlking's palace—the route the killer had used to enter—and the person who'd taken the Erlking's talisman had jumped him from behind.

No witnesses remained... except for one. Where was the Erlking's sprite? I'd have to go back to the clearing to search for him, assuming the killer hadn't chased him off or worse.

Footsteps sounded behind me. I eased a knife from my belt, wishing I'd forsaken all the rules and brought my iron blade, and pressed it against the intruder's neck.

Darrow hissed out a breath. "I *knew* you stole a security talisman. Have you no value for your life?"

"I could ask you the same question." I lowered the knife. "You must have guessed following me would paint a target on your own head."

"Yes, and you aren't the only person who had concerns about Lord Kerien's final moments," he said. "It's not your duty to pry into matters that concern the Sidhe and not yourself, and it certainly isn't wise of you to put your position of Gatekeeper in jeopardy."

Annoyance sparked inside me. Last night when he and I had fought the false Erlking together, I'd thought he'd started to relax his insistence on tailing me everywhere and let me work alone. Apparently not.

"You don't get to make that decision for me," I said. "Besides, I happen to know the enemy wants the Gatekeeper to live, and at the moment, so do most of the Sidhe. You, on the other hand, aren't even from this Court. Are you sure you aren't worried about your own position and not mine?"

His mouth flattened. "If that's the case, you shouldn't care what happens to me."

Way to go, Hazel. Guilt and anger surged in a churning

tide, tempered by relief to see him leaving. His retreating footsteps rang through the empty manor as I looked down into the gutted hole in the centre of the Seelie Queen's entrance hall. This was where Lord Kerien had met his unfortunate end, and yet no traces remained of his presence. Just the collapsed ruins of a tunnel beneath a trapdoor choked with weeds. If I used my magic, I might be able to clear the path, but who was to say the killer wasn't still lurking down there in the dark?

Maybe I shouldn't have been so quick to send Darrow away. I felt like a complete arse, not to mention a hypocrite, because I didn't really believe he'd come here out of concern he'd lose his job. Two Sidhe had died here, and he didn't want me involved for the same reason I didn't want him to butt in on my investigation. I'd been set apart from everyone else for so long that stepping in to face danger alone had become second nature, and now I'd driven away one of my only allies.

The sound of rustling leaves came from outside. *Darrow?* I stepped out the door, opening my mouth to speak. Darrow, however, was nowhere to be seen.

A slithering noise followed, making the small hairs rise on my arms. Then, a web of shadows peeled away from the bushes, coalescing into a semi-transparent formless mass. A sluagh: part spirit, part corporeal, and ugly as hell. The being slid right past me, sending a shudder deep into my bones.

And it wasn't alone. More beasts slithered and hissed along the paths outside the Seelie Queen's estate, formless and shadowy.

Darrow.

I turned my back on the house and broke into a run,

but the sluagh filled my vision, surging out of the forest all over the Erlking's territory.

"Hello, ugly," I murmured to the nearest, palming my sharpened blade. "What are you supposed to be?"

The sluagh made a wet noise like a troll treading on a snail. Had the murderer left them here to deter anyone else from looking into Lord Kerien's death?

I halted behind the gates, my stomach turning over. A sluagh's shadowy form swamped the green glow surrounding the spear-sharp points, slithering around and underneath the gate, heedless of its magic. At least one had made it through, into the Court, and Darrow would have no idea they were right behind him.

Drawing a knife, I ran for the gate and pushed it open. At once it closed behind me, but the sluagh continued to slide around and beneath it. Oh, god.

I spotted Darrow heading down the path ahead of me, and broke into a full-on sprint.

"Hey!" I shouted. "There are Vale beasts in the Erlking's territory. They're coming to invade the Court."

He turned around, his eyes widening. "What?"

I jabbed a finger at the shadowy mass coalescing over my shoulder. "They were hiding in the forest, and they got through the gates without opening them. Warn the Sidhe."

"I will." Without another word, he broke into a sprint so fast the leaves on the ground flew into the air in a rustling dervish. Shadows whispered over my shoulders. He might have taken my warning to heart, but he'd also left me alone with the enemy.

Fine. Maybe I could thin down the enemies before they reached the Sidhe. I turned on the spot to find a larger sluagh looming over me. It took the form of a humanoid creature with sinewy wings and a beak-like mouth.

I aimed my blade at its flank, but the sluagh turned incorporeal and my blade passed right through it. Catching my balance, I swung again, my blade snagging mid-strike. I tugged, hard, but the blade stuck. A black viscous substance dripped from where the blade had sunk in, pooling on the leaf-strewn path.

With a firm tug, I freed the blade. A wave of shadow lashed at me in return, locking around my legs and slamming me onto my back. Shadowy tentacles yanked the blade from my hand. Cursing, I raised my hand in defence, and to my surprise—and disgust—my fist sank into shadowy flesh. Ugh.

The beast reeled, shrieking. Frowning, I looked down at my hand and spotted the iron band on my wrist. It wasn't powerful enough to count as a weapon, but it gave me an opening.

With a lunge, I grabbed my weapon from where it'd fallen to the earth. Then I spun on the spot and stabbed the sluagh in its head. A horrible popping noise ensued, and black blood spouted onto the forest floor. Above, more sluagh swarmed into the Court, a black mass intent on chasing down their prey.

The sluagh came from the Grey Vale. And there was only one way they could have got into the Erlking's territory was if the doorway had been hidden somewhere in the forest. As long as it remained open, the sluagh would continue to swarm into the Court.

I broke into a run for the ambassadors' palace, skidding to a halt behind my family's gate. Beside it lay a shredded hole in the universe through which I could see grey trees, grey paths, and a horrible emptiness that sucked at my bones.

The Grey Vale.

"No." I gasped. "Mum—"

A knife pressed to my throat from behind. A low, melodic male voice said, "Don't move, human, or I will kill you where you stand. You traitorous humans have allowed the outcasts into our Court."

Shit. "It's a setup," I said. "Someone opened a way into the Vale beside the gate to frame my family."

"Can anyone prove it?" asked the Sidhe behind me.

"Someone has been moving my family's gate around without my permission," I said, between breaths. "I haven't used it since this morning. It's the truth."

"You're not the only person who has control over that gate," said the Sidhe. "And the other Gatekeeper has been seen entering the Court without an invitation."

Mum. *No.* "She's not responsible. She can't open a way into the Vale. None of us can. Only the Sidhe—"

His knife moved against my neck, and warm blood trickled onto my collarbone. "There she is."

Mum stepped through the gate, accompanied by Darrow of all people. *Shit.*

"Let my daughter go," Mum said, her voice quiet, dangerous.

The Sidhe's hand twitched on the knife at the warning note in her tone. "Do you deny that you used the gate to enter our Court without your daughter's knowledge?"

"No," said Mum. "But you're making a mistake. I am not the killer, nor did I open that doorway into the Vale."

The question was, who had? Only Sidhe who held a talisman could open doors between realms. It'd bet it was the same person who'd opened the other doorway in the Erlking's territory, trying to throw the Sidhe off the trace. Perhaps they'd intended me to take the blame, but I'd screwed things up for them when I'd gone to the Erlking's territory instead of coming back here. But Mum hadn't denied his accusation. Had she really been using the gate to get into the Court without telling me?

"The former Gatekeeper will be taken into the jail to await trial," said the Sidhe. I twisted around to give him a glare and recognised him as the same Sidhe who'd tried to threaten my family before. *Fucker.* "If she is found guilty, she will be executed."

"Damn you," I spat. "There's another doorway into the Vale open on the Erlking's territory, and a swarm of sluagh coming this way. If you don't believe me, they'll be here soon enough."

"Why were you on the Erlking's territory?" His tone dripped with disbelief, as though I was hardly worth bothering with.

"Because the Erlking himself sent me a note after his death asking me to investigate his murder." There was no point in concealing the truth now. "He wouldn't have done that if he'd believed any members of my family were guilty. Darrow can confirm it—"

"Why should I trust the word of three mortals?" said the Sidhe. "Darrow, see to it that she doesn't intervene."

Darrow took my arm. In the same instant, the Sidhe spoke an inaudible word, and the doorway into the Vale closed, winking out of existence. A heartbeat later, he and Mum vanished in a flash of green light.

I twisted in Darrow's grip. "Let go of me."

Small wonder he hadn't jumped to my defence, after

what I'd said to him in the forest, but it was just one more failure to add to the heap. On top of that, I'd left the Erlking's note at the Lynn house, and the Sidhe were more likely to give me the crown than let me go home and retrieve it.

The gates opened, and Ilsa hurried over to meet me. "Hazel!"

I yanked my arm away from Darrow and ran to embrace my sister. "I'm sorry. The killer opened a way to the Vale near the gate—they took Mum."

"I know," said Ilsa. "River is here, and he can help us."

River walked to her side. While his short blond hair and green eyes painted him as a Summer half-Sidhe, he still wore his necromancer uniform, indicating he'd run here straight from Edinburgh. "I promise to try, but I can't work miracles, and neither can my father. Normally, the decision would go to the higher Sidhe, but without the Erlking—"

"Please." My voice cracked. "They won't listen to me. I don't know who moved the gate here and opened the doorway to the Vale, but as soon as I mentioned finding another doorway in the Erlking's territory, they fixated on that and not the swarm of sluagh coming this way. They wouldn't believe the Erlking asked me to investigate, and I left the note at home."

"What, this note?" Ilsa stuck her hand in her pocket and pulled out a scrap of paper etched with the Erlking's seal. "Thought you might need it."

I hugged her again, taking the note. "You're a lifesaver."

Not that I could make heads or tails of the Erlking's words, but nobody would be able to deny his seal was genuine. Releasing Ilsa, I turned to Darrow, but he wasn't there. A knot twisted in my chest to know I'd fucked up majorly, but Ilsa and River would help me fix this, and I'd mend things with Darrow later. If we all survived.

"I'll talk to the Sidhe," River said. "I haven't been here in weeks, so they can't pin the blame on me for any of the recent events."

"Whereas I have a reputation." I gave a humourless smile. "We need to make sure the Sidhe sent someone to close the Vale entrance on the Erlking's territory, too."

"You were on the Erlking's territory again?" asked Ilsa.

"Yes, I was. I think if I hadn't been, I'd have arrived here right in time to be framed for opening the doorway into the Vale. That, or been slaughtered by whatever's waiting on the other side." As it was, Mum was the one who'd taken the fall. "Are the other Sidhe in the palace?"

"Some of them are," said Ilsa. "Do you want to talk to them, or…?"

"I think I'll pay a visit to Lord Raivan. I have a favour to ask him."

The only way to get the truth was to go back to the source. In other words, the Summer Court's jail. I'd ask to visit my mother… and pay a little detour to find the Seelie Queen.

I *hope I'm not too late.*

At this point, I'd trust River and Ilsa to handle the situation a damn sight more than anyone else here—including Darrow. I hardly believed he'd let Mum take the fall for someone else's crime. Even if I'd been a bitch to him, my mother was innocent, and he knew it.

I needed to clear her name and figure out who'd really opened that doorway, but I remained as far from catching the culprit as ever. Which left me to use the last tool at my disposal: annoying the shit out of the Sidhe.

I came to a halt at the meadow, where a carpet of vibrant yellow flowers swayed in the warm breeze. Lord Raivan paced through the grass, a bored expression on his face, waiting for any humans who might come here with requests. Considering I could count the number of humans who had dealings with Faerie on one hand, it must be a dull job, despite the pleasant scenery.

When he spotted me, his boredom shifted to annoyance. "What do you want, human?"

I pulled the Erlking's note from my pocket. "I have a note from the Erlking he sent me after his death, implying he wanted me to investigate his murder. The other Sidhe have arrested my mother for a crime she didn't commit and are refusing to listen to me." *So it's your lucky day.*

"A note from the Erlking?" he repeated. "What nonsense is this?"

"Read it." I thrust the note under his nose. "That's his seal."

"It is." His bright green eyes rounded. "The Erlking asked *you* to investigate his death? Why did you wait until now to show me this?"

"Because the note implies the killer is still in the Court," I said. "And because whoever the killer is, they just opened a doorway into the Vale and framed my family for it."

"If the Sidhe call for your family's blood, you took a great risk in coming to me," he said.

"Perhaps, but you know the Seelie Queen has good reason to want my family locked up or worse." I also had it on good authority that he'd set foot in the land of the outcasts once before and immediately fled in terror. "I should also tell you there's another passage into the Vale open over on the Erlking's territory, and even if the Sidhe have closed it, the sluagh have probably spread all over the Court now."

The blond Sidhe's angular features paled. "What?"

"Yep." I let my gaze pan across the meadow as though checking for ghostly fae lurking in the corners. "The sluagh love to prey on the living. I bet they can't resist a wide-open space like this meadow. If you ask me, my mother is probably safer in prison."

Lord Raivan's mouth pressed together. "I will take you to the jail, but I cannot promise the guards will let you in."

"If the Erlking's seal doesn't do it, nothing will."

The field warped around us, turning into a path leading up to a large, grim building which appeared to have grown out of the surrounding trees. Branches and roots met in the middle to form walls, while a Sidhe guarded each side of the entrance. As we strode up to them, two pairs of green eyes raked me up and down.

"Gatekeeper," said the Sidhe on the left, a female dressed in dark armour who wielded a long spear. "What do you want?"

I held up the note. "The Erlking sent me this before his death. It implies there are two traitors in the Court who were responsible for his assassination. My mother doesn't fit either description."

"The human is not to be released. We have our orders."

"Then I'd like to pay her a visit." I lowered the note with another pointed flash of the Erlking's seal. "The Erlking would never have wanted you to execute the former Gatekeeper without proof of her guilt."

She jerked her head towards her companion, a male guard with blue-black hair and the same armour as his partner. "Take her in. Don't let her out of your sight."

The second guard beckoned me to the door, formed from branches fused together. As he tapped it with his spear, the branches retracted into the door frame, allowing us into a dimly lit hallway. He used the spear to open another door on the right, which led into a corridor lined with cells formed of similar interlocking branches.

"Is this the human section?" I asked. "Or do you just imprison people wherever you feel like it?"

"We don't typically imprison humans."

I bet they didn't. If a human crossed a Sidhe, they didn't survive to see the inside of a cell. With one exception. I scanned the corridor, eyeing the dimly lit cells. "Doesn't look very secure."

"It is," he said. "Prisoners either have their magic bound or are otherwise incapacitated before imprisonment. The high-security area elsewhere in the prison allows no magic to enter aside from our own talismans."

"I should hope so."

The cells had no windows or doors, just thin gaps between the interlocking branches to allow in a minimum of natural light, which made it impossible to see their inhabitants. I opened my mouth to ask how the guards knew who was in each cell, then spotted a row of symbols carved into the branches above each door. Must be some kind of numbering system.

The guard halted in the middle of a corridor lined with cells. "Talk to her from here."

I leaned where he indicated, but the thick branches of the cell grew so closely together that I couldn't make out Mum's features on the other side. I edged closer on the pretext of speaking to her in a whisper.

Then, I spun on the spot, blasting the Sidhe with magic. Thorny stems shot from my hands, turning to ropes that wrapped tightly around him. He opened his mouth to shout, and I directed the ropes to cover his face, too, leaving an inch for him to breathe. The spear, which had fallen from his limp hand, rolled to a halt at my feet.

"Hazel." Mum's voice was faint. "What are you doing?"

I picked up the discarded spear. "Looking for the real murderer. Where are they keeping her, do you know?"

"Third corridor, behind the magic-proof barrier. I heard them talking." She knew precisely who I meant.

"Thanks. I'll come back for you later, I promise."

The Seelie Queen would be under the tightest possible security, so I threw on a glamour to make myself look like the female guard I'd seen at the entrance and followed Mum's directions.

I went through four doors before I reached the magic-proofed high-security area. The instant I passed through the entrance, pressure pinned me on all sides, as though a strong wind buffeted me from four directions at once. The spell on the cells must suppress the magic of anyone in here, which was the closest substitute in Faerie to building everything out of iron. I looked down to find my glamour had melted away when I'd entered. Damn. I'd need to move fast.

I walked swiftly through the corridors, checking each cell for any signs of the former monarch of Summer. At the sound of footsteps behind me, I darted into an alcove, pulling out the note from the Erlking in case I needed to flash the seal at anyone.

Then my gaze fell on the last line of text. The meaningless string of symbols.

When the footsteps faded, I stuck my head out and read the code on the nearest cell door. It matched the arrangement of symbols on the Erlking's note exactly.

I walked down the line of cells, checking them against the note. Two corridors down and I found the cell that corresponded to the symbols, tucked away into a corner and concealed behind a web of branches.

"I wondered if I'd ever see you again, Hazel Lynn," said

the Seelie Queen's voice from behind the wall of branches. "Or should I call you Gatekeeper now?"

"Feel free," I said. "I don't think we've ever spoken a word to one another." I might have asked how she knew I was here, but she'd have heard them bring in my mother and figured that I wouldn't be far behind.

"No, but your mother and I had quite the interesting rapport," she said. "It's a shame she won't be in here for long."

"How do you keep updated on what's going on outside?" Even the most powerful woman in the Summer Court wasn't a mind-reader, and she had no access to her magic in here.

"Sprites. Hobs. Messengers. There are always those willing to do my bidding in exchange for the continuation of their miserable lives."

Ugh. "You're the reason my mum's facing execution for a murder she didn't commit."

"I'm afraid I cannot claim responsibility for that, Hazel," she said. "It sounds like she is the one who implicated herself in my ex-husband's death."

"Like we don't both know you did it." She wasn't lying, of course, but that didn't prove anything. "And my family and I wrecked your last scheme."

"Yes, you did," she said. "Quite thoroughly. The Gate-keepers... I had to admit, I never thought of you as a potential threat. Until my husband had the nerve to send your mother into the Grey Vale in search of a way to strip me of my powers. I had to put a stop to that."

"Because you want his power for your own," I said. "You want his talisman."

"The talisman?" She gave a low laugh that raised the

hairs on my arms. "You think that's what this is about? The crown is all I desire."

"You'll never wear it." My hands clenched. "And I will see to it that you'll never see the outside of this cell again. I want you to tell me who your conspirators are."

"There's no need." Her voice dropped to a whisper. "They should be arriving soon."

Crap. She means it. Backing away from her cell, I broke into a fast walk, retracing my steps. I was glamour-free, but the Sidhe had bigger problems than a rogue Gate-keeper, and *I* had bigger problems than being caught. Mum was trapped behind bars, with no weapons or any other way of defending herself.

Turning right, I ran smack into Darrow. "Hazel, you have to leave."

I swore. "The Seelie Queen told me her conspirators are on their way here right now. What the hell are you doing? Come to gloat?"

"No," he said. "You should know, I warned your mother not to come through the gate, but she insisted on making sure you were safe. As for me, I came here to ask the Sidhe to reconsider her sentence, but more beasts broke through the Vale opening in the Erlking's territory before the Sidhe were able to close it."

A tremendous roar rattled the whole building. *Vale beasts.* They'd come here to help their Queen break out.

Not on my watch.

I ran past Darrow and towards the doors, which lay open. Further down the path, the Sidhe guards did battle with a huge troll. Its knuckles and feet were covered in crudely stitched gloves tipped with metal spikes. *Iron.* While it was big and dull-minded like most trolls, even a graze from iron would severely incapacitate any Sidhe. Including Darrow.

A Sidhe warrior ducked under the troll's arm, spear twirling and piercing its fleshy upper arm. Blood sprayed from its grey skin, but the blade remained stuck. Iron punched the Sidhe's armoured chest, sending him flying back a good ten metres. Two more Sidhe lay crumpled in pools of blood, their armour crushed and their silky hair matted with gore.

"Stay back!" I warned. "I'm gonna take it out."

I ran closer to the troll, my weapon at the ready. One swift thrust snagged its wrist but didn't break the skin. Its arms were thick as tree trunks, its skin tougher even than the illusion Darrow has conjured. The Vale had honed it into a vicious killing machine—bigger, sharper, and equipped with lethal iron.

Darrow ran to my side to help, his blade in his hand.

"I meant you, too," I said. "That's iron, in case you haven't noticed."

"It can crush your skull as easily as mine." He moved in a blur, slicing at the beast's thighs. The troll bellowed in pain. The iron must be hurting it, but trolls were low-magic and could still fight while impaired. If anything, the agony had only made this one more pissed off.

Thrusting upwards, I skidded underneath the troll's outstretched arm and caught the metal braces on the edge of my blade. Then I grabbed the underside of its wrist and propelled myself onto its arm. The beast tried to shake me off, but the chains prevented it from moving its arms high enough to grab me. Under the iron, layers of skin peeled off, flecked with blood.

Climbing onto its shoulder, I thrust the spear I'd

stolen clean through its throat. Blood slid in rivulets from the wound, and the troll let out a gurgling cry. Several Sidhe jumped aside from its body as its knees hit the earth. I leapt to the ground, hurrying to Darrow's side.

"I have to get my mother out, Darrow," I said. "While the Sidhe are distracted. I won't get another chance."

Then we'd really be on their shit list, but I couldn't bring myself to give a crap. I'd make sure the people I loved were safe first and worry about the rest later.

"I can't promise they won't come after you, but I can buy you time." He approached the fallen Sidhe, who had begun to gather the injured and dead, while I ran back into the jail.

An unconscious guard lay outside Mum's vacant cell, bearing the unmistakable imprint of one of Mum's brutal punches on his face. Had she been planning an escape from the start? If so, it would have been nice if she'd clued *me* in on it. I hadn't the faintest idea where she'd run off to, but I had to trust she'd make it out of the Court in one piece.

I backed out of the jail and snapped my fingers at the small group of surviving Sidhe. "Pull yourselves together and get more guards outside that jail before you have worse than a troll on your hands."

I didn't see Ilsa or the others, but they'd likely be back at the ambassadors' palace. As the Sidhe began to argue with one another, I ran into the forest, leaving the jail behind. Darrow caught me up on the path, falling into step alongside me.

"You should have stayed," I told him. "They need someone with sense to help them out."

"I'm more concerned with the intruders," he said. "Your mother wasn't in the jail?"

"She ran for it. I don't blame her." I shook my head. "Mum probably won't be at home, not with the Sidhe watching out for her, but my sister is back at the ambassadors' palace with the gate."

We moved swiftly through the trees, the haunting cries of the sluagh forming a chilling backdrop. Both of us kept our weapons out, but we didn't encounter a single person until we came to the ambassadors' palace. Outside stood two Sidhe: Lady Aiten and Lord Veren. I beckoned to Darrow and we veered down another path to where Ilsa stood next to the gate to the Lynn house, arguing with Lord Raivan.

"That's my home," she was saying. "I live on the other side of that gate. I need to get back to—"

"Lord Raivan," I said. "Vale beasts just attacked the jail, and they're working for the Seelie Queen. More might be on their way here. I'd focus on that, not my family's gate."

"It's the truth," added Darrow. "I was there. Hazel needs to leave before the killer targets her next."

"Uh, no she doesn't," I said. "I'm going after the—"

"Hazel," Ilsa said, her eyes on Lord Veren. "That guy? He's dead."

Everyone turned her way, then to Lord Veren, who gave a slow blink, not speaking a word. Despite the shiny veneer of his glamour, there was something oddly still about the angles of his face and the green light of his eyes.

Ilsa's spirit sight allowed her to see souls. It never steered her wrong. Not even in Faerie.

How can he be dead? He's still breathing.

One breathes without life...

He was one of the conspirators.

"Lady Aiten," I said. "Step away from that man."

In the same instant, Lord Veren's glamour fell away, revealing a face ravaged with scars, rotting strips of skin peeling away. His blade made a *snick* sound as it plunged into Lady Aiten's chest.

Lady Aiten gave a startled gasp, then fell to the ground. Lord Veren withdrew his blade in a smooth motion, his face expressionless. Lord Raivan lunged at him, but Lord Veren blocked Lord Raivan's strike with ease. Two quick slashes later and Lord Raivan fell back, bleeding heavily from his right arm. Lord Veren retained his supernatural speed, despite his condition. *How is that possible?* He was dead—still breathing, but no longer alive…

He must have touched the Erlking's talisman. Its magic somehow allowed him to exist in that ghastly half-alive condition, rotting from the inside and outside alike.

Magic sprang to my palms and slammed into Lord Veren in a whirl of green energy. Ilsa ran to my side to help out, and Darrow's blade met his with a jarring crash. My heart climbed into my throat, watching him and Lord Veren struggle against one another. When Lord Veren went on the offensive, I conjured magic to my hands and struck him from behind. He seemed to feel no pain, and my attack fizzled out without doing any damage.

The Sidhe's knife flashed, sinking deep into Darrow's chest. A gasp tore from my lungs. *No.*

Lord Veren withdrew his blade. "Find me in the Vale, Gatekeeper."

He turned and walked away, leaving Darrow bleeding

at my feet. He groaned, thick blood pulsing from the wound in his chest. He'd die if I didn't get him to a healer.

"River!" Ilsa shouted. "We need help!"

River came through the gate to the palace, his eyes widening at the sight of the fallen Sidhe. "Who did this?"

"Lord Veren," said Ilsa. "He was the traitor, and I think the Erlking's talisman turned him into some kind of zombie. We need a healer."

"I can't use my magic to heal others," said River, white-faced. "I'll fetch my father."

Lord Raivan stirred, his face ashen, but his wounds weren't deep. He'd live. Lady Aiten, however, had fallen unconscious. And Darrow…

"The grove," I said to Ilsa. "I have to take him there."

"Mum would kill you," said Ilsa, biting her lip. "And the enemy might be behind the gate."

I glanced down at Darrow. He'd gone icy pale, but his eyes flickered open when I crouched beside him. "You're not going to die, do you hear me?"

His voice was a low rasp. "Call my sprite, Humming-bird. He'll get me to a healer."

The magic in the grove could heal any injury, but Ilsa was right—the enemy might well be waiting on the other side of the gate. If I wanted to save Darrow, I had to get him out of here. I was damned if I lost anyone else.

I stood, calling out, "Hummingbird, I need your help. Darrow—"

Before I finished speaking, a sprite appeared above Darrow's inert body. Ilsa shouted my name, but a torrent of light descended, bearing us away into oblivion.

19

I blinked, disorientated, and found myself crouched on an earthen floor. The sprite flew around Darrow's prone body, making agitated noises. The packed earth forming the domed ceiling and the tunnel-like corridors branching outwards put me in mind of the Gatekeepers' training grounds. The luminescent fungi glowing in clusters on the walls and floor, not so much.

Where the hell are we?

Before I could quite get a grip on my senses, several fae ran into the room. Sidhe, judging by their vibrant green eyes, but their plain black-and-green attire was unfamiliar to me, as were their carved weapons.

I rose to my feet. "I didn't hurt him. Darrow's sprite brought us here because he's dying. He needs a healer."

A sharp voice from behind the Sidhe said, "Take care of him. I will deal with the Gatekeeper."

The Sidhe parted to allow the speaker to pass through: a female Sidhe with ivory-white hair dressed in armoured clothing in rich shades of brown and green and marked with jewelled studs like twinkling stars. As I took in the angles of her face, her glamour struck me like a solid blow, knocking the breath from my lungs.

"Have you no voice, Gatekeeper?"

I licked my dry lips. "I'm sorry, but I have no idea where I am."

"You are in the realm of the Aes Sidhe, and I am Etaina. Come with me, Hazel Lynn."

The *Aes Sidhe?* No wonder Darrow had been so tight-lipped on the subject of his Court. They were supposed to have died out before the Erlking had even taken Summer's throne.

My legs moved jerkily as I walked after the Sidhe woman into the tunnel, down a narrow passage lit by more luminous groups of bright fungi, and through a wooden door into a surprisingly modern-looking office. My eyes took in the elegant wooden furniture, the carved desk, the bookshelves, but my brain refused to process the woman in front of me.

"I thought the Aes Sidhe died out," I said. "Centuries ago."

"It's easier for us to let the rest of Faerie believe that," said Etaina. "We broke from the main Courts countless years ago."

Holy shit. From the way she spoke, it sounded like she'd been *alive* then. That made her as old as the Erlking himself.

"Why did you send Darrow to Summer, then? As a spy?"

"I suspect you know that already." She gave me an appraising look. "You put me in a difficult position, Gatekeeper. No outsider has crossed our boundaries in a long time, and Darrow swore to tell nobody of this place."

"He didn't break his word," I said. "He told me to call his sprite to bring him to be healed. The traitor who killed the Erlking stabbed him, and he wouldn't have survived if he hadn't come here."

Etaina's lips thinned. "I told him not to interfere in Court affairs. I should have guessed the Gatekeeper would force him to do otherwise."

"Whoa." I raised my hands, still soaked in Darrow's blood. "I didn't force him to do a thing, and besides, I'm not Gatekeeper yet. How can I get back into the Court from here?"

"You'll leave when I say so, Gatekeeper," she said. "Many would prefer not to let you leave at all."

"That would be inconvenient." Not that the Sidhe would be falling over themselves to send a rescue party after the chaos I'd left behind in the Court, but the last thing I needed was to perish in some unfamiliar Court below the earth. "I saved Darrow's life. You're his queen, right?"

She turned to me, clasping her hands in front of her chest. "Tell me how Darrow came to be injured."

"The Erlking was murdered by an assassin, which I imagine he's probably told you," I said. "The killer opened several gateways into the Grey Vale in the Summer Court. When we caught one of the conspirators, Darrow fought him and was stabbed in the process."

"I find it hard to believe that my ambassador would fall so easily."

"He didn't." Did she even know about the Erlking's talisman? The last thing I needed was this secret Court taking the side of the enemy. "His adversary used magic to make himself unable to feel pain."

Her gaze sharpened." The assassin took the Erlking's talisman."

"You *know—?*"

"Of course I know," she said. "It is, in part, the reason the Aes Sidhe split from Summer. I know its magic well."

Shit. How could that be possible? Even the current generations of Sidhe didn't know the truth about the talisman—or they hadn't, until his death. She must be from the same generation which had fought the old gods, banished them from Faerie, and claimed their magic. Which made her far older than the Gatekeepers.

"Then..." I curled my bloodied hands into fists. "I know you don't like my family, though I don't understand why, but if there's anything you can tell me about how to fight against the Erlking's talisman, it might save a lot of lives."

The Erlking had had to live in isolation for his entire reign order to keep the talisman's magic from harming the rest of the Court, and as far as I knew, it couldn't be destroyed. The Erlking would have known that if the Court had abandoned the talisman in the land of the outcasts, anyone might have been able to steal it and use it against the Court. He'd been backed into a corner, and I had no doubt he'd tried every alternative before claiming its magic as his own.

Etaina's bright green eyes brightened, and tendrils of magic brushed against me, alien and sharp. I held still, my heart hammering, as the threads of magic touched the symbol on my forehead.

The breath punched from my lungs, and a wave of

cold terror washed over me as images of yawning chasms and starless skies flashed before my eyes. Her magic, like Darrow's, might well be exempt from my protective shield—and had the power to remake reality however she saw fit.

She could make me worship her, bow down and serve her for the rest of my existence.

"So it's true," she murmured, half to herself. "The Gatekeepers' magic endures."

"What...?" I forced out the words. "What are you talking about?"

"Your vow remains intact, even with the Erlking's passing and his wife's betrayal," she mused.

"Yes..." The knot in my chest loosened a fraction when the tendrils of magic lifted from my forehead. "What does it matter to you? Didn't you leave the Court before my ancestor even set foot in Faerie?"

"The tale is well known among my people," she said. "The tale of Thomas Lynn, a human who wormed his way into the realm of the Sidhe and stole their magic."

My mouth parted. "That's not the story I grew up with. Thomas Lynn was kidnapped by a Sidhe and tricked into signing his entire family into a lifetime of servitude to the Courts."

Darrow had thought I'd volunteered for the job. That I'd *wanted* the faeries' power. It was starting to make sense where he'd learned it.

"Etaina." Darrow's hoarse voice came from outside the door. "Let Hazel leave. She has no quarrel with us."

"Darrow." My heart jumped in my chest. He leaned against the door frame, his face pale and streaked with blood, but the wound was no longer bleeding, and his gaze was steady. "You shouldn't be walking."

"Hazel," he rasped. "Thank you for saving my life."

"See?" I gave Etaina a pointed look. "I don't want to fight you. I need to get back to the Court and get that talisman away from the enemy. I don't expect you'll ever see me again, so if you won't help me, please—let me go."

Darrow drew himself upright. "I will go after her as soon as I am able. For now, I would advise you to aid her goal. The Court can ill afford to lose a Gatekeeper as well as a king."

He was asking her to help me? Accepting help from a strange Sidhe was a great way to end up entangled in a blood debt, but I had no chance of getting that talisman back alone. Not without ending up the same way as Lord Kerien.

"I will see if my fellow Sidhe agree," she said. "You go with Darrow, Gatekeeper."

I opened my mouth to argue, but Darrow swayed unsteadily against the door frame, prompting me to take his arm. "You won't be following me back to the Court in this state."

"The healing spell's effects will kick in soon," he said. "My wounds have already sealed."

So they had. The vicious stab wound had vanished, though his shirt was soaked through with blood. "At least go and lie down somewhere."

He turned right and walked down the corridor. Since I had no idea how to get out of this place, I followed his lead, until he halted at a wooden door, pushing it open to reveal a sitting room lit by clouds of glittering fireflies hovering below the earthen ceiling.

Darrow peeled off his bloodied shirt, then walked through a door into the neighbouring room. The sound of running water came through, and I glimpsed a bathroom with modern features behind the door.

"Do you live here?" I asked.

"This is the only place we're unlikely to be disturbed."

"Look, Darrow," I said, "I'm no use hanging around here while my siblings are stuck in Faerie, my mother is on the run, and the Summer Court is under attack."

"The Sidhe should have sealed the entrances to the Vale by now," he said.

"So you do know of the Vale." I sank into an armchair, tiredness tugging at my bones. "I suppose nothing you say should surprise me now. The *Aes Sidhe.*"

He was probably right in that the Sidhe would have dealt with the outcasts by now—with the exception of Lord Veren. *Meet me in the Vale, he'd said.* He was waiting for me to find him. He could wait a little longer.

Darrow entered the room, free of bloodstains and wearing a clean shirt. "What did you want to know?"

"Your Court split from Summer," I said. "How did you end up with both Summer and Winter magic, then?"

"The Aes Sidhe still maintain enough of a connection to the Seelie Court that our magic aligns with them. My other parent was half-Unseelie."

And two of his grandparents must be human. "Etaina isn't a relation…?"

"No," he said. "She is… I would call her our Queen, but she dislikes that title. Our leadership is not hereditary."

"No wonder she doesn't like the Courts," I murmured. "She just spun me a story about how my ancestor supposedly *stole* the Sidhe's magic. Is that why you hate me so much?"

"I don't hate you," he said. "As for your ancestor, I know what I was taught about him, and that's all."

"It's total bollocks," I said. "Even if Thomas Lynn *did* sign a deal with the Sidhe on purpose, my family sure as hell didn't volunteer for this. Believe me, if not for the Erlking's murder, I'd hoped to break the curse as soon as I figured out which Sidhe actually put it on my family in the first place."

His mouth parted. "You did?"

"So?" I said. "It doesn't matter. I've lost my Gatekeeper's position several times over at this point, and I'll be dead by the day's end assuming I ever get out of here. You might as well tell me everything you know."

"You aren't going to die," he said. "As soon as my wound has fully healed, I'll come with you to hunt down that traitor."

"This isn't your fight." I looked down at my bloodied hands. "I told you, if the murderer doesn't kill me, the Sidhe will, and you'll be labelled as guilty by association if they catch both of us together."

"We are still bound, Hazel, until you complete your training," he said. "Besides, the Sidhe will know by now that you didn't open the paths into the Vale, and Lady Aiten is still bound not to harm you."

"That's if she survives." My mouth tightened. "Are you hiding any secret tricks to dealing with the Erlking's talisman, then? Etaina knows of it, and I'm taking a wild guess that she told you before you came to the Court. She knew the Erlking before he took over Summer."

"She did," he confirmed. "As for the talisman, I've

never set eyes on it, and know little of it aside from its power."

"You didn't see the Erlking's death coming?" I asked.

"No." He shook his head. "I didn't know of the Seelie Queen's betrayal before my arrival in the Court, either. I believe Etaina did, and that's why I was sent in to gather intelligence."

"I wish you'd told me earlier, so I wouldn't have suspected you of being involved in his murder."

"I was vow-bound not to tell you of my mission. That vow lifted the instant my sprite brought us here."

I tilted my head. "So you weren't just being cryptic for the sake of it."

"Maybe a little." The merest hint of a smile touched his mouth. "You were determined to press me for answers, and I have to admit, I wanted to know what you'd try next."

Heat seared my neck. He'd seen through my attempts to ply him with alcohol and lessons in resisting seductive glamour.

"You didn't mind?" I said. "Not even when I set off your glamour and almost revealed your secret? You could have… you could have done more than you did, couldn't you?"

His eyes darkened. "I don't use that skill any more than necessary."

"You talked your way into Summer, didn't you?" I went on. "No wonder they don't mind someone from another Court running around their territory. That's why they gave you the job and why nobody asks which Court you're from. Am I right?"

He looked away. "My talent comes with a cost.

Namely, it's difficult for me to get close to people. If they saw through the base level of my glamour, then I'd have to choose whether to risk them finding out the truth. It's not permanent, and it would have been inconvenient to keep using it on you. Besides, people would have noticed if you suddenly started worshipping me."

Another wave of heat washed over my cheeks. "Why did you decide to train the Gatekeeper, then?"

"It was the obvious choice of position for someone who wanted to keep an eye on the Erlking's pawn."

His words smacked me in the chest. "Pawn? You still think I'm just a tool with no free will of my own?"

"When I first came to the Court, I knew no better," he said. "It wasn't I who trained your cousin, the Winter Gatekeeper, and I hadn't met your family before then. My opinion was based on rumour, not fact."

"And now?" *Dammit, Hazel, who cares what he thinks of you?*

It shouldn't matter, and yet a significant part of me expected to die today. Was it so terrible that I wanted confirmation that there was one thing I hadn't screwed up?

"Now?" he said, his voice soft. "I know you're brave, strong and loyal, and you're the most interesting thing that's happened in my life in a long while."

I snorted. "You make me sound like some kind of freak accident or natural disaster." Despite my flippant tone, my heartbeat kicked into gear.

Especially when he leaned closer to me, letting his mouth brush mine. "Is it not obvious why I helped you?"

There was a sharp rap on the door, and he broke away from me. "Who is it?"

The door opened, revealing Etaina's tall, angular figure. "I have come for the Gatekeeper. My fellow Sidhe and I have decided that we will allow her to return to the Summer Court."

"Oh." I walked to the door and opened it. "What's the catch?"

"You will then come here to meet with me after the threat is dealt with, and we will discuss your options."

"You seem confident I'm going to survive," I said. "If I don't, the Vale outcasts might well come here next."

"That's the only reason I'm giving you this." She handed me a round stone. "This will provide protection against the effects of the Erlking's talisman as long as you are holding it. I will send you directly back into Summer. Darrow will stay here until his injury has healed."

His aquamarine eyes looked into mine. "Stay alive until then. Think of it as your last Trial."

The Trials didn't matter, not anymore. It was time to follow the outcasts right into the Grey Vale and get the Erlking's talisman out of their hands. Whatever it took.

20

The light cleared, leaving me on the path outside the ambassadors' palace. Pocketing the stone, I walked to the oak doors and opened them.

Coral gasped, then she ran over and tackle-hugged me. "Hazel!"

"You're okay." I hugged her back. "What are you doing here? I thought you were back at the Gatekeeper's training grounds."

"I was looking for you," she said. "The Sidhe said your mother is on the run from jail, and they think you helped her escape."

"They're dead wrong on that one." I should have guessed they'd come to that conclusion. "Mum escaped on her own when the Vale beasts attacked the jail. Have you seen my sister?"

Her eyes widened. "The other human is your sister? I thought you looked alike. She ran out of here with a half-Sidhe about half an hour ago."

"Her boyfriend," I explained. "River. His father works

for the Court, so they came here to plead on my mother's behalf. Have I missed anything else?"

"Chaos," she said. "Those sluagh monsters got to the Gatekeeper's base, but we managed to fight them off. I *think* the Sidhe killed the rest, but I'm lost on where they came from in the first place. I heard someone mention the Grey Vale?"

"Yeah." I grimaced. "Lord Veren opened a doorway into the Vale and framed my family for it. He's the one who stole the Erlking's talisman, and I need to go into the Vale to find him. If anyone asks, Darrow is recovering from his injuries and hasn't deserted his post. I might not come back here for a while."

Lady Aiten and Lord Raivan had both been injured, but Lord Raivan ought to be back on his feet by now. I hoped so, because I needed a Sidhe to open a doorway into the Vale for me.

"You can't go to the Grey Vale," she insisted. "Didn't you say it's where the outcasts who attacked Earth came from? There's worse than sluagh in that place."

"I've been there before." I scanned the hall for any signs of the Sidhe. "I'll see if I can ask Lord Raivan to take me there, assuming he's awake."

Her jaw dropped. "You've been to the Vale?"

I nodded. "It's how I became Gatekeeper. The Erlking sent Mum on an important mission to the Vale, and the Seelie Queen didn't like that. She took my mum hostage and tried to use our gate to summon the Sidhe's old gods to attack the Courts. The same gods whose power is in the Erlking's talisman. Believe me, as long as Lord Veren has it, we're all fucked one way or another, so I might as well go down fighting. You should warn the Sea Queen to prepare for a potential attack from the Vale. I don't think this is going to stop with Summer."

Her mouth gaped open. "Hazel…"

"Coral!" Her brother entered the hall, his dark cape swirling behind him. "I heard the Court was under attack. You have to come with me."

I looked between them. "Who told you that?"

Cliff turned my way. "You're alive?"

"I assume I am, since I'm standing here." Something wasn't right. "Why are *you* here? Shouldn't you be with your Queen?"

"I thought my sister was dead." His eyes narrowed at me. "You've done enough harm. Come, Coral."

She flashed me an apologetic look. "Cliff, it wasn't Hazel's fault. She's about to risk her neck for all our sakes."

He walked forwards. "What happens in the Courts is none of our concern. Come back home with me."

I moved between them. "Hang on a second there. Cliff, who exactly told you the Court was attacked? And why did you abandon your Queen during a time when the Courts are under threat from an outside force?"

His body tensed, and out of the corner of my eye, a glamour flickered under his cape.

"What are you hiding?" I took one step closer. Then my hand snapped out, grabbing his glamour, which shattered—revealing the bow strapped to his back.

Coral gasped. "You stole our mother's talisman."

"Of course I did," said Cliff. "The Sea Queen uses it as an ornament, not the weapon it's designed to be. You didn't think I'd come here unarmed, did you?"

"You expect me to buy that bullshit?" The Erlking's

words hit me. "You don't need to breathe underwater, do you? You're the one who shot him."

"No!" Coral shook her head. "Cliff, tell me you didn't—"

"The Erlking planned to absorb our Court into Summer," said Cliff. "We would have been reduced to nothing. You would never have been Queen."

"Oh, don't pretend you did this for unselfish reasons," I said. "You wanted your mother's crown for your own, didn't you?"

Coral shook her head again. "My brother wouldn't do that. He's loyal to the throne."

"Unless he was offered something better than a throne."

Something like a prime position in whatever Court the Seelie Queen planned to set up after she escaped jail.

Cliff's mouth thinned. "Get out of my way. I was told to leave you unharmed, but you're trying my patience."

Told by who? The Seelie Queen wanted me alive, as far as I knew, but I didn't trust her people one single bit.

"Nobody said the same to me." I pulled out one of my blades. "Easy way or hard way."

Coral gasped as her brother hefted the bow onto his shoulder, an arrow already nocked. "No—*no.*"

"I claimed its magic long ago," said Cliff. "Our mother, in her fragile state, didn't even notice."

"And were you responsible for that, too?" I queried. "I find it a little callous that you left her unprotected to join a coup in another Court."

Coral's expression turned from horrified to incensed. "You caused her sickness, didn't you? That's why you wanted me out of the Court. You supported me going to

Summer because you knew I'd figure it out right away if I stayed at home."

His mouth opened and closed, his hands trembling on the bow. "I did this to protect both of us, Coral, I promise."

She raised her fist and delivered an impressive right hook to his jaw. He staggered under the bow's weight, and Coral hit him again. The talisman slipped in his hands as he scrambled to adjust the arrow. If he fired it by accident, either of us might die.

I blasted him in the chest with magic. The bow's weight combined with the momentum sent him staggering back into the wall. At once, I directed my magic at the vines growing from the floor, which wound around his ankles, ensnaring him. He swore, fighting their grip, and I plucked the talisman from his hands and pointed it at his chest.

"The talisman will never serve you, human filth," he spat.

"I don't *want* a talisman." The bow was heavy as hell and awkward to carry, but it made an impressive cracking noise when it collided with Cliff's skull. He crumpled, the vines looping around his ankles like ropes.

Coral let out a sob. "The Sidhe will murder him for this. What was he *thinking?*"

The palace's oak doors flew open and Ilsa ran into the entrance hall. "Hazel? What the hell is going on?"

"We found the second traitor." I indicated Cliff's unconscious body. "He's the one who shot the Erlking. With this."

Her eyes widened at the sight of the bow. "Damn. We need to hand that over to the Sidhe... but I didn't know you were here. You just vanished into thin air. Is Darrow with you?"

"He says he'll be right behind me when I go after Lord Veren into the Vale."

Ilsa shook her head. "You aren't going in there alone, Hazel. Have you seen Mum?"

"I literally just got back, so no." Wait. *Please tell me* she *didn't go into the Vale.* I should have guessed Mum would never be content to let the murderer go free. "We need to make sure this guy faces justice and take the bow straight to the Sidhe."

"He claimed it?" Ilsa guessed, eyeing Coral's grim expression. "Okay, I'll take that bow. Lord Raivan was behind me, but he was staggering around with his injuries still half-healed."

"Are no other Sidhe in here at all?" I asked Coral.

"No." Her lips trembled. "Hazel, if I let you go into the Vale, I'll be breaking my vow to bodyguard you."

Dammit. Bloody Sidhe and their vows. "Then guard him." I indicated Cliff. "If you stop him from coming after me, you'll be keeping your word. And watching the bow, too."

Her gaze clouded. "All right."

"I'll be back, as soon as I can." I gave her a brief hug. "Is Lord Raivan close? I need a Sidhe to open a door into the Vale for me." Getting out would be another battle entirely, but I'd confront that one later.

Ilsa pulled out her own talisman. "I can open a way through with this—"

"Not a chance," I said. "I need you to stay back here and warn the other Sidhe that Lord Veren will keep attacking the Court until he manages to break the Seelie Queen out of jail. I'm going to find Lord Raivan."

"What is it now, mortal?" Lord Raivan entered the hall. He was pale and unsteady on his feet, and his gaze went from Coral, to the bow, to Ilsa, and me. "I thought you abandoned us, Gatekeeper."

"Not quite," I said. "I need transportation into the Grey Vale. The Erlking's murderer is there, and I'm going to kill him."

"I can make one trip," said Lord Raivan. "But I cannot guarantee your safe return."

"I'll risk it."

Lord Raivan unsheathed his own sword, which glimmered with green light. Despite the paleness of his iron-damaged skin, his features were regal and impressive as he raised the talisman and a flash of light sent me reeling back.

The light turned grey, eerie, and I landed on my feet on an equally grey path bathed in silver and silence. I'd reached the land of the outcasts.

21

More paths extended on either side of me, flanked with silvery trees, bleached of colour. A faint glow streamed through the canopy, reflecting on the fallen leaves and wreathing the trees in a strange, misty light.

Gone were Summer's vibrant colours and fragrances. This was the realm to which traitors were banished, stripped of their magic and left to fight over any scraps they could find.

What the Sidhe had failed to take into account was that the same gods they'd banished from their realm had left traces of their magic here in the Vale, and when that magic had wound up in the hands of Faerie's worst criminals, Earth had paid the price for it.

And now the Courts might, too.

My footsteps made no sound as I walked along the path, rounding a corner. In the Vale, the world rearranged itself depending on whether the person in control wanted to be found or not, so I could guarantee Lord Veren wouldn't be far off—along with the Erlking's talisman. And while I'd like nothing more than to leave it to rot here in this empty realm away from the Courts, one day, a rogue Sidhe might successfully win it over. That weapon, in the hands of the outcasts, would easily do as much damage as a second faerie invasion. Earth and the Courts alike would crumble.

I wouldn't allow it.

I reached into my pocket and touched my fingertips to the cool stone Etaina had given me. If she'd intentionally given me a dud, I was royally fucked. Putting my faith in strangers ran counter to everything I'd learned about surviving in Faerie. Mum would be pissed at me.

Speaking of Mum…

I rounded another corner and heard shouting up ahead. A human figure circled a giant beast—another ogre, by the looks of things—and wielded a sharp iron blade in her hands.

I ran to meet her. "Mum, what the hell are you doing?"

Her blade sank into the ogre's padded chest. She might be vulnerable without her magic, but she was still holding her own. Not surprising, since unlike me, she hadn't had her iron weapons taken away. The blade withdrew with a sharp noise, and blood fountained onto the grey-silver path. The beast collapsed into a bloody heap at Mum's feet. "Hazel, you shouldn't be here."

"You brought iron," I said. "Wish I could say the same."

"Here." She handed me her blade, then drew a second one from her belt. "It'll be more useful than your magic in this place."

I didn't doubt that. "Where is the Erlking's talisman, do you know?"

"Close," she said. "It was Lord Veren who betrayed the Court."

"I know," I said. "Ilsa figured it out. She saw he had no soul—or a damaged one. I think that talisman is slowly killing him, if it hasn't already. You can't go near the talisman, Mum."

Why had she come here? She knew there was no way out if you didn't have faerie magic. Then again, so did I. If we both died here, Ilsa would use necromancy to find us in the afterlife to give us a tongue-lashing, I just knew it.

"I could say the same to you." Mum shook her head. "Hazel, I know this realm."

"And I have this." I removed the stone from my pocket. "It will protect me from the talisman's magic."

Her breath hissed out. "Where did you get that?"

"The Aes Sidhe. I'll tell you later." I turned on the spot, my skin prickling. "I think we're being watched."

Cold fingers trailed down my spine, and a cloud of darkness coalesced above the silvery path. Outlined in stark blue magic, it formed a vaguely humanoid shape.

A wraith. The ghost of a Winter Sidhe, if its blue glow was any indication. When a Sidhe died in the Vale, they had no afterlife to move on to, so many of them remained trapped in the form of concentrated magic and rage, equipped with all the powers they'd had when they'd been alive. Unlike the sluagh, it held no physical form, so stabbing it wouldn't be effective in the slightest.

"Mum!" I shouted. "Get back."

A wave of magic hurtled towards me, ricocheting to the side and slamming into a tree. *Thank god.* My magic-proofed shield worked on the dead. I blasted the wraith with a handful of bright green energy, but my magic alone was no match for a living Sidhe's, let alone a dead one.

I bared my teeth and drew on every ounce of the Gatekeeper's magic I possessed. The circlet's light grew to a blinding greenish white, pushing the wraith out of range. My hands glowed, forming a shield around me.

"Stay back," I snarled. "Get out of my way."

The wraith's magic hit my shield and ricocheted away into the trees. I beckoned to Mum. "I'll hold up the shield. It can't hit either of us."

I hope. I found myself wondering if the Erlking's talisman would have any effect on it. While its magic destroyed the living, not the dead, it also targeted magic, too. Not that I'd seen any sign of it yet. The wraith pummelled my shield, over and over, drifting behind Mum and me like an angry shadow.

"Wonderful," I said. "We have a ghostly stalker. Where the hell is that Lord Veren? I thought he was desperate for me to come and find him."

"Hazel." Mum pointed ahead. Fog wreathed the path, peeling back to reveal a large stone construction which blended into the surrounding grey.

"Why is it always castles?" I remarked. "I mean, it might be an idea for the next power-hungry Sidhe to make their palace out of a tree house or a tent, just for variety. Like the Sea Queen's ship. Castles are so... medieval."

I had zero doubts that the place would be booby trapped halfway to hell, but I relished the challenge. Hefting my iron blade, I stalked forwards, ignoring the chill breath of the wraith on my back.

Mum swore under her breath. "Hazel, the talisman isn't inside the castle. It's a magical creation."

I stopped walking. "Shit."

The Vale had led us in the wrong direction. But the castle clearly belonged to *someone*. And since there were no friends here, I'd go with 'foe'.

Sure enough, a Sidhe stepped out in front of the castle. Tall and lean, he had blue-black hair and pointed features that looked oddly lifeless. His eyes were pale, leached of colour. Most outcasts had no magic, but the castle hadn't sprung up out of the ground.

Frowning, I glanced at him out of the corner of my eye. At once, his glamour peeled back, revealing a face mottled with bruises. "You touched the talisman, didn't you? Where is it?"

"It's mine," he said, his tone monotone, his eyes glassy.

"Uh-huh." A chill settled between my shoulder blades. "Listen, I'm in a rush. I'm also being stalked by a wraith, so it'd be really helpful if you dealt with that. Where is the talisman?"

"It's mine," he repeated.

"Right. We already established that." Given his appearance, he was well and truly addled. "Never mind. We're leaving. Enjoy your... castle."

The Sidhe gave a cold, empty smile. "But you haven't met my pet. Let me introduce you."

A deafening boom shook the path, and Mum and I raised our blades. A gigantic troll shambled around the corner, its skin grey and flaking. Half a chain hung from its ankle, suggesting someone had unsuccessfully tried to chain it up like the other troll which had attacked the Court. *Just wonderful.*

"Pleasure to meet you, but we've gotta run." I whirled around, and the wraith loomed in my way, icy magic chilling me to the bone.

"Do you mind?"

The wraith's icy magic coasted straight at us, bouncing off my shield and hitting the troll in the face. The troll staggered under the assault, icy shards flying in all directions. With a furious bellow, it charged.

Mum spun to the side, avoiding the troll by a hair's breadth. I, meanwhile, ran straight through the wraith. A chill of icy energy shot straight to my core and I staggered on the other side—but the ogre's charge didn't slow. It hadn't quite grasped that its target was incorporeal.

Mum lunged at the ogre, dealing a vicious cut to its thigh. The chain swung around, knocking Mum clean off her feet.

"Dammit!" I ducked another attack, forced to the side to avoid the troll's charge. The wraith's icy magic sent the beast reeling. I'd much rather leave the two of them to fight it out, but Mum had landed right in their path.

I dove at the troll, my blade sinking into its meaty thigh. The troll bellowed but didn't slow, its fist swinging at my head. I ducked and rolled, forced to let go of the blade to avoid the chain. Mum had backed up, slowly, but she was bleeding from a nasty-looking cut on her forehead.

I gave a lunge in an attempt to retrieve my blade, but it remained lodged in the ogre's thigh. A beefy hand caught my shoulders and lifted me into the air, holding me in the way of the wraith's attack. The fucker was using *me* as a shield.

"Hey!" I kicked out, my boots making the same impact

as a pebble against the troll's thick arm. Another icy attack from the wraith bounced off my shield, striking the nearest tree. "Mum, run!"

Breaking free of the troll's grip, I landed on my feet in time for the chain to swing directly at my head.

22

I flung myself onto the leaf-strewn path. The chain grazed my shoulder, missing my head by a hair's breadth. The troll's foot came down, and I rolled onto my back to avoid being struck by the blade wedged in its thigh.

Raising my arms, I snagged the blade's hilt with my fingertips and gave a tremendous heave. The blade came free with a spray of blood, but the troll hardly seemed to feel it. It turned on me, having decided to abandon the wraith in favour of live prey.

A wave of magic slammed into the ogre, green-blue tendrils sending me flying head over heels. I landed on my feet, the impact jarring my knees. *Ow. What the fuck?*

Only one person's magic could get through my shield.

"Darrow." I straightened upright. "I told you *not* to follow me here."

Instead of answering, he ran into the fray, magic sparking from his hands, a combination of both Winter and Summer. The wraith reeled back, while the troll bellowed in rage.

As it charged, I leapt at the troll from behind, grabbing the back of its chained arm. Climbing one-handedly, I pulled myself onto its shoulders. With a wild lunge, I sank the point of my blade into its neck.

The ogre threw back its head and roared, and I held on grimly. Darrow whirled to the side in time to avoid being crushed, but not far enough away to avoid being splattered from head to toe with blood.

"Oops." I yanked out my blade and jumped off the dead troll's shoulders. "First mud and now blood. You're welcome, by the way. Did you kill that wraith?"

He wiped blood from his face with his sleeve. "I don't think so. I just stunned it."

"Wonderful." I scanned the undergrowth in search of Mum. She was still on her feet, but blood matted the side of her head. "Mum, are you okay?"

"I'll be fine, Hazel," she said. "The wraith disappeared."

"Told you they were bastards," I added to Darrow.

"How did you kill them last time?"

"I didn't. My sister did."

Laughter echoed through the trees, drawing our attention to the male Sidhe standing unsteadily in front of his castle. "You make an admirable fighter, for a human."

"Go away." I waved a hand at him. "We're not interested in you. We're looking for Lord Veren."

"Him." His manner switched from manic to furious in the blink of an eye. "The thief. His blood will turn to ashes and his skin will rot from his flesh. I will take the talisman from his decaying fingers—"

Darrow's magic lashed out, knocking the Sidhe off his

feet. "Tell me where he is," he demanded. "I want that talisman, and I'm going to get it one way or another."

Shock punched the air from my lungs. He hadn't come back to help me at all, but because Etaina had sent him to bring the talisman directly to her.

Dammit, Hazel. Had I seriously thought he'd risk his life in the Vale if there was nothing in it for him? Etaina might have given me the stone, but she'd sent Darrow in to ensure the talisman ended up in her hands no matter the outcome.

Perhaps she did know more about the Erlking's talisman than I did, but if the Erlking had taught me one thing in the short time we'd known one another, it was that none could truly claim to understand the power of the gods.

Someday, you're going to thank me for this, Darrow.

"You know what, let's just leave them to it." I took Mum's arm and pulled her off the path into the trees. "Come on, Vale, sort your shit out. Take me to Lord Veren and the talisman he stole."

The tree's branches rustled, and a group of Sidhe emerged with silent steps. They must have been watching our fight from the woods, unseen by anyone, even Darrow. His eyes widened in alarm, and Mum's grip on my arm tightened.

Fuck. I can't fight all of them at once.

"Move aside," Mum said sharply. "If you're conspiring with the Erlking's murderer, you'll face the wrath of the Court and the Gatekeepers alike."

"We have nothing to fear from you, Gatekeeper," said a female Sidhe with ice-white hair and oddly pale eyes. "Take them."

I raised my blade in warning, but the Sidhe didn't seem afraid of the iron at all. Hands grasped my blade—rotting hands, half-dead. I gripped tighter, slicing off a Sidhe's hand, but he made no sound. They must have all stepped within the talisman's orbit, and the Erlking's staff had turned them all into something beyond death.

Darrow spat out a curse, his blade sinking into a Sidhe's chest. Mum grappled with another, but his hand closed over the edge of her sword, but he didn't bleed when he yanked it away from her and pointed it at Darrow.

The Sidhe spoke in a raspy voice. "If you don't stop fighting, he dies."

Darrow paled, the light of his magic fading. *Why did you come here?* I already knew why, but while he might have ulterior motives, I didn't want him to die in the land of the outcasts.

"This one isn't human," said another Sidhe. "What is he, then?"

Darrow replied in the faerie tongue with an epithet which implied one of the Sidhe's parents had fornicated with a troll. I choked on an unexpected laugh which turned into a gasp when the Sidhe struck him over the head with the hilt of Mum's iron blade and pressed it to his neck. "Hand me your weapon, Gatekeeper."

I extended my blade, turning it at the last second and severing the Sidhe's wrists. Mum's blade clattered to the ground, and she grabbed it, beheading the Sidhe who held Darrow. He pulled himself free and regained his balance, but the iron's touch had leached the blue-green shine from his eyes.

"That's enough," came a cold voice. The Sidhe parted

to allow Lord Veren to walk through. "Are you incapable of subduing a simple human, even after I gave you a taste of the talisman's magic?"

"What did you expect when you turned your allies into zombies?" I said to him. "You should know, I have two necromancers as siblings. Chopping body parts off dead people is second nature to us. What did you do with the Erlking's talisman?"

If he carried it, I'd be able to sense its life-sucking magic. Had he seriously left it lying around where anyone could pick it up?

"The talisman has no wielder anymore." He stepped over the beheaded Sidhe, uncaring of his fate. Mum and I raised our iron blades in unison, while Darrow gave Lord Veren a defiant stare.

"Take care of these two," Lord Veren told the Sidhe. "I will handle the Gatekeeper myself."

"Like hell you will." I plunged my blade into a Sidhe's throat. Blood gushed out, yet his hands grabbed me, unfeeling and oblivious to the iron I carried.

The other Sidhe swarmed between our group, circling Mum and Darrow and cutting me off from them. Darrow's face was bleached white, while Mum's hands trembled on her weapon. *I have to do something*—but the Sidhe were beyond fearing death. They'd fight until they fell apart.

Lord Veren faced me, and I glared into his dull eyes. "I hope you know nobody in the Court will actually care that you've captured me. If you think you can use me as leverage against Summer, you're dead wrong."

"Oh, I'm not under any illusions that you're of value to anyone, Gatekeeper," said Lord Veren. "Except, perhaps, for the Seelie Queen. You'll have the honour of serving as the first Gatekeeper in the new relationship between Sidhe and humans."

"I'd rather eat dirt."

His hand moved blindingly fast, striking me across the face. Blood filled my mouth where I'd bitten my tongue, and I spat at his feet.

"You will speak with respect."

"Nobody respects zombies where I come from." I leaned out of the way of his putrid stench. "Besides, why settle for less? You have the most powerful talisman in the realms at your disposal, yet you still want to bow to someone else."

Unfortunately, I'd bet that's why the outcasts had lasted this long without murdering one another. They were united in the belief that the Seelie Queen was the rightful leader. But they wouldn't live long enough to see her plans come to fruition.

"The Seelie Queen has earned the crown by right," he said. "She will lead us to greatness."

"I hope she'll also lead you to a bath. You smell like a rat that's been dead for a week."

He gave me another slap. "If it were up to me, I'd hang your corpse at the entrance to our new Court as a warning."

"But it isn't." Question was, why did she want to keep me alive? "Is she afraid the vow binding me to the Court will rebound on her if she kills me?"

Her fears might not be unfounded. Usually when a participant in a vow died, the vow winked out of existence. But the vow binding my family to the Court had endured through generations and survived even the Erlking's passing. There was no stronger form of magic the Sidhe possessed. Perhaps the Seelie Queen feared that if she killed me, the backlash of the broken vow would ricochet straight back into her face.

"When we rule the Court, the old vows won't matter," he said. "We will live free of obligation, and it is a great honour for you to be invited to join us."

"To be honest, you lost me when you shot the Erlking dead and set that talisman loose in the world," I said. "You left me with no choice but to kick your arse into next week."

The circlet's glow bathed my face in light. Magic blasted from my hands into his decaying face, and his skin peeled back from his skull. He staggered, and I elbowed him aside, running through the trees.

My feet pounded against the earth, heedless of the Sidhe giving chase. With any luck, they'd leave Mum and Darrow alone in favour of pursuing me.

I sent a silent plea to the Vale. *Take me to it. Take me to the Erlking's talisman.*

The path warped and changed before my eyes. I skidded to a halt at the edge of a clearing. The entire area was barren and lifeless, trees reduced to husks, and in the centre stood the Erlking's staff. Power curled around its base, threads of shadow stirring the leaves on the ground. The talisman had even eaten through the meagre threads of magic remaining in the Grey Vale, leaving nothing but emptiness behind.

Gripping the round stone Etaina had given me in one hand, I walked towards the staff, and my own fate.

23

The Sidhe's footsteps faded into the background. Magic rippled outwards from the talisman, and I gripped the cool stone in my pocket, hoping it *wasn't* a dud.

Either way, it was too late for me to turn back. The staff's magic brushed against my skin, bringing the scent of earthen tunnels and empty landscapes bare of any hint of life—and beneath that, something that called to me, promising power. The lure of a talisman wanting to be claimed.

"Stay away from that, human." The Sidhe's voices sounded further away than they should. I risked a brief glance over my shoulder, where the group of Sidhe had halted outside the clearing.

Aha. If they took another step, the talisman's magic would hit them... which meant I was already within its orbit. The protective magic of the stone had kept me from harm.

With swift steps, I closed the distance between me and

the staff. The talisman came up to my shoulder, carved from wood that would never break, and wisps of magic clung to its base. My fingers curled around the middle of the staff, and magic tickled my skin, tingling with static. *Okay. Don't fail me now.*

The sound of footfalls came from my shoulder. Wheeling around with the talisman in my hands, I raised it as a shield before me.

The Sidhe who'd crept up on me reached out a hand almost bare of skin, muscle and sinew gleaming beneath. His face was sunken, his eyes unseeing, his legs decaying as he walked.

"I really wouldn't," I told him.

The talisman's magic tingled from my hands to my arms, wisps of smoke encasing the Sidhe's outstretched arm.

His hand dropped, lifeless, his body decaying, and the talisman's light grew brighter, as though it drew strength from the lives it took. Bile coated the back of my throat. If not for the stone in my pocket, the talisman would have eaten the skin off my bones and peeled the Gatekeeper's mark from my forehead until the vow winked out of existence.

I held the talisman towards the other Sidhe. "Last chance to run. All of you."

Magic rippled out from the talisman, and the Sidhe recoiled. Threads curled up my arm, and a gasp escaped as the sharp tingling sensation grew stronger. Too strong.

Shit. Does the immunity have a limit?

Darkness poured from the staff, encasing me like a cloak. My heart kick-started with a jolt. The talisman thought I was trying to claim it. Since it couldn't destroy me, it wanted to own me instead.

"Stop that." I held it at arm's length, willing the shadows to go away. Two Sidhe dropped where they stood, their skin peeling off their bones, blood evaporating, organs shrivelling to nothingness.

"Let go of that staff, Gatekeeper!" Two Sidhe ran at me, and the talisman's magic hit them in a wave, turning them to dust and brittle bone.

I kept moving towards the Sidhe, panic rising at the sensation of the talisman's magic curling around me, penetrating to my very soul. The talisman sought someone to harness its power, and thanks to the effects of the stone in my pocket, it deemed me worthy. *Stop that. Stop it.*

Magic raced through my veins, spilling out of my fingertips. Darkness spread across the ground, shadows filling the space around me. Trees collapsed, turning to husks. The Vale itself quaked and trembled beneath the talisman's power.

Power only the Erlking had been able to control.

Lord Veren lunged at me with a roar of fury, but his body collapsed into dust before the talisman made contact. Magic filled the gaps in my fingers, clawed up my throat and out of every pore. An inhuman sound tore from my throat. I ran at the surviving Sidhe, who turned tail and fled into the surrounding forest.

Then a familiar voice shouted my name. The talisman faltered in my grip when Mum reached the path. "Hazel."

"Stop!" I backed towards the clearing. "Don't come near me. I need to get rid of this thing."

"You can't." Her mouth pinched, her face pale beneath the bleeding cut on her forehead. "It's claimed you, Hazel."

I can't wield the staff. I'm Gatekeeper. Not even the Erlking had been able to stop its magic from destroying everyone it touched, and if I kept it, I would never be able to set foot in Faerie again.

I'd never see my *family* again.

"You can control it, Hazel." Mum looked me in the eyes. "You have power over the magic, not the other way around. Ask your sister."

"Ilsa's talisman isn't like this." Her magic might have the same source, but she wasn't driven to destroy everyone she touched.

Had Etaina known this would be a side-effect of the stone? I should have known it'd have a sting in the tail. Too bad for her, because Darrow would be stuck here along with me for the foreseeable future.

Unless...

I glanced down at the shadowy magic curling around the staff's base. "I can open a way back to the Courts now I have this."

Wielding a faerie's talisman gifted me with the ability to cross between realms. I could drop Mum and Darrow off at home, and then... stay here. Not an appealing option, but neither was reducing the Summer Court to dust and doing the Seelie Queen's job for her.

"Hazel." Mum's voice was soft.

I drew in a ragged breath. "Mum, fetch Darrow and get ready to run. I'm going to open a way back into Faerie next to the gate to our home. As soon as you're through, ask a Sidhe to close the doorway behind you. Don't tell them I have the Erlking's talisman, or they'll come here and rip it from my fingers."

And then? The Courts would fall, one way or another. I understood why the Erlking had held the secret close to his chest for centuries. The Sidhe—prideful, rash, arrogant—would bring about their own end.

"You aren't staying behind, Hazel."

"This isn't about me." I looked her in the eyes. "Don't make this any harder than it needs to be."

Her lips pursed. "What if I told you there's a way to keep that talisman secured?"

"I'd say you might have told me that earlier."

"There were… circumstances." She glanced behind her. "The talisman will be safe in the Inner Garden's grove."

The Inner Garden. "You think the healing magic in there will counter the effects of the talisman?"

She might well be right. The only Sidhe immune to the talisman's magic was the Seelie Queen, due to her super-charged healing abilities. But I didn't dare let that hope bloom, not until I saw it for myself.

"Trust me," Mum said. "I won't allow the talisman to harm anyone. I promise you that."

"You'll have to keep your distance when I open the doorway," I told her. "Where is Darrow?"

"He's unconscious from the effects of the iron."

"Probably for the best." After all, he'd wanted the talisman himself—or rather, for Etaina. She'd be wanting her stone back, come to that, but I wouldn't relinquish it yet. If she found out I'd claimed the talisman, she'd assume I'd done it on purpose. She might well ask Darrow to steal it from me, and the talisman's magic would destroy both of us.

Mum returned to the path, carrying an unconscious Darrow in her arms. I didn't dare look at him. My chest tightened, and I crossed my fingers and toes that he didn't wake in time to see what I'd done.

"Ready?" I extended the talisman, picturing our family's gate in my mind's eye. The Vale's grey path turned transparent, and a square-shaped doorway opened in mid-air, revealing the path outside the ambassadors' palace.

"Damn," I murmured. "Guess it really is as easy as the Sidhe make it look."

I stepped away from the doorway to allow Mum to take Darrow through. She strode into the doorway with no hesitation, unafraid of the talisman's touch. I wished I shared her confidence. She couldn't possibly have known I'd end up with the Erlking's staff in my hands, could she?

Mum leaned out of the doorway. "There's nobody here, Hazel. Be quick."

I kept an eye on her, mentally calculating the distance. When I was certain she was out of range, I stepped through the doorway and into the Summer Court.

The instant my feet touched the ground, the grass wilted under my feet, and dead leaves dropped off the nearest plants. Alarmed, I headed for family's gate, shedding leaves as I did so.

"Ilsa!" Mum called through the gate to the ambassadors' palace. "Tell the Sidhe to close that doorway, won't you?"

"You what?" Ilsa's head popped up from behind one of the large-leafed plants outside the palace, and her eyes bulged. "Hazel. Is that—?"

"Don't come any closer." I ran towards Summer's gate,

wincing as another wave of dead leaves fell over my head. "Mum, I really hope you're right. I don't know how long I can keep its magic reined in."

"You won't need to for long," she insisted. "Go on, Hazel."

I hurried out into my family's garden. Grass died beneath my feet, each strand shrivelling in the earth. Flowers wilted in their beds, while the hedges shed their leaves, turning brown and disintegrating into a fine mist.

"The Erlking must have done a shit-ton of damage when he first claimed this thing." I backed up from the gate so Mum could get through without falling within range of the talisman. Green leaves turned brown, vibrant magic sucked into the torrent of shadow wrapping around the staff.

Cursing, I ducked through the narrow opening in the hedge into the Inner Garden and the grove. My gaze fell on the glittering waters within... where, on top of the water, cocooned in a protective shield, lay the Erlking's crown.

I forgot all about the staff. "What the hell is that doing in there?"

"Put the staff down," Mum said from behind me.

I was too stunned not to obey, so I let the staff fall into the healing waters of the grove. It floated on the surface, shadows coalescing around it, yet the water's glow remained intact.

"Fuck me." I sank onto the grass. "Okay, seriously. How much of this did you plan?"

The crown glittered above the water's surface, its tips gleaming with silver-green gems. *Mum had it all along?*

"Less than you think," she said. "I suspected the Sidhe

had a traitor in their midst. The staff was already gone, so I persuaded the Sidhe to allow me to hide the crown here until the killer was caught."

I pressed the heels of my palms to my eyes. "So Lady Aiten accused us because you really did steal the crown."

"Lady Aiten was not thrilled with my idea, but I had her guarantee of protection from the other Sidhe, and she kept them from searching the house."

"She kept checking up on you. That's why the gate moved to the ambassadors' palace." I pushed to my feet, my hands trembling. "And as part of the act she pretended to accuse you and yelled at me a lot. I think she enjoyed that part."

"Believe me, Hazel, I wish I could have told you the truth, but I couldn't guarantee the other Sidhe wouldn't have pulled the information out of you."

"That doesn't explain how you knew I could safely store the staff here in the grove." I marvelled at the sight of the shadowy form of the talisman floating atop the water. Seemingly harmless.

"I didn't," she said. "I guessed, based on what I knew of the staff and the Seelie Queen's ability to resist its magic. I didn't expect you to claim it, but I had this marked out as a safe place to hide it, should we manage to get it away from the killer."

I whistled. "That's one hell of a gamble. Did you find out who the heir is?"

"Not yet, but I was asked to look into that, too."

"I knew it," Ilsa said from outside the grove. "I *knew* someone from the Court put you up to this."

"Did you know about that?" I pointed to the crown.

"No." Ilsa peered through the grove's entrance. "I think

it's safe for me to come in here as long as the talisman is in the water."

"But it probably isn't safe to give me a hug." Shadowy magic wreathed my arms, wrapped around my body. Both outside and inside. A chill settled on my shoulders. I'd brought the talisman to safety and prevented it from causing a war—but how long would it be before the Sidhe realised the Gatekeeper had claimed it?

24

When I left the grove, the grass outside was already growing again, the flowers returning to their former vibrancy.

"You can't leave it in the water forever, Mum," Ilsa said, echoing my thoughts. "You also can't leave the crown in there. The Sidhe will want it back."

"I'm aware of that," said Mum. "I'll give them enough time to jail the surviving conspirators and recover from their injuries. Once Lady Aiten is back on her feet, I'll give her the crown back."

"Presumably without letting her look in there." I pointed to the grove. "The magic is still inside me. Is there any way to un-claim a talisman once you have it?"

I could hardly believe that my own *mother* had been more devious than the Sidhe had, yet now the shock had worn off a little, my worries about the talisman reared their heads again. Currents of shadowy magic tingled up my arms, while I didn't dare touch anything in the house in case the talisman's effects caused our family magic to short-circuit.

I shuffled after Ilsa and Mum into the kitchen. The lights came on, then died with a hissing noise. I wrapped my arms around myself. "This isn't going to work. I'm a literal walking anti-magic plague."

While the majority of the magic remained inside the talisman, part of it rested in me, alongside my Gatekeeper's powers. Impossible to hide.

"Try holding something made of iron," Ilsa said. "It counters most magic."

"This isn't faerie magic, though." I picked up a knife from the kitchen sideboard. "It's like yours."

Similar to faerie magic in almost every way... except its origins were from a time before the Sidhe had ruled, when gods had walked among them, wielding magic deadly enough to tear reality to shreds.

My throat went dry. Darrow would think I'd betrayed him when he found out. I wouldn't be able to keep it a secret forever. The instant a Sidhe set eyes on me, they'd know.

"It might not be as strong once you're back in the Court," Ilsa said. "Not if you leave the talisman in this realm, anyway. Most Sidhe are weakened when they aren't carrying their talismans."

"They'll still sense it," I insisted. "And I'll always know it's here."

I knew Faerie. One taste and you wanted more. The talisman belonged to a race that even the Sidhe had feared, and inch by inch, its magic would infect me until it claimed me, body and soul—or cast me aside like an old coat to seek a new wielder.

Mum pressed her lips together. "You could have the magic stripped from you, but only the Sidhe can do that."

I put down the knife. "Like they do to exiles right before they send them into the Vale? Would that work?"

"I would think so," Mum said. "There's a spell for stripping a talisman's magic from a wielder, but I suspect only a Sidhe can perform it."

"I can find out." Ilsa left the kitchen, no doubt in search of a book.

"Why am I not surprised." A smile tugged at my mouth. "I'm carrying the embodiment of the apocalypse inside me and she still insists on looking it up in a book."

"Come on." Mum beckoned me into the living room. "Look—I'm this close to you, and the talisman isn't hurting me."

So she was. Didn't mean I wanted to risk getting closer, though. "All right."

I made for the living room and slumped on the beaten-up old sofa. At the very least, it wouldn't be a tragedy if it collapsed underneath me.

"I left Darrow at the ambassadors' palace," she added. "He didn't wake, so he doesn't know you have the talisman."

"Good." I pulled out the stone Etaina had given me. "I need to return this, but it's also the only way to counter the effects of the talisman's magic. Guess there's no point in me carrying it around with me. Maybe you guys should take turns passing it among yourselves in case I accidentally step within range."

Mum shook her head. "If it was given with the expectation of being returned, then keeping it might have side effects. Who—"

"Got it." Ilsa walked back into the room with a text-book in her arms, interrupting me before I could figure out how to explain what I'd learned in the realm of the Aes Sidhe. "An Invocation can be used to remove the talisman's magic. I thought so, but I just wanted to double-check."

"I should have known," said Mum. "Can you do it?"

I frowned, uncomprehending. Then it hit me. A human couldn't speak an Invocation without losing their mind, but a human who carried the magic of a god was another thing entirely. Which included Ilsa herself... and now, me.

"I can," said Ilsa. "If you trust me, Hazel."

"What kind of question is that?" I said. "I'm not asking a Sidhe to do it, that's for damned sure."

Ilsa grinned. "I thought not."

Ilsa could strip the magic out of me herself, unbind the link between the talisman and me. Hope bloomed in my chest, and I pushed to my feet. Magic coiled around my fingertips, itching to hold the staff again and wield its power, but I pushed it aside. "I'll have to be holding the staff for it to work, I think. I'll also need to guarantee we won't be interrupted."

"I'll take care of that," said Mum.

"Are you sure?" Ilsa said. "You were injured—and you're exhausted, Hazel."

I shook my head. "If I delay, it might get worse. I don't want to wake up and find the house has collapsed overnight."

What we'd do with the staff long-term, I'd deal with later. I would never be able to live my own life as long as I held that talisman. The Gatekeeper's curse was more than enough for me.

The pool of water remained in the same condition as earlier, unchanged by the presence of the staff. The crown hovered above it, encased in a protective shield.

"I can't believe Mum swiped the crown." I reached for the staff, pulling it out of the water. Cold tendrils ensnared my arms, whispering dark promises, and I stepped around the pool to prevent its magic from touching Ilsa.

"Nor me." Ilsa stood at a safe distance away. "Devious, for sure. I'll be having words with her later."

"Save your words for the Invocation. I think you'll need them." Worry fluttered behind my breastbone. Invocations were dangerous even in Faerie. It seemed fitting that the language that had originally belonged to the gods would be the only force capable of removing the talisman's influence from me.

Ilsa opened the book and sat down on a rock beside the pool. "I've never done this before, but I assume it won't remove your Gatekeeper's magic, too."

"Don't tell me about the downsides." I rested the staff on the ground, holding it with both hands. Shadowy magic coiled up my arms, and I tightened my grip to resist the impulse to lift it into the air. *Nice try, but you won't get me that easily.* "Quickly—please."

"All right." Ilsa took in a deep breath. Then she spoke.

Words slammed into me one at a time, echoing around the clearing. Their meanings filtered through my mind, but didn't stick, their magic too much for my human mind to handle. My hands shook, the earth trembled and the talisman's rage bubbled to the surface.

Pain ripped through my body from head to toe, searing my skin from the inside out. Frayed shadows leaked from my hands, and a loud, furious roar sounded, vibrating through my bones and blood.

My vision blurred, and the waters of the grove rose to catch me as I fell.

———

"At least you had a soft landing," Ilsa said later, when we were back in the living room.

I wrapped the blanket around myself, sneezing. "I think I might have the dubious honour of being the first human in existence to have a talisman's magic forcibly ripped out of me."

"Sorry," Ilsa said. "I didn't want to hurt you, but—"

"I'd take the pain ten times over as long as I can walk around without killing everything I touch." I fingered the edge of the blanket. "I don't know how the Erlking stood it for hundreds of years."

"He must have found a way to deal with it," said Ilsa. "Perhaps he left instructions behind."

"Along with his cryptic message?" I scowled. "I don't see why he couldn't just *name* the traitors."

"Perhaps he feared for your safety," said Mum. "And he was right to worry."

"Lord Veren wanted me alive. So did the Seelie Queen." I pushed a handful of damp hair out of my face. "She wants me to rule at her side. Personally, I think she's afraid of the Gatekeeper's vow backfiring on her... do you think that might be it?"

Mum's lips compressed. "Perhaps. Even the Gate-keepers don't know everything about the vow."

"Which explains why Etaina got such wild ideas about Thomas Lynn."

"Speaking of which," said Ilsa. "What does she want the talisman for, do you know?"

"Supposedly to keep it safe." I'd told her and Mum about Darrow's Court after they'd carried me out of the grove. "It sounded like Etaina knew the Erlking before he even claimed the talisman."

Ilsa leaned forward. "So these… Aes Sidhe… they're not part of Summer. They split *before* the Erlking became the king. No wonder they aren't in our books, except in a historical sense. They're thought to have died out."

"That's worrying," said Mum. "I have to confess, my knowledge of the Aes Sidhe isn't extensive. They guard their secrets well. It sounds like this Darrow is the same."

"Yeah, if he hadn't been unconscious, I might have had to fight him for it." I grimaced. "That Etaina *really* doesn't like the Gatekeepers."

Too bad I couldn't go back and question her again without her calling in the favour I owed for the stone.

The click of the gate opening came from outside. Mum was on her feet a moment later. "The Sidhe."

"Wonderful." I pushed to my feet, my body protesting. "Have they come for the crown? That didn't take long."

I reached the back door first, but it wasn't the Sidhe. Instead, Coral hurried towards the house across the field.

"She's an ally," I told the others. "Her brother betrayed the Sea Queen—which I think makes *her* the heir to the Sea Kingdom. I'll have to help her deal with that."

"Later," Ilsa said sternly. "You're not responsible for dealing with everyone's problems, do you hear me?"

"I don't know about that," I said. "I'm on a roll at the moment. If you need me to come to the necromancer guild and yell at someone, just let me know."

I waved Coral over, and she wrapped me in a hug. I squeezed her back, relieved to be able to hug my friends without the talisman's magic attacking them. "Hazel, I thought you were dead. When you didn't come back…"

"I'm sorry," I said. "I should have come to check up on you right away."

"I know you needed to see if your family were okay." Her brow wrinkled. "Why are you all wet?"

"Went for an unplanned swim," I said. "Speaking of which… your brother?"

"The Sidhe took him to their jail." She bit her lip, her eyes glittering. "Since he committed crimes against the Summer Court, he'll be tried and executed in Faerie, not at home."

"I'm sorry." Not for him, but for her, and everyone his selfish pursuit of power had hurt.

"He made his choice." She blinked tears from her eyes. "I'll never understand it. My mother will be devastated."

I gave her another hug. "I understand if you don't want to stay here in Summer."

"I still have a job to do." Steel entered her expression. "I'm not going to let you die at the final hurdle."

I raised my brows. "I'm not sure I *can* be Gatekeeper after this. I disobeyed orders. Majorly."

"You also helped save the Court," she said. "Lord Raivan and Lady Aiten are telling everyone you were the one who killed the traitors."

I shot Ilsa an accusing look. "Did you put River up to that before you left, by any chance?"

"I may have said something to that effect," she said. "It's true, isn't it?"

"Yes, but I assumed they'd want a statement from me before they believed anything we said. Since Mum broke out of jail, I broke *into* the jail, and… I've lost track of all the other laws we broke, to be honest."

"Lady Aiten permitted me to defend the Court by any means necessary," Mum put in. "You're still Gatekeeper."

For now. With the talisman out of the enemy's hands, all that remained was to crown a new monarch. Afterwards, I'd be free to consider my old promise to break the family curse and free future generations of Lynns from a lifetime of obligation to Faerie.

———

The Sidhe gave us a week to recover. While it seemed generous of them, the time difference with Faerie might have been a factor. That, and Lady Aiten had needed time to fully heal from her wounds. She'd been lucky to survive.

Mum and I were in the middle of a sparring match when the gates to the Summer Court opened and Lady Aiten walked out onto the lawn, at full power once again. Dark hair coiled down her back and vibrant magic the same shade of green as her cloak shone from her eyes.

"You." I kept my voice cold. "Thanks for telling me you knew my family was innocent all along."

"I hoped that I wouldn't need to deceive you," she said, "but events forced me to."

Was being stabbed by Lord Veren part of your plan? I held my tongue, somehow. "You came for the crown."

"I did." She turned to Mum, who gave me a look telling me to keep her busy so that she wouldn't see what else was in the grove.

"Mum will handle it." I laid down the practise sword. "Why did you decide not to trust me? You knew I wasn't going to betray the Court."

"What happened to the rebels?" she asked.

So much for an apology. "Dead. The talisman killed them."

"And the talisman itself?"

"Lost in the Vale." Mum and I had discussed our cover story over the last week and decided it was best to go with the Vale story. "I don't think anyone will miss it."

Her green eyes bored into mine, but I held her stare. I'd never been gladder of my mortal ability to lie. "We have closed all the doors to the Vale, and all the rebels are accounted for. That leaves the crown."

"Here." Mum approached us with the crown. Sharp silver points glittered with studded gemstones, while green light wreathed its edges. "My vow is fulfilled."

Of course there'd been a vow involved. I should have guessed. "You're not going to force us to find the heir on pain of death?"

"The heir?" Lady Aiten frowned. "No. I merely advised your mother to keep an updated record of the Erlking's relations. We're still searching for any clues behind left by the king himself."

Hmm. "Don't look at me. He didn't send me any notes except for the first one, and we caught all the conspirators. Is the Seelie Queen safe in her cell?"

"She is," she confirmed. "But I'll be displeased if I find you're keeping any more secrets from me, Hazel Lynn."

"Noted." I gave her a smile. "Be careful with that crown, won't you?"

We'd never be friends, but between us, we'd caught the killer, quelled a rebellion, and returned the crown to the right hands. Or the only hands for the job, in any case. And I wasn't bound to a murderous talisman, which was always a bonus. With the talisman gone, the Sidhe would be free to elect a new heir without fear of the outcasts obliterating their new monarch before they'd even taken the throne.

I'd had a taste of its power, and despite my best intentions, I'd wanted more. Like faerie magic, it called to a dark, primal part of me who craved to walk down the same path my ancestor had. A path that would lead to me the same fate as those poor suckers in the Vale.

No thanks. I'd leave the power-hungry avarice to the Sidhe.

———

The following day brought another knock at the front door, when Ilsa and I were in the middle of sorting some of Mum's notes on the Erlking's family tree.

"Expecting someone?" asked Ilsa.

"Not that I'm aware of." I got to my feet and walked into the hall, peering through the spy hole behind the front door. Well, well.

"Darrow," I said, opening the door. "To what do I owe the pleasure?"

"I'm here to remove the binding mark," he said. "You passed your Trials."

I raised an eyebrow. "You're implying my battle with the outcasts was supposed to be a test?"

"Not a planned one," he said. "But you demonstrated all the skills necessary to be Gatekeeper of the Summer Court. Now, all there is to do is arrange the ceremony."

Uh-huh. I knew better than to believe that was why he was here. "I assume Etaina sent you here to check up on me. Not the Summer Court."

"The Sidhe are occupied at the moment. I heard they got their crown back. Did they get the staff, too?"

Aha. I'd guessed right. "There is no wielder," I told him, truthfully. "The Summer Court will elect a new heir, and then they'll decide how to proceed."

"And do you trust them with this decision?"

No. "It's not up to me. It's up to the Erlking, or his successor."

"I heard some odd rumours," he said. "About the way you returned to the Court after the events in the Vale. No Sidhe accompanied you, yet only Sidhe can open doorways into the Court."

"Not quite," Ilsa put in from behind me. "You're Darrow, aren't you? I'm Ilsa Lynn."

"Hazel's sister." His gaze slid between us, as though taking note of our similarities and differences. Ilsa scowled. She hated when people did that. "You mean to say you know where the talisman is?"

"No, but I know where mine is." She gave a smile. "Want a demonstration?"

"Ilsa." As much as I wanted to get rid of Darrow's curiosity, opening the gates of Death on the doorstep was

a step too far. "She doesn't mean that. But yes, my sister's talisman can enable inter-realm travel. It can also summon the dead, so I wouldn't tell Etaina about it unless you want an unexpected visit from a troop of zombies."

His brows climbed into his hairline. "Etaina isn't concerned with all talismans, just the Erlking's. Besides, I came here to see you."

"Uh-huh." I heard Ilsa retreat, her part done, and irritation prickled at me. "Get to the bloody point, Darrow. I prefer it when people are upfront with me, and I like it even better when they don't pretend to have been sent here by the Summer Court when they're actually here to gather intelligence."

I wasn't a complete fool. Whatever had happened between us didn't change the fact that we belonged to different Courts. My duty was to Summer, and once my Trials officially came to an end, there'd be nothing keeping him here.

"I did come to remove the mark," he said. "You can't blame me for being curious about how you found a safe place to store the talisman, assuming you still have it."

I'd never been more relieved I hadn't been able to take him to the grove to be healed after he'd nearly died. Even if my visit to the Aes Sidhe had brought Etaina's presence into my life. "Trust me when I say it's safe, and better off out of anyone's hands. You know if anyone had that talisman, they'd never get a moment's peace."

"I agree." He tilted his head. "Etaina does as well. We would be more than happy to take the talisman under our watch. We would see to it that it doesn't fall it into the wrong hands. If you don't mind telling me where it is."

"No, I don't think I will. Give Etaina my regards." I

held out the stone. "She can also have this back, if she promises not to use it as leverage."

"You didn't swear a vow to her, so it should be fine." He took the stone, but before I could withdraw my hand, he caught my wrist.

My heart jerked against my ribcage. "If you're planning to use force, then prepare for a world of pain."

He pulled me against him, his lips brushing my ear. "Oh, I'm not. I have other ways to convince you."

I caught my balance, startled by his sudden closeness. *What in hell is he doing?*

Magic sparked up my wrist, and the binding unravelled with a sudden jolt that jerked me forward off the doorstep and into his arms. Currents of magic buzzed between us, setting my heart racing.

"You did that on purpose." I took a firm step back. "Also, I'm not convinced yet. Sorry to disappoint you."

With a voice filled with promises, he said, "Until next time, then."

Then he turned and walked away.

"Hazel?" Ilsa stepped up behind me. "Are you okay?"

"I think," I said, "I may be in trouble."

ABOUT THE AUTHOR

Emma is the New York Times and USA Today Bestselling author of the Changeling Chronicles urban fantasy series.

Emma spent her childhood creating imaginary worlds to compensate for a disappointingly average reality, so it was probably inevitable that she ended up writing fantasy novels. When she's not immersed in her own fictional universes, Emma can be found with her head in a book or wandering around the world in search of adventure.

Find out more about Emma's books at
www.emmaladams.com.